Hi Pri

C000069756

WHAT DREAMS WE HAD

Happy reading!

Ruth

WHAT DREAMS WE HAD

PHILL FEATHERSTONE

Opitus Books

Everyone dreams, but not equally. Those who dream by night in the dusty recesses of their minds, wake in the day to find that it was vanity: but the dreamers of the day are dangerous, for they may act on their dreams with open eyes, to make them possible.

T.E.Lawrence

I have had a most rare vision. I had a dream, past the wit of man to say what dream it was... The eye of man hath not heard, the ear of man hath not seen, man's hand is not able to taste, his tongue to conceive, nor his heart to report, what my dream was.

A Midsummer Night's Dream, Act 4 Scene 1

PROLOGUE – AWAKE

1

Elena was the first in the band to realise that things were going wrong. The number was called California Rock Chick. The lyrics were hers and the tune was by DJ, but that hadn't stopped Alex from introducing it as his own. Joey started a driving 2/4 beat on the drums and Alex shouted the words.

Cool house, big pool, and her own hot car
She don't give a shit about who you are
She turns all the heads when she walks on the beach
She's a queen, she's a dream and she's outa your reach
She's a California rock chick rock chick rock chick
California rock chick
Rock chick

Because it was a school prom, they'd changed 'don't give a shit' to 'couldn't care less'. It didn't matter; what was coming was far worse. The school banned alcohol, but Alex had managed to smuggle in a water bottle full of vodka. That and the weed he smoked at the break were enough to do it. At the end of the first chorus he stood up, clapping his hands, and began to chant.

A group of lads at the front who had been told off by a teacher for moshing couldn't believe their luck. This was payback time. They took up what Alex was yelling with gusto, more at the back of the hall joined in, and the noise grew until it seemed that the entire school was shouting as one.

California cock chick
Cock chick cock chick
California cock chick
Cock chick cock chick

The teachers went berserk, although some of the younger ones found it hard not to laugh. DJ had the presence of mind to kill the mics, and Joey stopped drumming.

Steve Sutton, the Deputy Headteacher, leapt onto the stage. He was furious, scarlet with rage. He snatched Elena's microphone and jabbed a finger at DJ to turn it up.

'Silence!' he bellowed into it. 'Silence!' Raggedly and slowly the racket ebbed. 'You've had your fun. Now it's over,' he yelled, glaring at the boys at the front. 'This prom is done. Finished. You're all to leave. I want this hall cleared in two minutes.'

The students began to file from the room. Some were gleeful, many looked crestfallen, and from one quarter there was subdued booing. Several of the girls were in tears because the opportunity to get the most out of the outfits they'd worked so hard on had been snatched from them. Eventually, the teachers managed to herd everyone

2

out, but it took longer than the two minutes Sutton had demanded.

As the last few left through the rear doors, he turned to the band. 'You too,' he said. 'Out.' Joey started to undo the cymbals. 'Leave it,' he snapped. 'Leave the stuff here. You can sort it out tomorrow. I want all of you in my office at 8.30 in the morning. I hope you're pleased with yourselves.' He stamped off to supervise the rest of the evacuation.

'You idiot!' DJ snarled at Alex, advancing on him. 'What the fuck were you thinking?' Elena thought he was going to thump him.

Alex didn't answer. He'd sunk onto a chair and he looked a greasy white, as if he was about to throw up. Joey hooked Alex's arm over his shoulders and helped him down from the stage. Elena followed.

~

It wasn't the Deputy Head they saw the next morning. They were outside his office in good time, but he immediately led them to the room of Gina Meredith, the Headteacher. She sat behind an enormous desk and the four of them lined up in front of it. Sutton sat on a chair to the side. On the wall behind him was a large, illuminated copy of the school's crest. The motto beneath it read, *A pure mind served by a pure heart*. Oh shit, thought DJ.

They'd decided on their story the night before. Or rather Elena, DJ and Joey had; Alex had been completely out of it. The line they'd agreed was simple. The

3

chanting had come not from the band but from a group of boys. Sorry, they hadn't seen exactly who started it and couldn't name them. It was a lie but, as Elena pointed out, it was justified for self-preservation and it was morally acceptable because it didn't hurt anyone else.

Meredith appeared sceptical. 'Is that your reading of what happened, Mr Sutton?' she said, turning to him.

He thought for a moment. 'I honestly can't say,' he said. 'The band may not have started the obscene chant but my impression is that Alex at least joined in.'

Alex was about to say something but Elena gave him a warning nudge, and the four waited in silence.

The school had a problem. The incident could be seen as the deliberate promotion of disorder, an attempt to sabotage one of the major events in the calendar. It had resulted in the prom, which many students looked forward to, being cut short. Already there had been complaints from parents. Suspension would be the obvious punishment. On the other hand, three of the band–Alex, DJ and Elena–were A* students, almost certain to do very well in their exams next year. Besides that, Alex's father had only recently made a substantial donation to the school's development fund. Finally, because it was so nearly the end of term suspension would be pointless.

At last Meredith spoke. 'Your explanation doesn't convince me,' she said. 'If I was certain that one of you was the instigator of this appalling behaviour I would have no hesitation in punishing you severely. However, you assure me that it was none of you and we have no one who can say it was, so I must give you the benefit of the doubt.'

Despite this exoneration, they were in some disgrace. However, less than a week later the school closed for the summer break, and by the time DJ, Alex, Joey and Elena returned to begin the new term the occasion seemed to have been forgotten. Except that the band wasn't invited again to play at school events. Instead, another group from a year below who called themselves *Vampire Slaves* took over. They wore black and were heavily into fangs and fake blood, but worse than that was their music: repetitive covers badly played, with no original material at all.

Not long afterwards, the band lost its name; or rather, it lost them. They used to call themselves *The Green Men*. That was after The Green Man pub that Elena's parents run, where they had their first few gigs and the only ones for which they were paid. They'd needed a name quickly, jumped on that and it had stuck, but it had never been right. Elena, for one, had never been happy with it.

'We're not all men,' she'd grumbled. 'I'm a girl.'

Joey had suggested *Green People*, but Alex thought that sounded as if they were aliens. 'Green has other associations too,' he'd said. 'Like unripe. Or immature. Or green with envy. It's just not cool.'

'It's cool when it's to do with conservation,' Elena had said.

'And what's belting out rock to a roomful of people got to do with conservation?'

The discussion had got nowhere, but now they have to come up with a new name because Alex had found the others that lunchtime and given them some astonishing news.

'Meredith just sent for me,' he told them. 'Guess what. She wants us to play at the end-of-term awards.'

'Never!'

'What?'

'Really?'

'Yes, really. She said she's taking a risk. She said that in a few days we'll be leaving. She said we could,' and he made air quotes with his fingers, '"repeat the anarchy of last year", or we could put on a great show and ensure everybody has a good time and that we leave in a blaze of glory. She said I was to talk to you all about it.'

'Why did she send for you?' DJ said.

'She assumed I'm the band leader.'

'You?' DJ was irritated. 'We don't have a fucking leader. We're a democracy.'

'Democracies have leaders,' said Alex.

'Well it's not you,' said DJ.

'Okay, okay,' said Alex, shrugging.

So they are to play, and they need a name, and time is short.

They've gathered around the table in Elena's kitchen. Her parents are in the bar. In the middle of the table is a box. When they started the business of choosing they brainstormed, writing ideas on slips of paper and dropping them into it. Elena picks out another one.

'*To Be Continued*,' she says.

DJ, Alex and Joey receive the suggestion in silence. They've been at this for some time now and they're weary.

DJ is the first to respond. 'It's not bad. It kind of gives the idea of forward momentum, like we're at the beginning of something.'

'Yes, and it implies that we're not done, that there's more to come from us,' says Joey.

They wait. What does Alex think? If they're honest, none of them is taken with this one but the pressure is mounting to settle on a name, and soon.

Alex says nothing for long seconds, then, 'I suppose it's got something, but there's kind of an unfinished vibe to it. It sounds as if we're a work in progress. We don't want people to think we're playing stuff we haven't properly worked on. Like we haven't rehearsed.'

DJ feels a stab of irritation. Every proposal that comes out of the box is rejected by Alex but he makes none of his own. He picks out another slip. '*Rainbow Avenue*,' he reads. 'How about that?' It's a suggestion that's come from him and he quite likes it. He can see the spectrum logo on Joey's bass drum.

The faces of the others aren't encouraging.

'Yuk,' says Alex.

'No,' says Elena. 'We can't. It's too LGBT. They've kind of appropriated the rainbow, so it's hard to use it for anything else. I mean I don't mind people thinking we're gay,' she adds hurriedly, 'but we're not gay, so why should we give people the idea that we are.'

'Yeah, but it's also a symbol of the NHS,' says DJ.

'Remember when all that Covid stuff was going on and there were NHS rainbows everywhere? People put them in their windows.'

'What do you think, Joey?' says Elena.

Joey doesn't pause to think. He has an idea that he's been mulling over because it comes out straight away. '*Persons Unknown*,' he says.

Alex makes a sound somewhere between a sigh and a raspberry. 'It wasn't in the box,' he says. 'We're only considering ideas that have been put in the box or we'll be here all night.'

This isn't a rule they'd agreed to, and DJ resents Alex suddenly inventing it. He feels compelled to give Joey's suggestion a run. 'Mm,' he says, thoughtfully. 'It's a possibility. It's got a kind of mystery. Hey, we could dress in black and wear masks, like Anonymous.'

'Are you serious?' says Elena. 'Dress up as anarchists and remind people of the last time we played at a school prom? Good idea!'

'Anyway, we don't want to be unknown,' Alex says wearily. 'It's the absolute opposite of what we want.'

'So it's kind of ironic?' says Elena.

They all look at each other. It's another no.

DJ goes back to the box. '*Strip Mall Psychos*,' he reads. 'Who the fuck came up with that one? Have we gone completely punk or something? Is this your writing, Joey?'

'Hey,' says Elena. 'The first rule of brainstorming is that all ideas are unattributed, and all get considered.'

'That's two rules,' says DJ. 'Anyway, is anybody backing this one?'

They all shake their heads. Nobody owns up to putting it in the box.

Mia watches. She's been sitting apart, pretending to be doing something on her phone but listening to the discussion. She's not a member of the band and she wasn't at the prom last year. She realises she has no say in what they decide to call themselves, but she's DJ's girlfriend so she thinks she should have. It scarcely matters though. The band hasn't much life left. If their exam results turn out to be what their teachers have predicted, in a few weeks two of them will leave home to start courses at different universities. Alex, who's taking a year off, and Joey, who's starting a job in a local restaurant, will still be here but Elena and DJ will go to opposite ends of the country. The band will split, it has no future. They only need a name for now.

She puts her hand up and coughs loudly. The other four look towards her. 'How about *Friendly Fire*?' she says.

There's another silence.

'Hey, I like that,' says DJ. 'Fire gives a feeling of energy and passion, and Friendly chimes with the sort of music we play and the image we want to promote.' He waits for Alex to disagree, but this time he doesn't.

'Yeah,' he says. 'Fire's also aggression and attack, but Friendly tones it down and stops it being too negative.'

'It's an oxymoron,' says Elena. 'I like it.'

'Who are you calling a moron?' Alex and DJ chant in unison, repeating the old joke that always came up when they did parts of speech in class.

They all laugh, even Joey, who remembers the word

cropping up in an English lesson once but has long forgotten what it means.

'*Friendly Fire* it is then,' says DJ.

'Terrific,' says Mia. 'Thank God you've managed at last to agree on something. I'll start right away on the posters.'

2

Alex is late. The other three aren't surprised; he's been late for nearly all the band practices. They'd agreed to meet in the music room at 3.30. It's now nearly 4.00 and Elena, Joey and DJ are filling time. DJ is working on a riff he came up with the previous day. It's only half a dozen notes and he's extending and elaborating it. Elena's listening and in her head forming a few phrases which she thinks fit the shapes DJ is making and may grow into lyrics. Joey is practising drum patterns, trying to get faster.

Elena is annoyed about Alex's lateness. He's once again treating them all, and especially her, with disrespect. It's as if he doesn't care. Over the time that she's been going out with him, she's come to the conclusion that deep down the only thing that Alex cares about is Alex. He can irritate her so much that sometimes she wants to tell him to sod off and never see him again, but there are things she really likes about him, and when he's in the mood he can be charming.

'At last,' she says as he comes through the door.

'About fucking time,' says DJ.

'Sorry,' says Alex. 'Something cropped up.'

DJ snorts. 'It always does. Man, you're the one who wanted to meet at 3.30.'

'Yeah, I know. I was on my way here and I would have been on time but then I ran into Steve Sutton.'

'And?'

'Well, he stopped me and gave me a lecture on how important it is that we play our very best at the awards, "for the good name of the school". I said of course and then he said that there's going to be a very special guest.'

The others, who were getting bored with yet another Alex excuse, are now interested.

'A special guest?' says Elena. 'Did he say who?'

'Yes, he did.' Alex sits down at the keyboards, smirking.

'Well fucking who?' says DJ.

Alex plays an arpeggio and leaves a long pause. Then he says, 'Theo Vasilias.'

'What, *the* Theo Vasilias?' says Elena.

'Well as far as I know there is only one.'

'Theo Vasilias!' Elena squeals. She's as excited as a schoolgirl - but of course, that's what she is, at least for the next few days.

'Who's he?' says Joey.

Alex sighs. 'Jesus, Joey. The Blackbirds' new striker? I know you're not into football, but I would have thought even a dick like you would know about your local team's record signing.'

'Oh, yeah,' says Joey. He does know who Vasilias is,

12

but a complete lack of interest in the game that appeals so much to the other three is part of the detached persona he cultivates. Besides, he knows it niggles them.

'How come?' says DJ.

'Charlie Dodds,' says Alex, referring to the Head of PE, 'knows Bruno Sylvani, Theo's agent. Charlie asked if he could get him to be guest of honour at the school awards, and he said yes.'

Elena crosses her arms and gives herself an excited little squeeze. 'He said yes.'

'Fine,' says DJ wearily. He's irritated by Elena's little girl behaviour. Mia might get away with it, but not Elena. She's anything but a little girl.

'Well aren't you excited?' she says.

'Why?' says DJ. 'I can see Vasilias at any home game at the Park.'

Elena sighs. 'Yes, but you can't meet him there.'

'And,' Alex says, 'if he likes our music it could lead to other things.'

'Such as?'

'Use your imagination. He's a Premiership footballer and he's dating a TV celeb. He must know no end of important people – other players, personalities, stars. If we impress him enough for him to talk about us, some of them might want us to play for them too.'

DJ is unimpressed. 'It's not like he has anything else to do. Like score goals, for example.'

'He's taking time to settle in,' says Elena, who's a fervent fan.

'Taking time!' says DJ. 'Joined United in January, paid 183K a week, and yet to get his name on the score sheet.

How much time does he need? Fuck me, I could do better!'

'A hundred and eighty-three thousand pounds a week!' says Joey. 'Wow. Lucky dude. That must be,' he thinks for a moment, 'nine point five million a year.'

Elena, who's not good with numbers, is impressed by Joey's mental arithmetic.

'Does he really get that much?' Joey says.

'He certainly does,' says Alex, 'and that's just what United pay him. There's sponsorship and merchandise on top of that. Although it's chicken feed compared with what guys like Messi and Ronaldo get. They're up to a hundred million or more.'

'Unbelievable,' says Joey. 'And you say he hasn't scored?'

'And he won't,' says DJ, ''cos the season's finished. So you can see why he's not too popular with the fans.'

Elena understands the frustration, but she doesn't think it's all the player's fault. 'It's the way he's been used,' she says. 'He needs space. When he was at Juventus they let him run all over the field, he was everywhere. That's the way he's used to playing. Here it's like they've drawn a line across the pitch and he's not allowed to go behind it. It makes it too easy for the opposition to mark him.'

'Hark at super coach,' says Alex.

'She's right,' says DJ. 'And he's missed some games. He was out with groin strain for a few weeks in the spring.'

'And speaking of groin strain,' says Alex, 'I wonder if he'll be bringing his tart with him.'

Elena makes a sound of disapproval and punches him hard on the arm.

'Hey,' he says, rubbing the spot. 'What's that for?'

'Sorry,' she says. 'Did I interrupt your lurid speculations?'

'Who's he mean?' says Joey.

Elena shoots him a pitying glance. 'Oh Joey, you're such an innocent. He means Theo's girlfriend, Lita Jordan.' Joey looks none the wiser. Elena shakes her head. 'You must have heard of her. She's a celeb, an influencer. Don't you watch TV?'

'Not much,' says Joey.

'She was in the last series of *Love Shack*. Her picture's everywhere. You must have seen her.'

'Oh,' says Joey.

'She might come with him,' says Elena. 'They're supposed to be getting married soon.'

Alex looks at his watch. 'We need to get started.'

'Says the guy who was late,' says DJ.

The practice begins well, working through their setlist. It begins with a cover of *Let's Dance*. They take it a bit faster than Bowie's original and it makes a good opener. Next is the first of their originals. It's called *Saturday Girl* and it's a complete contrast. It's in slow two-four time with occasional missed beats, which conveys a mood of yearning and loss. It opens with Elena's vocals, very soft.

I was the Saturday girl
I don't come round here any more
I heard what you told me
Don't come knocking on your door
Saturday girl stay away
You know the score

There's a lyrical middle section from Alex on the keyboards and an aching guitar solo from DJ. Then Elena's voice comes in again, husky and wounded as the melody glides into a minor key before closing on an unresolved chord. The words are by Elena and DJ wrote the tune. Everyone agrees it's one of the best things they've done.

After that, they need to liven things up again and have chosen *Sultans of Swing* as their second cover. They segue from that into another number in the same key and at the same tempo. It's called *Party Hard* and is as bouncy as the title suggests. Joey puts in some aggressive drum work and Elena brings a raw edge to the vocal. It finishes with climbing chords from Alex and a spectacular drum climax. As it ends Elena whoops and DJ clenches his fists in the air.

'Well if that doesn't get the hall rocking I don't know what will,' says Alex.

'Great vocals, Ellie,' says DJ. 'And the keyboard and drums? Awesome.'

'Let's do it again,' says Joey.

'We'd better get on,' Elena says. 'We don't have much time. And besides, if I do that again it'll kill my throat.'

There are a few minutes while they get their breath back. Then Alex says, 'Time for something completely different.'

They're halfway through the setlist, and it's now that the row starts. At the last rehearsal, Alex persuaded them to leave the middle slot for something he was working on. They agreed, but as it wasn't finished none of the others have heard it. Now it's done and Alex plays it, singing the lyrics and accompanying himself. He hasn't got a very strong voice and sometimes he doesn't quite hit the note, but the style suits the song because the effect is to create an unpleasant mood of tension and awkwardness. He looks up as the last notes die. The others are silent.

'It's called *Mr Molester*,' he says.

DJ is the first to respond. 'Okay. Yeah. Some deep stuff there, man. It's very meaningful but, I don't know.' He turns to Elena. 'Do you think it's right for this sort of do?'

'Why wouldn't it be?' says Alex.

DJ is treading carefully. He wants to keep things on an even keel if he can, so he says gently, 'It's an awards evening. It's a celebration of achievement. Isn't it a bit, you know, serious? People won't want to think about the stuff in your song. Not there, not then.'

'Well they should,' Alex snaps. 'Life isn't just sugar and spice, you know.'

To Joey that sounds rich. Alex's parents are among the wealthiest in the town. Sugar and spice are probably all he's ever known.

Elena joins in. 'I think DJ's right. It's a great song,' she adds hurriedly, reading the expression on Alex's face. 'The message is very powerful and I'm sure we should add it to our list. We can put it out on YouTube, but I don't think we should play it at the awards.' Alex says nothing but glares at her. She goes on, 'There are girls at our school who I know have been groomed, or they've got experience of men attempting to groom them...'

'Then they'll know what the song's about,' Alex interrupts. 'And for those who don't it will be a warning.'

'Being groomed is horrible,' Elena continues.

'Starting with something you think is going to be wonderful and exciting, and before you know what's happening being manipulated into doing things that you don't want to do, that's awful. And when you find out what's really going on, well, that's the worst part of all. It can turn a girl over, affect her for years.'

'All the more reason for playing my song,' says Alex. 'Right here, in the middle of the set. You can have your saccharine and candy floss, then *Mr Molester* to bring people down to earth and make them think, then some more saccharine and candy floss to finish up.'

Elena slowly shakes her head. DJ is looking down at his hands.

'Anyway,' Alex says, 'what about *Saturday Girl*? That's about somebody being abused.'

'It's about somebody being dumped,' says DJ. 'Don't you ever listen to the lyrics?'

Alex turns to Joey. 'What do you think?'

Joey doesn't hesitate. 'I think it's a social event, not a social studies lesson.' Joey isn't usually so forthright and his answer surprises them all.

'Three to one,' says DJ.

Alex's anger explodes. He jumps up, tipping over his chair so that it falls with a clatter. 'Thanks a bunch,' he snarls. 'Heaven forbid we do anything that might have some connection with real life.'

'It's not that,' says Elena. 'It's just that after the last time we don't want to upset anybody. We don't want Sutton shutting us down again.'

'Fuck off, all of you.' Alex stamps out, slamming the door.

There's a silence. Quite a long one.

Then, 'Right,' says DJ. 'That went well.'

'It was you, Joey,' says Elena. 'Alex was expecting you to be on his side because he thinks you're the serious one.'

Joey shrugs.

'He also thinks he can push you around,' says DJ.

Joey shrugs again.

DJ starts packing his gear. 'Are you working tonight?' he says.

'Yes,' says Joey.

'I'm picking Mia up from Gym52. I can drop you at *The Golden Bough* on the way.'

'Thanks.' Joey is pleased. It will save him a long wait at the bus stop.

'Do you want me to give you a lift to Alex's?' DJ says to Elena. 'I think he needs talking down. I can go that way if you like.'

She shakes her head. 'No, it's okay. I'll catch him later.'

'Fair enough.'

DJ and Joey go. Elena sits at the keyboard and tries a few chords. She had some piano lessons when she was younger and she got on well, but as she moved into her teens schoolwork, boys and a busy social life took precedence over practising and she dropped them. She plays with one hand the hook from *Mr Molester*. It's catchy, an earworm. What a pity Alex came up with such savage, bitter words to go with it.

She puts on her coat and leaves.

3

Leavers' proms used to be dull and predictable. For most of the girls it was an opportunity to show off their ideas of sophisticated evening wear. The preparations started early – buying, trying, experimenting, exchanging, parading, often with a lot of input from mums. For the boys, it was a chance to show that they were at last breaking free from the traces that had for so long bound them. They too dressed up, most of them in suits and a few even in dinner jackets. Many assumed an air of detachment and spent the time looking with disdain or amusement on the antics of the rest.

Two years ago a new head arrived at the school. Gina Meredith's aim was to make the occasion more of a landmark. Inspired by the high school events she'd seen on her study tour to the U.S.A. she took a fresh approach. There were to be refreshments, made in home economics lessons by students and served by the teachers. There were to be tables and chairs grouped around the edges of the room, with a space for dancing in the middle. And there were to be awards, presented by a guest of honour.

So tonight the sports hall is decorated, there are lights, and two stages are installed. The bands set up their gear and do their sound-checks. The students preen and perfume. The awards night begins.

Vampire Slaves are on first. Alex has been going around all week referring to them as "the support band". That has annoyed them and they feel the need to make an impact. Lacking the ability to do that through their music they rely on fangs and a lot of stage blood. They play what DJ calls "thrash trash", which involves guitar discords and a lot of work on the cymbals. Some of the students hate it and they hang around in sullen groups. However, others love it, and giving up on attempts to dance to the erratic beat they congregate at the front of the hall in a messy crowd.

'I suppose if you can't play, all you've got left is to clown about,' Alex says loudly as the *Slaves* leave the stage.

The halfway point marks the arrival of the guest of honour. There's an expectant hush and attention switches to the main entrance. The sea of students surges forward. Everyone's quiet, some of the girls push to the front while others strain and crane from the back. The doors open, there's a cheer from those who can see, and Theo Vasilias enters with his partner.

'Will you look at that!' Alex gasps. Everyone is already looking. The whole school is mesmerised. Students and staff, male, female and everything in between, fifteen hundred pairs of eyes are all riveted.

"That" is Lita Jordan. Her appearance is different now from when she was on *Love Shack*. On TV she'd been blonde, her skin the colour of honey. Now she's dark and pale, sheathed from neck to ankle in black satin. Jewels glitter at her throat, sparkling with the lustre that can only come from real diamonds. Her eyes are startling, wide with long lashes, on a canvas of green make-up. The multi-million pound Premiership footballer beside her is reduced to a sideshow.

'What a doll,' says Alex, in awe.

'Yes, Barbie,' says Elena, who's annoyed that her boyfriend is salivating so unashamedly over another female.

'And some,' says Alex. 'I wouldn't mind getting my hands on her.'

DJ shakes his head. 'You really are a jerk, you know,' he says to him.

'What do you mean?'

'I mean show the woman some respect. What would you think if people talked about Casia like that?'

'Casia doesn't go flashing her tits on national TV. Anyway, who are you? The bloody vicar?'

DJ sighs. 'By the way, your girlfriend is standing right here. Maybe you can spare some attention for her?'

'Now, now, boys,' says Elena. 'But thanks, DJ. And just for the record, I agree with you.'

Lita's dress looks modest until she walks forward, then it makes its impact. It's slit to her thigh, and open at the back to show a deep V. She has a tiny tattoo, a butterfly, between her shoulder blades. She walks to the stage alongside Theo on four-inch heels no thicker than a pencil. Students are banned from wearing stilettos because of damage to the sports hall floor, and Charlie Dodds winces visibly at every step Lita takes. She makes her way onto the temporary stage and Theo leads her to a chair. Five hundred phones click.

The awards ceremony takes time. There are a dozen prizes, and for each one the nominees are read out. Then the final selection is announced and that person has to emerge from the hall, make their way through a throng of friends who all want to give their congratulations, come to the stage, accept the award, and be photographed with Theo. It's boring. Most of the students aren't within missile range of an award, and some of them are getting restless. Alex consoles himself by watching Lita. She maintains a cool detachment, looking directly ahead most of the time and politely clapping when each award is made. Once she glances up and catches Alex's eye. There's a moment's hesitation, then she smiles softly before looking away. Alex's pulse races.

Eventually, it ends. The winners have all been applauded and Theo has presented each of them with a certificate and a small statuette of a boy and girl together holding aloft a flaming torch. It's time for *Friendly Fire*.

Joey does a few experimental drum shots, DJ tweaks his tuning, Alex cracks his knuckles, Elena clears her throat, Steve Sutton gives them a cautionary look, Alex counts them in and the set begins: *Let's Dance*.

Joey excels, his driving beat creating pure energy. After the first number, he rips off his jacket and throws it to the back of the stage. 'Rock and roll,' someone in the crowd yells.

The band is at its best. Elena is in fine voice, creating in *Saturday Girl* a husky, wounded tone which is both sexy and sad. DJ accomplishes the tricky riff in *Sultans of Swing* with aplomb. Alex is in top form, his fingers running smoothly over the keys, alternately bending over the keyboard and smiling out at the throng. There are plenty of dancers, staff as well as students, and a large group forms in front of the stage. Everything draws wild acclaim, the band's original numbers as much as the covers.

They finish and the crowd wants more. They've called an uneasy truce over *Mr Molester* and Alex has accepted that it won't be included in the set. That only leaves *California Rock Chick*, which they daren't do, so they play *Let's Dance* again. They would have repeated one of the other numbers too but Sutton calls time and the crowd slowly starts to leave.

Elena hugs Alex and DJ. She tries to hug Joey, but it's difficult with him still behind his drums and anyway, he's embarrassed. All of them are sweaty and exhausted.

The hall is emptying. Mia joins them on stage and kisses DJ, a big one full on the lips. 'You were fantastic,' she tells them.

'Great set,' one of DJ's friends calls as he walks past the stage.

'Terrific gig, guys,' somebody else shouts. It's one of the *Vampire Slaves*. Alex gives him the thumbs up.

'Theo and Lita stayed till nearly the end,' says Mia.

'Did they?' says Alex, although he knows they did. He'd watched them constantly, twice caught Lita's eye, once got a smile from her, and he had seen them leave.

He'd hoped that Lita might glance back over her shoulder as she went out but she didn't. He doesn't think it at all absurd that he, a nineteen-year-old nobody, might try to flirt with a celebrity beauty five years his senior, who's engaged to a handsome Premiership footballer and millionaire. Or that he already has a kind, generous and thoughtful girlfriend in Elena.

Charlie Dodds, who'd left the hall with Theo and Lita, is now back. He's talking to a man Alex hasn't seen before. He's older than Charlie and wears a striped suit. His silver hair is tied in a ponytail. There's something about his manner and bearing that makes Alex think he's important. One of the Governors? An influential parent?

'Well done, folks.' It's Steve Sutton. 'Thank you. You did a good job. The Head has had to go but she asked me to pass on her congratulations and appreciation.'

DJ opens his mouth to answer but Alex gets in first. 'No problem,' he says. 'It went well, didn't it?'

The Deputy nods and smiles, and goes to deal with the stragglers in the foyer.

DJ bites back the surge of annoyance he felt when Alex answered. He doesn't want to spoil the evening but there will come a time when Alex has to be put in his place. He unplugs his guitars, puts them in their cases, packs his pedals and coils his cables. The amps, keyboard and drums belong to the school so they stay. Joey has already gone.

'Hell's bells, he left fast,' says Alex. 'Did somebody shout fire?'

'His mum's working and his sister's on her own.'

'Christ, I'm thirsty,' says Elena. 'I've got a throat like a belt sander. You coming?' she says to Alex.

'No, you go, I'll see you in a minute.'

The others leave and Alex stays on the stage, pretending to fiddle with the keyboard lid. He's interested in the man Charlie Dodds is talking with, who's looked several times towards the stage and now points. Charlie and the stranger come towards him.

Four of them are sitting at a table. Elena has coke, Mia has an energy drink, Alex and DJ cappuccinos.

'Joey can't come.' Elena looks glum.

'Why not?' says DJ.

'It's his job at *The Golden Bough*. They want him to start straight away.'

'Mean buggers. Won't they let him have a holiday?'

'It seems not.'

'It's okay though,' says Alex. 'We can manage.'

Elena frowns at him.

'Well we can,' he says. 'If it was me or DJ, or you, there'd be a problem. But I can synth drums on the keyboard, so we don't need Joey.'

The other two stare at him.

'You can be a heartless bastard sometimes,' says DJ.

'But it's true,' Alex persists. 'We can manage.' He stares back at them defiantly.

Alex had been alone on the stage when Charlie

Dodds came over with the distinguished-looking stranger.

'Alex, this is Bruno Sylvani,' he said.

The name rang a bell and Alex thought he ought to know him. A politician? An actor? Somebody on TV?

'Bruno's an old friend of mine,' Charlie had explained. 'He owns S.I.R., Sylvani International Representation. He's Theo's manager.' Alex remembered then. 'It was Bruno who persuaded Theo to be tonight's guest of honour.'

Bruno gave a slight bow and extended his hand. Alex took it and winced. Bruno's grip was firm, on the verge of being painful. His hand was held longer than he expected, and he got a whiff of Bruno's fragrance, masculine and spicy.

'Oh, right,' said Alex, taking his hand back. He waited. Was he supposed to say more? 'Right. Thank you.'

'Theo enjoyed your performance,' said Bruno. 'Lita too. She likes your music.' His voice was rich as chocolate, his words voiced with precision and a marked Italian accent.

'Oh, good,' said Alex, wondering what this was about.

'Bruno has a proposition, a request,' said Charlie. 'I told him it might not be possible, that you probably all have plans for the summer, but... I'll let him explain it to you.'

'Certainly,' said Bruno. He moved a little closer and dropped his voice slightly. 'It's not yet generally known, but Theo and Lita are to be married.'

Not generally known? thought Alex. Elena knew it.

'In fact, the wedding will take place very soon, in a

couple of weeks. I should like to invite *Friendly Fire* to come to Italy, your visit to coincide with the wedding.' Bruno said it with a flourish, like a conjuror whisking away a cloth to reveal a surprise. Alex was lost for words. 'Naturally, you won't attend the wedding itself. Theo is a devout catholic and the ceremony will be in church, with only family and close friends.'

Charlie was almost as excited as Alex and joined in. 'The wedding's low key but there'll be a huge reception, five hundred guests. Bruno's been telling me some of the people who'll be there. Amazing.'

'Although everything, of course, is to be kept top secret,' Bruno had cautioned. 'We wouldn't want the press to know too much about either the occasion or the attendance.'

Alex could find nothing to say and Bruno had seemed to take his hesitation as reservation.

'If you can, if you will,' he said. 'All your travel expenses will be met and you will live on the property. There will be no payment, but my PA will handle the arrangements and if you act as her link you will receive a fee for your time and trouble.'

Some trouble, Alex thought, getting everyone to a gig in Italy. And what a gig. A celebrity wedding. Who knows who they might meet? He had wanted to accept at once, but Bruno insisted he consult with the others. 'The invitation is for all four of you,' he said.

When he'd put it to the rest of the band there had been no discussion. Elena had been wildly excited. She followed Lita on Instagram and as far as she was concerned they were best buddies.

DJ, too, had been keen. 'You mean we get a trip to Italy for nothing?' he said.

'Yes,' said Alex. 'Apparently, Theo's got this big house and there's what Bruno says is a luxury villa in the grounds. We can have the run of it. Cool, or what?'

'Definitely cool,' said DJ. 'It's a no-brainer.'

'And there won't be anyone else staying there? What about the wedding guests?' said Elena.

Alex shrugged. 'Maybe they'll be in the big house, but Bruno did say we'll have the villa to ourselves.'

'And we can stay for as long as we want?'

'Yes. Well no, not forever, obviously. But he said we could get there a few days before the wedding, and we can stay on for a bit after if we like.'

There had been one difficulty: Mia. She wasn't in the band but she was DJ's girlfriend. It turned out to be easily settled. Alex had explained the situation to Bruno's PA and asked if Mia could come as well. She phoned back later the same day. Signor Sylvani would be delighted for this young lady to join the party, and her fare would be paid too. It couldn't be better.

Except that now they've hit a snag. Joey hadn't gone to the green room after the gig. Alex had called him the next morning to give him the news and he'd seemed okay with it; now Elena's reporting that he says he can't go.

'What's the problem?' says Alex.

'He's got no cash,' says Elena. 'I mean none. Zilch. You know what things are like with him. His mum's paid peanuts at the care home and his dad's left them in the lurch.

'But it's all accounted for,' says Alex. 'Theo's covering the travel and our keep.'

'Maybe,' says Elena, 'but he can't go to Italy with no money at all. Could you? Even with everything provided, he's going to need cash to spend on the way. And if he wants to buy anything while he's there, souvenirs or something.'

'I'll lend him some,' says DJ. 'In fact, I'll give it to him.'

'He wouldn't take it,' says Elena. She knows very well that Joey's family may be poor but he's proud. He'd find a handout too embarrassing, and he could even see the offer as an insult. 'Anyway, it's not just the money,' says Elena. '*The Golden Bough* are being arsey. They want him to start working there straight away, now all his exams are over, and they're not happy about him putting it off.'

'It'll only be for a week, ten days at the most.'

'That may be, but they still don't like it.'

'He should tell them to go fuck themselves,' says Alex.

Elena sighs, and not for the first time is struck by Alex's complete failure to understand what it means to be in a situation like Joey's.

There's silence.

'We can't go without Joey,' says DJ. 'He's part of the band.'

'What? So just because Joey can't go the rest of us can't either? If he can't, none of us can? Is that what you're saying?' Alex is outraged because he feels that the opportunity for the trip is due to him and he can see it slipping away.

Elena puts her foot down. 'We can't leave Joey behind,' she says. 'We're all going off in different

33

directions in a few weeks. It might be the last chance we ever get to spend time together.

'Can't Joey tell these restaurant dudes he's already booked to go away?' says DJ. 'They've got to let him have a holiday. He can't go straight from school into work without a break.'

'It'll be okay,' says Alex. He's getting used to the idea of there being no drummer and he quite likes it. If he provides the rhythm from the keyboards it will give him more control over the band's output, their tempo, attack and overall sound. 'We'll miss him, 'course we will,' he adds hurriedly, seeing Elena's expression, 'but we'll manage.'

'No we won't,' says Elena. She folds her arms. 'If Joey doesn't go, neither do I.'

Alex has seen this body language from Elena before. He knows she means what she says. 'It's a pity we're not getting paid for it,' he says. 'If we were that would solve his problem. Well, one of them.'

'Hey, there's an idea,' says DJ. 'You say Joey won't take money from us. So tell him that Bruno's changed his mind and Theo's going to pay us. If each of us puts twenty-five quid in the kitty, that will be a hundred. Tell him that's his share. It should keep him going.'

Mia is silent. She's not as badly off as Joey, but money has never flowed as freely in her home as it seems to do with DJ, Elena and Alex, and it's never treated casually. Finding twenty-five pounds for Joey will make a hole in what she was hoping to take for herself.

Elena seems to know what she's thinking. 'Not Mia,' she says. 'It's not fair to ask her because she's not in the band. Let's us three make it thirty each. That will give Joey ninety, and that should be enough.'

'Right,' says Alex. 'So assuming Joey can fix it with the restaurant, that means we can go. Have you told your folks yet?' he asks DJ.

'No. You told yours?'

'Mine won't give a shit,' says Alex. 'What about yours?' he says to Elena.

'They're paying me to work in the pub for the holidays, but I'm sure I can talk them into letting me go for a week or so.'

'So they should,' says Alex. 'Playing at a celeb wedding. How cool is that?'

There's silence while the three think about the amazing world that has just opened to them. They don't know then how much it's going to change them.

5

Elena is unloading the dishwasher and stacking the glasses on shelves. It's part of the routine she's taken over now she's working in the bar.

'So it will be you, DJ, Alex, and Joey,' says her father.

'And Mia. They've agreed to pay for her too.'

'Have they now? Theo must be pretty keen to have you there, then.'

'And pretty loaded too,' says her mother. 'It will be nice to have another girl to talk to.'

'Talking won't be a problem,' says her father. 'It's shutting her up that's the hard bit.'

Elena throws a bar cloth at him.

'Anyway,' says her mother, 'it will be a good opportunity for you to practice your Italian.'

Elena nods. She's got a GCSE in Italian and has been to Italy before, once on a package to Rimini with her parents, when everybody spoke English and all they did was sunbathe on a very crowded beach, and once with the Year 11 languages group from school. They'd gone to Venice, but most of them had been far more interested in checking out the local talent than in speaking the language. And anyway, all the teenagers they'd met had wanted to show off their English.

'And you might meet a *nice* boyfriend. Then you can dump the one you've got.' Elena's mother has never liked Alex.

'Where is this Castle...?'

'Castelvecchio. Vecchia means old. It's in Tuscany, not far from Florence.'

'I've been to Tuscany,' says her father. 'Years ago, before I knew your mother. It's beautiful. Vineyards, olive groves, wooded hills, and some amazing houses. If this Theo guy owns one of those he must be doing something right, even if it isn't scoring goals for us.'

'Sounds lovely,' says her mother. 'You'll have to be sure to take something warm, though. The Tylers down the road went to Tuscany last summer, and Joyce said the evenings can get quite chilly in the hills.'

'Yeah, okay mum.' Elena gives her a peck on the cheek. 'I've got to go,' she says.

There's a silence after she's left. Then her mother says, 'What do you think?'

'About her going? I think it will be fine, don't you?'

'I don't know. Who is this Bruno? We don't know him, and he's inviting her to go with him to a foreign country.'

'It's not just Elena. There are five of them, and three are boys. And she's nineteen, not nine. It will be a great experience for her before she goes to university. The pub can struggle along without her for a few days.'

'You sound very laid back about it all. I'm not so sure. You hear such horrible stories.'

'Give them some credit for common sense. They're not kids. They're all old enough to vote. Jesus, they could even fight for their country. And two of the lads are big. I wouldn't want to mess with Alex, and especially not with DJ.'

'But don't you think it's strange that a celebrity couple would have a school band to play at their wedding?'

'I don't expect they'll be *the* band. That will be a proper group. They'll be more of a support act I expect. Anyway, they're good. They've got some good songs. A lot of people liked them when they played here. It's just that most of the regulars prefer folk music and weren't that struck, otherwise we'd have had them play a lot more.'

'And he's going to pay money to get them there? A support band?'

'Why not? Theo's got megabucks. Getting the five of them out there, keeping them and sending them home again will cost him less than half a day's pay.'

Elena's mum is still looking worried. 'Why don't we talk to the other parents?' she says.

'I don't know Joey's or Mia's parents. I don't think Joey has a dad, it's just his mum. We don't get on with Alex's folks and I wouldn't want to discuss it with them. But I'll phone DJ's dad if you like.'

'Yes,' she says. 'Do that.'

~

'We've talked about this,' says Alex's father. 'You've told us you don't want to start at Plymouth until next year, and that the university has agreed to hold your place for you. You did that without consulting us first, so why are you bothering to tell us about this Italian jaunt? Will what we say make any difference to you?'

Alex doesn't answer. He would have been wrong to accept Bruno's invitation without telling his parents, but now it seems he's wrong for telling them.

'You know the agreement,' his father continues. 'We've done the same for you as we did for your sister. When Casia got into Durham we put aside a sum to cover her fees, accommodation and living expenses for three years. It's worked fine for her. She went straight from school to university and she'll come out without any debts. We're not going to pay for you to hang about for a year. Whatever you spend now, on jaunts to Italy or anything else, you'll have to find yourself.'

That's twice his father has referred to the Italian trip as a 'jaunt'. It's obvious he sees it as something trivial, a pleasure outing rather than a new experience, an opportunity, and perhaps even the chance to meet some influential people. His parents hoped that he would join his father's accountancy firm. In their view studying Oceanography at Plymouth isn't at all an acceptable alternative. There have been many arguments about this and the message is clear and Alex is under no illusion: he's on his own. They don't care whether he goes to Italy or not, or even about what happens to him while he's there.

'He wants you to go where?' DJ's mother is sceptical.

'Castelvecchio. It's in Italy.'

'I guessed that.'

'It's Theo's place.'

'Oh, it's Theo now, is it? On first-name terms with an international footballer are we?'

His dad frowns. Not at DJ but at his mother. Her caution is for the boy's protection, he knows that, but it comes across as hostility.

'How long will you be away?' says his mother.

'Alex says we're invited to go there a few days before the wedding, to get ready, and then we can stay on a few days after. Probably about a week, maybe a bit more.'

'How will you get there?'

'We thought on the train.'

'*We* thought. You've discussed it.'

He ignores that. Does she think that the band wouldn't have talked about it? 'Bruno's assistant says it will be better to go by train because we'll have too much stuff to fly. That way I'll be able to take both my guitars.'

'Bruno?

'Bruno Sylvani. He's Theo's agent.'

'You've got it all worked out then.'

'What about the drums?' says his dad. 'And Alex's keyboards?' It's a practical question. His father has always been more interested than his mother in the band.

'This is the good bit. Castelvecchio used to belong to

some Italian rock star and it's got a proper recording studio. There's drums and keyboards and everything.'

'Sounds great,' says his dad.

There's a long silence.

'Well?' DJ says.

'If you've already arranged everything it seems a bit pointless asking us,' says his mother, with a shrug. 'Anyway, now you're eighteen we can't stop you.' She sounds resentful, as if she would stop him if she could.

His father reflects that they couldn't stop DJ from doing what he wanted long before he got to eighteen. His tone is more encouraging. 'It sounds terrific,' he says. 'I wish I could have a free week in Italy. And you might meet some interesting people.'

'You need to be careful,' says his mother. 'You don't know this man, so keep your wits about you.' She looks at her watch. "I must go,' she says, getting up from the kitchen table. In the doorway she turns back towards him. 'You'll have to use your own money,' she says.

It's her parting shot, a last attempt to exert some control over an event that half an hour before wasn't on her radar.

$\sim$

'And they're going to pay for you too? Are you sure?' says Angelina, Mia's mum.

'Yes. that's what Alex said.'

'Why on earth would they do that? You're not even in the band.' This is Ant, Mia's half-brother. He's two years younger than she is and on the verge of entering the 6th Form, but reluctantly and only because he can't think of anything else to do.

'Alex told them I'm a sort of super roadie, tuning the guitars, tightening the drum heads, making sure they all have the same set list, that sort of thing.'

'And do you do that?' says Angelina.

'Course she doesn't,' says Ant. 'It's a fucking con.'

'Language!' says Angelina, glancing at Lou, the youngest, who's sitting on the sofa colouring. She doesn't appear to be listening.

Mia is resentful of Ant's abrupt dismissal. 'Well, I did come up with the name for the band.'

'Did you?' says Angelina. 'What is it?'

'*Friendly Fire*,' says Mia.

'Crap,' says Ant.

'Take no notice of him, love,' says her mother. 'You go. It will do you good. You'd better watch the pasta, though. The Italians eat a lot of it, and you don't want to be carrying a load of lard when you start on your Sport Science.'

Mia's not worried about that. She eats what she likes and never puts on weight.

'Sport Science?' says Ant, mockingly. 'What sort of Mickey Mouse subject is that? What's sport got to do with science?'

Mia is used to this scathing response because it's an argument they've had before, but she can't help rising to it. 'Sport Science is about how your body works during exercise. Well, not yours because you never do any, but other people's. Studying the body includes Biology, Chemistry, Engineering, and Physics. How people behave when taking part in or watching sport involves Sociology and Psychology. The organisation of sport overlaps Sociology and Economics. All this may be easy stuff to a manly genius like you, but for a simple girl like me it's pretty scientific.'

Ant isn't impressed. 'Still sounds crap,' he says.

Angelina sighs. 'Now come on, you two, give it a rest. You don't have to be on at each other all the time.' Mia and Ant have never got on, not since he first arrived with Michael, her stepfather, a couple of years ago. 'I hope you have some fun,' Angelina continues. 'But you know I can't give you any money. You could ask Michael, he might have some. You've got a bit saved up, haven't you?'

Mia has a little earned from her part-time job at Gym52 but it's not a lot. She's not going to ask Michael for help, though. He's never laid a finger on her, but there's something in the way he stares at her that makes her think that it sometimes crosses his mind. The looks have become more obvious over the past year, particularly when he's been drinking. He's commented on her figure too, although never when Angelina's been around. Mia has now taken to locking her bedroom door when Angelina is working nights. She doesn't want to be in Michael's debt.

She kisses her mother's cheek. 'Thanks, Mum. The trip's all paid for and I won't need much spending money. I'll be fine.'

'Lucky cow,' mutters Ant as she leaves.

Joey is in his bedroom. He's at a small table he uses for his homework, or for what in the 6th Form was called "Independent Study". However, he's not busy with homework; exams are over and there's no more to do. He doesn't think he's done very well. His writing isn't fluent and he finds reading hard. He now knows he's dyslexic, but that wasn't spotted until he was well into secondary school. By that time he'd been labelled "thick" and it's been hard to shake it off.

He envies people like Elena who seem to find reading and writing so easy. If he tries, if he really concentrates, he can force some sort of order on the squiggles on a page, but it takes time. Luckily he has an excellent memory. He can remember recipes and he's good at mental arithmetic, easily scaling quantities up or down and converting measurements to meet what he needs for a dish.

The exams ambushed him. They were like Christmas; advertised a long way ahead, slow to approach, and then suddenly upon him and over. He doesn't think he's done well. Although there's no school homework any more there will be some theory work when his traineeship and college day release start. They told him at *The Golden Bough* that there'd be a lot.

'*The Golden Bough*,' his mother had said when he'd told her the outcome of his interview. 'I can't believe it. My lad working at a posh place like that.'

Joey is filling in a form. It's headed *Application for*

Unpaid Leave of Absence. The first section – name, address, date of birth, National Insurance Number – is straightforward. Then it gets more difficult. What dates will he be away? He knows when they're going because Alex has told him, but he's also said that the return ticket is open and can be used anytime. What should he put? He thinks a week. That seems a reasonable length of time, although when he'd asked permission to be away the manager hadn't wanted him to go at all. *Purpose of absence?* He can't say to play the drums at the marriage of a football star to a sexy celeb. He writes *To study Italian cuisine*. He practices his signature a couple of times and then signs the form. He examines the result. It seems such a grown-up thing to do, signing an official form. He puts the paper in an envelope and seals it.

He goes to the cupboard where he keeps his clothes and gets his passport out of the drawer. It's a child's passport and he looks a lot younger in the photo, but it's clearly him. He got it before his father left and the family was still together. At the time his father was earning good money as a plasterer and they'd gone to Disneyland for a week. The passport still has a year left. That's as well, because he can't afford an adult passport. Not yet.

He puts the passport in his backpack, then goes to the bathroom and locks the door. He kneels beside the bath and pops out the acrylic panel. He's done it before and it's easy now. He reaches underneath the bath and gropes until his fingers find a plastic bag. He takes out thirty pounds, thinks for a moment, and then takes another twenty. He's disappointed at the little that's left and he puts ten back. Forty pounds ought to be enough.

He reaches back under the bath and replaces the bag. He pops the panel back into place, then flushes the lavatory and goes back to his bedroom. There and then he resolves what he's going to do with his first wage from *The Golden Bough*; it's not hide it behind the bath.

6

Alex put the phone down. He thought for a moment, then Googled "Bruno Sylvani". The search brought up plenty of references – links to social media, press stories and of course Wikipedia. He clicked on that.

Bruno Enrico Sylvani (b. Ravenna, 25 March 1955) is the founder and owner of Sylvani International Representation (SIR), recently named by Forbes magazine as one of the three most powerful sports agencies in the world.

He is from an influential family with interests in property development, mining, and transport. He began his career as a football agent before extending into other areas, and he now manages the interests of a wide range of high-profile sportsmen and women as well as personalities from the world of entertainment and the media.

There followed a list of Bruno's clients. Some of them he hadn't heard of but a few were well known. There was a short account of Bruno's early career and the details of several large deals he'd brokered, then,

Sylvani's net worth is undisclosed but is thought to be over one billion dollars. He has homes in London, Italy, Monte Carlo and Los Angeles. He is married to Tania Incantare.

Alex clicked on Tania's name and was taken to the image of an extremely glamorous woman. The entry for her was much briefer. It told him that she had married Sylvani twenty years earlier and had a career in film and TV before moving into "creating events and experiences", which she calls "action art". There were the titles, in Italian, of some films she'd been in but Alex knew none of them.

He put her name in Google and clicked on images. There were photos of Tania taken from modelling shoots, together with stills from her movies. Some of the pictures looked like extravagant theatrical productions, with huge casts, elaborate settings, and lavish lighting. One scene was of girls dressed as nymphs being chased through the trees by creatures that were half man and half goat. He clicked on some of them to find out what they were, but all he got were captions such as *Extravaganza 119*, or *Entertainment for the Sultan of Brunei*. Further on were shots of her at events, usually with Bruno. She was very photogenic and had amazing eyes, which contributed to a disconcerting impression of mystery. Alex couldn't properly put it into words, but her expression was at the same time both intimate and distant; as if she knew something about you that you didn't even know yourself, but anyway didn't care.

~

He meets the others in *The Green Man*, all except Joey who is working at the restaurant. The back room is empty apart from two old men playing dominoes and they find a table. Elena fetches drinks but makes them pay.

'My parents run a pub, not a charity stall,' she says.

Alex tells them about looking up Bruno on Google. Elena checks on her phone.

'He seems a pretty important guy,' she says. 'And his wife, wow, she looks amazing. She's like a fairy. And those shows she puts on are incredible.' She turns her phone so that DJ and Mia can see. 'The thing I don't get is why us? With the money he's got they could hire professionals. I was reading that when Tony Coe got married last year they had Boy George.'

'Yeah, but that was fucking City,' says DJ. 'Anyway, who'd want Boy George?'

'It is strange,' Mia agrees. 'He hears you play once and then books you for a really important event. Not that you weren't very good,' she adds quickly, 'You were great but, well, it's surprising.'

'It was Lita who wanted us,' says Alex.

'We've got two choices,' says DJ. 'We go, or we don't go. Simple as that.'

There's silence. All of them have already got used to the idea of going. They've thought about it, dreamt about it, and have started making preparations. They've told their friends. The idea that they might not go is a non-starter.

'There's only one choice actually,' says Alex. 'We've got these.' He takes a fat packet from his backpack and tips out a collection of envelopes.

'What are those?' says Mia, picking up one of the envelopes.

'The tickets.'

'Jesus,' says DJ.

'Already?' says Elena.

'Came this afternoon,' says Alex. 'A courier brought them from Bruno's office, on a motorbike.'

'A courier,' says Elena. 'He must be keen.'

'These are train tickets,' says DJ, examining one of the envelopes. 'I thought we'd be flying.' He sounds disappointed.

'Bruno's assistant said we'd be able to take more baggage on the train.'

'We may not be flying,' says Elena, but have you seen this? We're Premier Class on Eurostar.' She flashes the tickets. 'You know, I bet this is more expensive than the 'plane. When I went to look round St Andrews it was cheaper to fly from Birmingham to Edinburgh than go by rail.'

'I think that settles whether or not he means it, don't you?' says Alex.

'We go,' says DJ.

That night Alex dreams of Lita. The voice is Elena's but the face and body are undoubtedly Lita's, provoked probably by the images of her he's been studying on his phone. The dream is intensely erotic, and he wakes up hot and clammy. He wriggles out of his shorts and drops them on the floor beside the bed. With a vague sense of guilt he thinks about Elena.

She's okay. No, she's more than that. She's warm-hearted and easy to get on with. She's thoughtful and generous. She's got a great sense of humour and she can see the funny side of most things. She's good company. She's super smart, predicted to get straight As in all her subjects, and likely an A* in two. Unlike other girlfriends he's had, she seems to care nothing for his family's money, which is a bit of a relief because he has no access to that.

He doesn't know anyone who dislikes her, but what does he himself feel? Really? He can't say. She has all these wonderful qualities, but somehow something isn't quite right for him and he's not sure what.

A mile away in another part of the town, tidy and well kept but nowhere near as spacious and affluent as the district where Alex lives, DJ is walking home. After he and Mia left *The Green Man* they went to his house. He spent the time learning to use a new guitar pedal, laying down some riffs that he then played over and added some effects. Mia lay on his bed, listening to him and reading. Then he took her home. The area where she lives has a dodgy side and he's not happy with her walking home alone; she won't hear of having an Uber, which she thinks is wasteful and emblematic of everything that's ruining both the climate and the economy.

They don't ever say much when they're together. For DJ that's a plus. He thinks a lot but he doesn't often share his thoughts, and he doesn't like girls who are always talking. Before he took up with Mia he used to spend a lot of time with Elena. He still likes her and they've been friends forever, but she was always going on at him to discuss things, to say more, to reveal parts of himself that he could barely put into words, let alone parade before someone else. His closeness to Elena was never what you might call a relationship, and it was already cooling when Mia arrived in the 6th Form from another school. They seemed to click straight away. Will a week with her in Italy take that to the next stage? He hopes so.

7

Elena was not the first person Mia met when she started at her new school, but she was the one who made the greatest impression in those early, unsure days.

Mia was emerging from a difficult and hurtful period. She had been a little girl when a teacher at her primary school spotted in her suppleness, strength and coordination the potential to be a high-performing gymnast. She worked hard, and her mentor put forward the possibility of her getting into the British Gymnastics Squad. She was invited to national development sessions and spent many hours in training. She was never quite good enough for the topmost honours but she stuck at it until, at thirteen, she was told she was too old. Too old at thirteen. The news was shattering, particularly as it came only six months after her father's death from cancer. Two years later her mother married Michael. It didn't mean a new father, it never could, but it did mean a new home, new siblings, and a new school.

Mia and Elena quickly became friends. Mia was drawn to Elena's steadiness, while Elena saw Mia's background as excitingly different from her own humdrum existence at *The Green Man*. They shared plans, dreams, secrets, hopes, and views of their world and the people in it. But seventeen is a time of flux when things change quickly. Elena helped out more at the pub. Mia got a part-time job at a local fitness centre. Elena started going out with Alex. Mia found herself spending more and more time with DJ. And of course, there were exams and the increasing imperatives of learning and revision. They met less, talked less, and shared less.

So when Elena suggests that they should hit the shops together to prepare for Italy Mia is pleased, but she's also cautious. She's pleased at the prospect of spending an afternoon with her friend but she's wary about how it might turn out. Elena sees herself as an arbiter of fashion, and her likes and dislikes are uncompromising. She invariably has opinions about what other people are wearing, and she isn't slow to share them. This makes Mia feel that anything she might choose to buy will have to pass Elena's scrutiny first.

There's also the question of money. Mia's job at Gym52 doesn't pay much and she's trying to save for university. On the other hand, Elena always seems to have plenty of spare cash. Therefore she's relieved when before they start Elena says, 'You spend what you like but I'm limiting myself. I've got some holiday stuff already, left over from last year, and we won't need much. We'll only be there for a week, won't we?'

She feels even better when Elena says that she always likes what Mia wears and will welcome her advice.

They go to the mall and begin to work their way through the hottest fashion stores. Elena buys a couple of tops, a swimsuit (one piece, 'So it hides my spare tyre'), some wraps and a pair of sandals.

'I need something to wear at the gig,' she says. 'I can't believe I'm going to be singing to a load of stars and celebs. It's got to be extra special for that.'

Elena is keen on some leather-look leggings and a puff-sleeve blouse. Mia has come to the conclusion that Elena is at least one size bigger than she thinks she is, and while the blouse is nice the leggings are not good. She finds her a corset mini-dress in black satin, in what she judges to be Elena's true size. It's not something Mia would choose for herself but Elena is delighted with it.

'It looks so good on you,' says Mia, 'it really does.' She's right. It pinches in Elena's waist, shows off her long legs, and makes the very most of her blonde hair and blooming complexion. 'Sexy and sophisticated. You'll be a sensation.'

They go for coffee.

'I wonder who'll be at the wedding,' says Mia.

'It's not the actual wedding,' says Elena. 'I mean, not the ceremony. That'll be in a church somewhere. It's a do they're having afterwards.'

'There'll be some soccer players there for sure,' says Mia.

'And some TV people. I bet there'll be some of the other contestants from *Love Shack*.'

'Maybe. Not Bobby Carroll, though.'

Both of them laugh. Mia is referring to Lita's screen partner in the TV show and the rumours in the tabloids of a liaison between them.

Elena becomes serious. 'I'm really looking forward to it, but I don't mind telling you the thought of playing in front of all those celebs is scary. I'm nervous.'

'No need to be,' says Mia. 'You'll be great.' Mia knows she will and is excited for her. 'What do I owe you for the coffee?'

'Nothing. It's on me. Let's get the bus.'

Mia has bought nothing but Elena doesn't seem to notice, and she realises as they walk to the bus stop that the trip was always intended to be for Elena's benefit, not hers. She doesn't mind that, and is relieved, and happy that her initial anxiety was unnecessary.

The boys' preparations are simpler. For Joey it's easy. He doesn't have many clothes beyond his school uniform and he has little money, so his kit is made up of his best two pairs of jeans, a few T-shirts, and underwear. Alex is something of a peacock, but he and DJ make similar decisions to Joey's, although for both of them the jeans are designer label, not factory shop.

Alex spends some time on the phone to Bruno's assistant to check on and finalise the arrangements. They'll leave from St Pancras on the Eurostar, and by what seems to be a complicated route involving several changes, arrive at Florence, where a car will pick them up at the station to take them to Castelvecchio.

The Eurostar is scheduled to leave just before noon, so they agree to meet at St Pancras at 10.00. Alex and Elena start the night before because Alex's uncle has a big house in Norwood and will put them up overnight. They're disappointed to find they've been given separate rooms, both with single beds. After a meal that seems to go on forever, they go upstairs and opt for Elena's room because it's bigger.

After a couple of hours, Alex gets up.

'What's the matter?' Elena asks sleepily.

'That bed's too fucking small,' he says. 'I can't get comfortable. Besides, you're boiling. It's like trying to sleep next to a furnace.'

'I thought you liked it that I'm hot.'

'I'm going next door. Anyway, it will be better if both beds have been slept in.'

'Better for who?' says Elena, but Alex has gone.

They rise early, pick at the over-elaborate breakfast Alex's aunt has prepared, leave as soon as they decently can and walk to Norwood Junction to catch a train to St Pancras. They don't say much on the way. Both are disappointed that their first whole night together wasn't more memorable.

When they get to the station the other three are already there, sitting in the Eurostar waiting area. Mia and DJ are close together, Joey a little way off. Mia and DJ have a large backpack each, and Joey has a smaller one. DJ has two guitar cases. Alex and Elena add their bags to the pile. Elena's case is by far the biggest. Mia remembers how when they were shopping together Elena had talked about not taking very much. Obviously, she's changed her mind.

'You look wasted,' Alex says to DJ.

'Thanks,' says DJ.

'When did you get here?' says Alex.

'About an hour ago. DJ's dad brought us,' says Mia.

'Good on him. What time did you have to leave?'

'Five thirty,' DJ says grumpily.

'Jesus,' says Alex. 'Okay?' he says turning to Joey, who nods. 'What's in the bag?' He's referring to a plastic carrier Joey's nursing.

'Sandwiches,' says Joey. 'My mam made them for the journey.'

'You won't need them,' says Alex. 'Lunch on the Eurostar is included with the Premier Class tickets. Chuck 'em.' He gestures towards the bin.

Joey can't bring himself to throw away unopened the food his mother had got up early to prepare for him so he stows the carrier in his backpack.

'Right,' says Alex, consulting the departure board. 'I think we can check in.'

He leads the way towards the desk, leaving Elena to struggle with her case. The others gather their belongings and follow. DJ is starting to resent the way that Alex seems to think he's in charge of everything, but he doesn't have the energy to challenge him.

All five of them are suffering from lack of sleep, and three of them from various degrees of hangover. Elena had brought a bottle of vodka from the pub and last night she and Alex drank most of it. Mia had gone round to DJ's. His parents had been out, and DJ had seen this and his imminent departure as an opportunity to reduce their stock of alcohol. Mia hardly drinks but DJ had enough for both of them, starting on his dad's beer and moving on to half a bottle of port he found in a cupboard. Joey hadn't drunk anything. *The Golden Bough* had insisted that he work his last shift to the end and he got home late, stone-cold sober.

There's a long check-in line but finally they're through to the platform.

'Well, here we go,' says Alex. He angles his phone and does a selfie, himself in the foreground and the others behind. '*Friendly Fire* on the road. I suppose you could call this our first international tour.'

'It's our first tour of any sort,' says Elena. She wonders if it will also be their last. Is there any future for the band? That might depend on what happens in Italy.

The carriage seems almost new and the seats are covered in soft, blue leather. There are neat tables, and a screen to inform passengers about the journey. There are four seats at a table and one across the gangway. Elena sees that Joey is moving towards the single seat and she doesn't want him to be on his own, so she gets in first.

'Do you mind if I have this one?' she says. 'I need to stretch out.'

'Oh. 'Course not,' says Joey, and he joins Alex, DJ and Mia.

'Hey, not bad,' says Elena, sinking into the seat and reclining it.

'Premier,' says Alex. 'Bit better than standard, eh?' He sounds as if he's responsible for it.

Joey's looking around, eager to take in everything. Eurostar is a new experience for all of them but Joey seems more impressed than the rest.

The train pulls away, easing along the track towards Stratford. Alex keeps up a commentary. 'Those are barriers to cut down noise,' he says, pointing at the tall panels that block the view in many places. 'See that? It's the Olympic Stadium. And that one there's the Aquatics Centre.'

'What's that between them?' says Joey.

Mia is listening politely, Elena is looking out on the other side of the train and DJ seems to be asleep. Alex is delighted that somebody's interested. 'It's the Orbit Tower,' he says. 'It was designed by Anish Kapoor.'

'Who?'

'He's a sculptor. It was put up for the 2012 Olympics and it's the largest piece of public art in the country. See, it's got a slide running around it. That's the world's tallest and longest tunnel slide.'

Joey is impressed but DJ isn't. 'For fuck's sake, Alex, are you going to go on like this all the way?' he says, rousing himself. 'What are you, some sort of guidebook?'

Alex assumes a sulky silence.

Lunch arrives on five trays. It's stuffed tomatoes, a roll and a slice of tart with some sort of topping. Alex was expecting more.

'Is there no choice?' he asks the waiter.

'The food is chosen from the online menu at the time of booking. These are all the vegan option.'

'Bruno's assistant must have decided on that,' he says to the table, 'without asking.'

'Probably sensible really,' says Elena, making peace. 'I suppose she was playing safe. Non-vegans can eat vegan food but not vice versa.'

'But none of us is vegan,' he says.

'I'm vegetarian,' says Mia.

'Oh yes. Right.'

'Tastes good, anyway,' says Elena, who's already started.

Alex pushes his away. 'You can have mine,' he says. The lack of choice over the food is a further affront, following hard on DJ's rejection of his tour guidance. However, he cheers up when the waiter returns with a bottle of Veuve Cliquot.

'This was ordered for your party,' he says, showing Alex the label and starting work on the cork. 'Included in the booking, with the complements of...' he consults a slip of paper, 'Mr Sylvani.'

He fills the glasses. Mia takes a sip and pushes her glass towards DJ.

'Don't you like it?' says Alex, astonished.

'It's all right,' says Mia. 'but it's not all it's cracked up to be. DJ likes champagne better than me, he can have mine.'

Alex looks towards Elena hoping that she might do the same for him but there's no chance. He raises his glass. 'Good old Bruno,' he says. 'Here's to him, and to our trip.'

'To our trip,' says Elena. 'It's like a dream.'

STAGE 1 - LIGHT SLEEP

When Elena had looked at the itinerary provided by Bruno's assistant the journey had seemed simple. It turns out to be not so. It's late afternoon when they arrive in Paris, where they have to change stations. That means a short journey on the RER before catching another train that takes them across central France. They go through areas whose names Elena has only seen before on wine bottles.

Three hours later they reach Geneva, where they have to change trains again. Already Elena's suitcase and DJ's two guitars are proving a nuisance, and they all pitch in to get them on and off the trains.

This leg of the journey is much slower than the previous one, and they trundle first around Lac Léman, along Lac Lausanne and finally into Bern. There they take the local line to Gare de Brigue and then another one to Domodossola. By now Elena is thoroughly fed up and regrets packing so much, and DJ is wishing he'd relied on the guitars Alex had said would be in the studio rather than bringing his own.

'What do we do now?' Joey says, looking at the deserted platforms.

Alex consults the schedule. 'We wait.'

'Jesus,' says DJ, 'I'm glad you've got all this written down. It would be a nightmare if we had to figure it out ourselves.'

'How long do we wait?' says Elena.

'Till...just a minute...four fifty-six,' says Alex.

'And what time is it now?'

'Just after one.'

'Holy shit,' says DJ.

'Do you think the rest of us could have copies of that itinerary?' says Elena. 'Rather than you keeping it to yourself?'

'Oh, right,' says Alex. 'Just wait while I get my portable photocopier out of my backpack and I'll do one for you.'

'Now now, children,' says Mia. 'You could take a piccy of it, on your phone.'

'Never mind,' says Elena, looking sulky. 'It's just that it would be nice if we were occasionally allowed to know what's going on.'

'Where are we?' says Joey.

'Why, we're here,' says Alex.

'He knows that, fuckbrain,' says DJ. 'He means what town.'

'Yeah,' says Joey. The wearisome journey is making them all irritable.

'Domodossola,' says Alex, gesturing at one of the station name boards.

'I never saw the alps,' says Mia, disappointed.

'No, it was dark,' says Alex.

Elena voices what they're all thinking. 'What are we going to do for four whole hours?'

DJ shrugs and looks around at the almost deserted station. 'Not much on offer, is there?'

'I think we should get some rest if we can,' says Alex.

Nearby is a door marked Sala d'attesa. 'I think that's a waiting room,' says Elena.

It is, but it's severe and uninviting, with slatted wooden benches and harsh, unforgiving lights.

'What a hole,' says Alex.

'Hey, it is what it is,' says DJ, 'and we have no choice.' He starts to bed down on one of the benches, using his backpack as a pillow and wrapping himself in his hoody.

'I've got a half bottle of vodka,' says Elena. 'Anybody else got anything?' None of them has. She passes the bottle around. Mia and Joey pass.

The station is desolate, everything closed. Mia gets out her purse, pink and in the shape of a heart, and goes to a clutch of vending machines. She buys a chocolate bar and a coke. Nobody else wants anything.

They wait. One by one they all fall asleep.

The next segment of their journey takes them to Milan, where they're due a little after six. By this time everyone is beyond grumpy. Their eyes prickle and they could do with a change of clothes. Mia furtively sniffs her armpit and wrinkles her nose. Elena's mouth feels as though a small creature has crawled into it and died. She wishes she'd put some mints or a tube of toothpaste in her bag. Her washing things are in her case and she can't be bothered looking for them. She rubs her teeth with her finger, trying to remove the fur. They're all wondering what possessed Bruno's assistant to send them this convoluted way rather than by air.

Ages ago, somewhere in France, DJ spilt milky coffee on his shirt. At first it wasn't too bad but now it smells. He's wondering if he has time to get a clean one from his backpack before they get into Milan when he becomes aware of Mia scrabbling in her shoulder bag. Something's bothering her.

'What's up?'

She doesn't stop but continues rummaging, becoming more agitated by the second. 'My purse. It's gone.'

'What do you mean, gone?'

'It's not there. It's missing. I had it at that last place we stopped but now it's gone.'

'It can't be.'

'It is.' She tips out the contents of her bag. 'Look.' She shakes the bag to show it's empty and pushes around the pile of contents on the table. Phone, keys, make-up bag, tissues, lipstick, tampon, travel mirror, two pens, notepad, bent postcard, paperback, half a tube of wine gums. No purse.

'You haven't put it somewhere else?' says Elena.

'Where else would I put it?'

'What was in it?' says DJ.

'Most of my euros. About a hundred and fifty.'

'Fuck me, why so much?' says Alex. 'I've only brought fifty. It's not as if there'll be anything to spend it on.'

'No credit cards?' says DJ.

'No, I keep them separate, thank goodness.'

'It must be somewhere,' says Elena.

'Well of course it is,' snaps Mia, who is close to tears. 'It's just not here.'

'Have you dropped it?'

They all search to see if it's fallen on the carriage floor.

'Somebody's nicked it,' says DJ. 'At that place where we had the long wait.'

'Yes, Domodossola,' says Alex. 'There was a scruffy-looking bloke hanging around the station, seemed like a homeless guy. He looked to be watching the waiting room where we were. I bet he saw you with it at the vending machine and waited till we were all asleep, then crept in and took it. Where was it?'

'In my bag.' Mia covers her face with her hands and begins to cry. DJ puts his arm around her. 'It's okay,' he says. 'It's one of those things.'

Elena, across the table, takes her hand.

Alex isn't so sympathetic. 'Don't worry,' he says, 'it's only money.'

DJ glares at him. It's the sort of crass remark that only a person who has never wanted for anything would make.

'We'll have a whip round,' says Joey.

Mia is touched. He's the one of the five of them who can least afford to do that.

There's no time for more because they're entering the station. They gather their things and tumble out onto the platform. Mia feels as though she's been mugged, and is kicking herself for not being more careful. She tries to remember. Did she fasten her bag? Where was it when she was sleeping? Why didn't she put the purse in her pocket? The fact that everybody, even Alex, is being especially nice to her somehow makes it worse.

Milan is an easy change and there's only a short wait before they settle down for the last lap, the two-hour journey to Florence. Mia is no longer tearful, but her eyes are red and her mouth turns down.

'Right, the final leg,' says Alex, settling into his seat. Elena snuggles up to him and rests her head on his shoulder. They both yawn. 'Don't fall asleep,' says Alex, 'you might wake up in Naples.'

Despite his warning, Alex himself finds it hard to stay awake. The long Lombardy plain south of Milan is flat, featureless and boring, and his eyelids are heavy. It's not until the line veers south after Bologna that the scenery becomes interesting, but by that time they're all too weary to care. They just want the ordeal to be over. Joey feels as though somebody has rubbed grit in his eyes. He rests his head against the carriage window but he's wide awake. Mia has slumped against him and her head is on his shoulder. He can feel her weight making his arm start to tingle. He doesn't mind. There's something wrong with the air conditioning and there's a wet, sweaty patch on his shirt where she lays but he doesn't mind that either. Her hand is close to his. Dare he take it? What would she do if he did? He hopes she and DJ stay asleep for as long as possible.

At a few minutes before nine the train approaches the picture postcard city of Florence, and at four minutes past, exactly on time, it shudders into the station of Santa Maria Novella.

Alex's instructions warn that the train doesn't stop for long and there's a scramble while they tip out their baggage. In the course of the changes they've worked out a system: Alex gets out first, DJ lifts the backpacks and guitars from wherever they've been stowed, Mia and Elena pass them along to Joey, who hands them out to Alex, who stacks them on the platform. Last of all is Elena's case, which is always left to the end because it's bulky and surprisingly heavy.

They stand on the platform stretching, sniffing the air. There's the smell of exhaust, of spicy food cooking, and an undercurrent of drains. The train pulls away and they walk out to the foyer. The first thing Elena sees is a *MacDonalds*. The next is *Victoria's Secret*. The familiarity of these outlets is in a way reassuring but it's also depressing. It's reassuring that here many things are the same as at home; it's depressing that after travelling for more than twenty hours they should be greeted by such ordinariness. Does economic advance mean everything becoming the same? Is this what's meant by "the global village"?

The driver is easy to spot. He's a young man, scarcely older than they are, in black trousers and a white shirt. He's holding a large card that says in big letters, *Mr Alex*, and in much smaller ones, *& praty*.

'Well that's you, Mr Alex,' Elena says, 'and I guess we're the praty.'

The driver is called Dino, and he loads their baggage and the two guitars into the back of a black Mercedes people carrier, swinging Elena's case as if it held no more than feathers.

Alex sits beside Dino, the others are in the rear. Dino has plenty of smiles but not much English. 'I shall be pleased that you are together,' he says.

Alex isn't sure what he means but it sounds friendly and so he smiles and nods. He turns to Elena. 'Ask him how long the journey will take,' he says.

'I'm too tired to struggle with Italian,' says Elena. 'Besides, if he thinks I can speak it he'll want to chat and I can't cope with that. It'll take as long as it will take.'

Dino turns on the radio. It's a woman speaking rapidly in Italian, much too fast for Elena to understand. He pokes the touch screen and brings up some music, *Christine and the Queens*.

Dino drives with nonchalance and flourish, weaving through slower traffic with easy skill. His attitude suggests that he believes the car to be protected by some kind of force field and that other vehicles will bounce harmlessly away when he comes near them. It's a characteristic of Italian driving that Elena witnessed when she was in the country before.

The sky is an impossible blue, the colours fervid and intense. They head out of the city towards the airport, and then onto the Autostrada del Sol. It's such an evocative, romantic-sounding name that Mia feels a choke in her throat when she sees the sign. She puts her hand on DJ's leg and he covers it with his. However, the scenery isn't at all romantic, being mainly factory units and malls. Gradually they thin out and the road starts to weave its way through patchy forest. The Merc slows and turns sharply onto a lesser road, and almost immediately begins to climb. There are fields planted with vines, but mostly the landscape is trees. The road winds, dips, climbs. The woods become denser. There's another turn, then another, and one more onto what is no more than a track.

'I hope we don't have to find our way out of here on our own,' says DJ.

The car hits a pothole and the jolt wakes Elena. 'Are we there yet?' she says.

'Almost,' says Dino.

Shit, thinks Alex, he does speak English after all. Did we say anything about him?

The lane levels, becomes smoother and turns into a wide, tree-lined avenue. Then, a hundred metres ahead, they see a building, ravishing in its Tuscan splendour. It's a square, classical villa with ochre walls, white window frames, red roof tiles, and a long white balustrade edging the front terrace. It looks down on them with haughty magnificence.

'Castelvecchio,' says Dino.

They expect him to drive them up to it but instead he turns sharply to the left, under a leafy arch and into a small courtyard outside another building. That, too, is a villa; much smaller but still imposing.

They climb stiffly out of the Mercedes. Emerging from the air-conditioned car is like walking into a roaster. They let Dino unload their bags and carry them inside while they take in the scenery.

'Should we tip him?' says Elena.

'No,' says Alex. 'It's what he's paid to do, isn't it?'

'Don't ask me,' says Mia bitterly. 'I'm skint.'

They can just see between the trees what must be the view from the terrace.

'Phew,' says Joey. 'Impressive, or what?'

Dino shows no sign of expecting a tip. He bows to the boys, smiles at the girls and hands Alex an envelope. Then he gets into the Mercedes and speeds away down the track, leaving a cloud of dust.

They go into a cool hall with white walls, terra cotta floor tiles, and a classical bust on a pedestal in the corner. There's a wide staircase of white marble in the middle of the room, and beyond a pair of large, double doors lead to a terrace with a view of hazy hills.

Beside the staircase, there's a table made of dark wood, with matching chairs. Alex pulls one out, sits down and opens the envelope Dino has given him. It's a single typed sheet.

'What does it say?' says DJ.

'Yes, read it out,' says Mia.

'It's from Bruno,' says Alex. He looks up and frowns. 'It's in Italian.' He sighs in exasperation. 'Irritating prick. He knows we can't speak Italian.'

'One of us can,' says DJ almost snatching the sheet from Alex and handing it to Elena.

'Only a bit,' she says, 'and only if it's not too complicated.' She puts the sheet on the table, flattens it out and studies it for a moment. She's gratified to see it makes more sense than she feared it might. 'It's not too difficult,' she says. 'It begins,' she reads, '*Miei cari bambini.* My dear children.'

'Children?' says Alex. 'What the fuck?'

'It's a friendly greeting, a term of endearment,' she says. 'He doesn't mean he thinks we're kids.' She reads on. '*Benvenuti a Castelvecchio*. Welcome to Castelvecchio.'

'You don't have to read out the Italian,' says Alex, irritably. 'Just the English will do.'

'Oh, right.' She goes back to the paper and runs her finger under the lines. 'He says, "Make this as it were your house." That must mean make yourselves at home. "Wander liberally." Wander liberally? I think that's go where you like. *Tuttavia*, that's "however"'. She frowns. 'I'm not sure about this next bit, but I think it says we're to take care in the forest because it's magical and mysterious, *un luogo di magia e mistero*.'

'A magical forest,' says Mia. 'Intriguing.'

'His assistant said don't go into the woods because of wild animals,' says Alex. 'She didn't mention magic. Does he say anything about the wedding?'

'Or the arrangements for the gig? Or when Theo and Lita will be here?' says DJ.

'No. Just *Salve. Ciao! Bruno.* That's all.' She turns the paper over. 'Oh, there's a PS, quite a long one. It's in English, thank God. It says that there's food and beer in the fridge, and Tuscan wine and the local liqueur in the store room. "The liqueur is Grappa di Castelvecchio," he says. "A speciality of the property and especially good. You must be sure to sample it. There is plenty." He also says that there's a cold supper for us in the kitchen and that from tomorrow a cook will come every day to prepare our dinner. "Her name is Gianna",' she reads. '"She has no English but in any case she is deaf, so you will not be able to communicate with her".'

'Great,' says Alex, 'so how do we tell her what we want?'

'I guess we don't,' says Elena. 'We just eat what we're given. Anyway, he also says that she's kind and reliable and has served the family for many years.'

'Right,' says DJ. 'Anything else?'

'Yes. "Tania and I will be with you in a day or so. Please do not approach Castelvecchio itself because it is heavily alarmed".'

'Okay. We'll consider ourselves warned off. Is that it?'

'There's a phone number, a mobile. His I suppose.' She tosses the paper onto the table.

'So,' says Alex, 'it seems like we're on our own for a bit. That's okay, it will give us time to rest up. I'm going for some of that food. I'm starving.'

'Not for me,' says Mia. The hours since Paris have been one long snack. They started with Joey's sandwiches and continued with a succession of chocolate bars, crisps, fizzy drinks, sweets, and biscuits. By the time they reached Florence Mia was feeling bloated and heavy, and the car journey hasn't helped. Now the mere thought of food brings on a sensation of nausea. None of the others is hungry either.

'I'm going to take a walk around,' says DJ. 'Anybody coming?' He looks at Mia but she shakes her head.

'I need a shower,' she says. 'And to wash my hair. It feels like a bird's nested in it.'

'It looks a bit like that too,' says DJ.

'Ha ha,' says Mia, drily. She's trying to put a brave face on things but she's still upset by the theft of the money, and even more by losing the heart-shaped purse, which had been a present from her father before cancer strode in and snuffed out his life.

'Me too,' says Elena. 'If I don't shower soon I'll become a biohazard.'

Alex comes out of the kitchen with a plate of salami in one hand. With the other, he's rolling the slices into tubes and stuffing them into his mouth. 'There's loads of food in there,' he says. 'All sorts of stuff.'

He goes through the doors to the terrace.

'See if there's a pool,' Mia calls after him. She and Elena climb the stairs.

9

The upper floor of the villa is a long, dim corridor with rooms leading off, three doors on each side. Mia opens the first one and Elena follows her in. The space they find is enormous and white, with a vast bed in the centre under an ornate chandelier. There are French doors that open onto a balcony overlooking the terrace. The view is stunning, across the forest to tawny, sunbaked hills. Ancient olive trees clump around red-roofed farms and fields are combed with vines.

Pictures line the wall over the bed. They're of mythical creatures – a satyr, a centaur, a basilisk, a nubile nymph losing the fabric that drapes her. On each side of the bed are wooden chests of drawers. They are clearly antique and shine with the deep lustre that only comes from years of polishing. Elena opens one. The smell of spices brings feelings of exotic mystery.

Mia opens a door in the wall opposite. 'Wow,' she says.

Elena joins her. It's a bathroom, almost as big as the bedroom. The floor and walls are tiled in creamy marble. In the centre is a Jacuzzi, semi-sunken, and beside it is a conventional bath, presumably so that bathers can flop between one and the other. There's an enclosure with multiple shower jets, and two vanity units, each with an upholstered stool. On one is what looks like the remote control for a TV. In an alcove are a lavatory and a bidet.

'Oh. My. God,' says Elena. 'You could have a party in here.' She wonders if people perhaps do. She picks up the remote and touches one of the buttons. To her astonishment the shower bursts into life, firing jets of water with the force of a fire hose. She touches it again and the room is filled with music, a string piece, soft and lyrically romantic. The sound is opulent and sensuous, the mellow darkness of cellos underpinning the glassy sweetness of violins.

Hanging beside the door are fluffy white bathrobes, soft as kittens. On a shelf is a neat pile of towels, each almost big enough to use as a bedspread. There are slippers. Mia opens a cupboard set into the wall. It contains a selection of washes and shampoos, some of which she's heard of and knows to be ridiculously expensive. There are colognes and creams and perfumes and deodorants and unguents and lotions and balms. The girls are lost for words and look on in wonder.

'Is this for everybody?' says Mia, looking around the room. 'I mean, I can't see a door apart from the one leading from the bedroom.'

'It must be an en suite,' says Elena.

'No way. It's vast.'

'Let's see.'

They go out to the corridor and try the room opposite. It's almost identical in layout and furnishing, although being on the shady side of the building the light is less intense. It too has a bathroom, equally opulent.

'I can't believe it,' says Mia. 'Just the bathrooms alone must have cost a fortune.'

'Are you and DJ sharing?' says Elena.

Mia looks at her quizzically. 'Aren't you and Alex?'

'Of course. I was just asking. In which case, which room do you want?'

'This one,' says Mia, choosing the shadier one.

'Sure?'

'Yes. Unless you're desperate to have it.'

'No. I wanted the sunny side anyway.'

'What about Joey?'

'He can have one of the others.' Elena moves along the corridor and opens the next door. It's another white bedroom, also lavish but not quite as large as the first two.

'Will he be okay with this?' says Mia. 'It's smaller than ours.'

'You bet he'll be okay,' says Elena. 'It's bigger than his house.'

The two girls go to their own rooms. Mia flops onto the bed. It's sumptuous and welcoming, with just the right degree of firmness. She stretches, loosening the crick she's felt in her neck since sleeping on the waiting room bench at Domodossola.

Domodossola, where she lost her purse. Or, rather, where it was stolen. The memory of that has never been far away, forgotten for a spell only to return and nag her again like a strained muscle or an aching tooth. A hundred and fifty euros! Why did she bring so much? There was no reason. She had no intention of spending anywhere near all of it, but she wanted not to be the poor friend, to be on a par with DJ, Elena and Alex. She gets up and goes to the bathroom. A hundred and fifty euros. A great deal of money to me, she thinks, but it probably wouldn't pay for so much as a tap in here. How can she make up for such a loss? There's a tanning salon at Gym52 and the manager has been trying to persuade her to work some shifts there. She doesn't want to because one of the other girls says it's boring and the manager is a bit of a creep, but probably now she'll have to.

She takes off her travel-stained clothes and drops them on the floor. Then she does a few toe touches and squats, turns on the shower jets, adjusts the flow and temperature, and steps in.

By the time DJ returns from his explorations Mia is out of the shower and standing on the balcony, wrapped in a towel. It looks in the opposite direction from Helena's, away from the terrace and up the slight hill towards the big house, Castelvecchio itself. She can see its terra cotta roof and sandy walls through gaps in the trees.

'You found the right room, then,' she says as he joins her.

'Elena put a post-it on the door,' he says.

Post-it, thinks Mia. Who brings post-its on holiday?

Well of course, Elena does.

'I wonder which is the magical part,' says DJ.

'What?'

'The forest,' he says, pointing across a grassy space to the woods that surround the villa. 'Bruno's note said to be careful because the forest is magical.' He laughs. 'It would be helpful to know which bit he's talking about.'

He puts his arm around her and they stand together taking in the view. Mia is shorter than he is and only comes up to his shoulder, so that when he turns to the side he's looking at the top of her head. The air is still and the woodland is dense. It's easy to imagine the trees concealing fantastical creatures.

'What did you find when you looked around?' she says.

'Loads. It's an amazing place. Downstairs there's just the kitchen, which is huge, and one enormous room full of brown furniture and shelves with loads of books. The terrace goes all the way across the front of the building and there are lots of places to chill. There's no pool, though. At least not here. There could be one up at the big house.'

'You didn't go there? Bruno said not to.'

'I didn't go right up to it, just part way. It's huge, much bigger than it seems from here. There are no signs of life though, it's all shut up.' He turns away and surveys the room. 'Quite a place, eh? And we've got it all to ourselves. For a week. Longer if we want.'

Mia will enjoy the week, but she doesn't want to stay for more than that. She needs to get home.

'Just think,' says DJ. 'For some people this is normal.

Some people live like this all the time. Have you been to Alex's place?' Mia shakes her head. 'Terrific house, but it's a hut compared with this.'

'Oh to be a millionaire,' she says.

'Billionaire, more like.'

'Millions, billions, what's the difference?'

'Hark at Miss Moneybags.' He kisses the top of her head. 'Fancy another shower? We could take one together.'

She smiles. 'Later,' she says. 'I just want to lie down for a bit.'

DJ goes into the bathroom, takes off his clothes and kicks them into a corner and stands in the huge shower cubicle. Above him is an overhead drench, a chrome disc the size of an LP. He experiments with the remote, adjusts the temperature, and stands while the grubbiness of the twenty-four-hour journey is rinsed from him. He shampoos his hair, lathers himself, and stands in bovine vacancy while the soap swills away. He touches a control and the water outlet switches from the drench to a pair of side-bars, hitting him with a force that knocks him sideways. He presses again, a pump cuts in and he jumps as the jets alternate rapidly between hot and ice cold. It's an incredible feeling, sensuous and invigorating. He leaves the shower, towels himself dry, and puts on one of the bathrobes.

Mia is lying on the bed facing away from him. At first he thinks she's asleep but she's not. He sits on the bed and gently rubs her back.

'What are you thinking about?' he says. She doesn't answer, but he can guess.

'I should never have come here,' she says, wiping her eyes with the heel of her hand. 'I've no reason to be here, I'm not even in the band.' Her voice is tiny, like a small, hurt animal. Mia is subject to depression and he feels sorry for her. He strokes her hair and she turns over.

'You have every reason to be here. I'm your reason,' he says. He stretches out beside her and draws her towards him. With one finger he traces the outline of her cheek, then puts his hand behind her head and pulls her closer. Their mouths meet.

'You smell good,' she says, as they separate.

He loosens her towel and scrambles free of his bathrobe. They kiss again, more fiercely this time. Limbs hook around limbs, like wrestlers seeking purchase. Hands grope and stroke. He caresses her thigh, her rear. Her fingers ruffle his hair, run down his back, and reach between his legs. Quickly he's inside her, too fast but he can't delay, and she wants that too. For an instant there's stillness as they lock together, her hands pulling him into her, her legs binding them tightly together. Their bodies are ablaze. Every perception is heightened, feelings and sounds razor-sharp. He hears the gauze curtains swish as the breeze picks up again. There's a voice, one of the others outside. In the distance a dog barks.

He holds her while the sensation of his climax ebbs and the throbbing in his head clears. They roll apart and lie side by side looking at the ceiling. For a long time neither moves, neither speaks. Then she says, 'I don't know how to say this.'

Say what? It was too quick for her? It probably was, but he'll make up for that later. Or... shit... she's pregnant!

They've done it a couple of times before without a condom, trusting to luck. Have they been caught out? He tenses.

What he doesn't anticipate is what she actually says. 'I think it was Alex.'

'What was?'

'Who stole my money. I think Alex took it.'

'What?' DJ sits bolt upright. Is she out of her mind? 'Why? What makes you say that?'

It's a moment before she replies. 'You know he said he hadn't brought much money with him, only about fifty euros?'

'Yes. He did say that.'

'Well, I saw him get out his wallet when he bought some drinks on the train. There looked to be a lot more than fifty euros in there.'

DJ could remember Alex paying. He'd seen him take a twenty note from his wallet, but he hadn't been in a position to see what it left behind. But it's unbelievable. He bends over her but she won't meet his eyes.

'It can't be,' he says. 'Why would he?' He thinks of Alex's house: grand, in its own grounds, hidden behind security gates, guarded by cameras; his dad's car, an electric Jaguar SUV on the drive, and his mother's, a Porsche 911, beside it. Maybe his sister Casia's Golf Gti too, if she's home. It's not possible. 'Even if you could believe that Alex is capable of that, why would he?' he repeats. 'His dad's got his own accountancy firm. They're rolling in it.'

She shakes her head. 'That scruffy guy at

Domodossola you thought might have taken it, I don't think it was him.'

'Why not?'

'He was still hanging around when we woke up and went to catch our train. Don't you think if it had been him he would have cleared off? He wouldn't have stayed there in case he was caught.'

'Maybe, but just because he didn't take it – and I still think it could have been him – that doesn't mean that Alex did. It's a crazy idea.' DJ thinks the most likely thing is that Mia lost the purse, that it fell out of her bag or the pocket of her jeans and she never noticed.

'But I saw what was in his wallet and it was more than he said.'

DJ can find no reply. He and Alex are mates. He's known him since they were both kids and they've spent so much time together. They started the band together. Although their musical tastes have drifted apart and sometimes they argue, DJ still considers Alex to be one of his very best friends. But then, so is Mia.

He shakes his head and wraps a strand of her hair around his finger. 'I'm really sorry you lost your cash,' he says, 'but you know I'll look after you. And you're wrong about Alex.'

She rolls away and they lie still for some time. The conversation has spoilt his mood. It's as if he's bitten on something rancid and he can't rid himself of the taste. That Alex has taken Mia's money doesn't make any sense at all, but Mia has convinced herself that he has and so now he feels obliged to find a way both to respond to her suspicion and to demonstrate his friend's innocence. But how can he possibly do that?

He feels a burst of irritation. If Mia had only taken the trouble to look after her purse this wouldn't have happened. And now what she's done risks souring the whole trip.

10

Joey is alone. He ought to go and find a room and clean himself up, but after the noise and bustle of the journey he's enjoying some time to himself. He's in the kitchen. It seems to have everything you could possibly need and he wonders if there'll be an opportunity for him to do some cooking in there. Perhaps this Gianna woman will let him help her. Although if she can't hear that might be difficult to arrange.

Next to the kitchen is a huge sitting room. It's dark and cool and crammed with furniture. Shelves stuffed with books line the walls. He thinks that Elena will be well suited if she can find something in English. All the titles he can see are in foreign languages. Of course, she'll be all right with books in Italian. Joey has always found English a challenge and admires people who can handle not only their own language but another one as well.

He doesn't like houses like this. It's too big and too posh for him. This is the sort of place that the customers at *The Golden Bough* come from ("diners" or "clients" the manager calls them, never customers). In the short time he's been working there Joey has concluded that many of them would be hard-pushed to make an omelette and don't know anything like as much about food and wine as they pretend. In fact on the whole the ones who talk loudest about what's on their plate are the ones who know least about it. But as chef says, they pay his wages.

He goes out to the terrace. There are sun beds that look new and expensive. He sits on the edge of one in the shade of a vine-covered pergola.

The villa is more or less square and surrounded by a broad swathe of grass so that it sits on an island of green. Beyond the grass are the woods. They must be very old because the growth is dense and there's no view or obvious path through. Joey doesn't know much about trees. He can recognise holly, and fir, and silver birch. He can't see any of those but he can tell that there are several different kinds of other trees.

Bruno's note said that the woods are magical. What does that mean? Does he mean magical like "amazing" or "wonderful"? Like, "Our evening at *The Golden Bough* was magical"? Somebody had written that on Trip Adviser and somebody else had printed it and stuck it on the notice board at the rear of the kitchen. He remembers that the note said the woods are mysterious too. That's the same as "strange" or "hard to understand". Magical and mysterious. It sounds a bit supernatural and Joey has no time for that sort of thing. His gran loves the paranormal, but not him. Of course, it could be that Bruno wrote it to scare them off going into the forest. If he did, that really would be mysterious.

He gets up and walks across the open area to where the woodland meets the grass, not more than fifty metres away. The trees are like a wall, as if they've been erected as a barrier. Even closer he can see no footpaths. The vegetation is dense, made up of dead branches and creepers that bar any way through.

He turns along the edge, thinking he might walk right around the villa until he gets to the track leading up to the big house. A dozen paces along he stops. A little way ahead there's a shape in the trees. He takes a couple more steps and recoils. Something lifeless is suspended from a branch. A rat? A squirrel? The flesh has been eaten till the white bones show through. It has a narrow body, long, boney arms, claws, and some sort of wrapper, a leathery sheath. They're wings. It's a bat, although much bigger than any of the bats he's seen before. It hangs motionless on a strand of grubby red twine.

Who would do that? Who would catch a bat and tie it to a tree? And why? He doesn't fancy going near it and he walks on. He's still pondering when he becomes aware of a buzzing. That too is coming from the wood, a little further along. He walks towards the sound.

It's another corpse. It's obvious what this one is because it's virtually whole. It's a rabbit, and it's hanging by its ears. The fur is a brownish grey, soft and unmarked. Its eyes are wide, as if locked in terror on whatever took its life. The buzzing is made by flies that rise in an angry cloud as he gets near. In going they reveal what was attracting them. There's a broad gash down the animal's stomach where glistening viscera ooze blood, and entrails teem with maggots. The guts look to have a life of their own, rolling to the churn of the grubs that feed on them. The thing stinks. The sight and the smell make him gag and he backs away.

What's happening? The bat's been dead a long time but the rabbit's a recent kill. Did one of Bruno's people put these things there as another warning to keep away from the woods, in case the written one didn't work? Is there any more of this weird stuff?

Yes, some other things are hanging in the trees, although in comparison with what he's just found these are vapid. He knows what the first is because his gran has one on a neck chain. It's called a pentacle, a five-pointed star inside a circle. His gran's is silver, but this one is made out of thin canes tied with string. His gran says the pentacle brings good luck and wards off evil.

Joey has got over the queasiness he felt when he ran into the two dead animals and now he's curious to see what else might be among the branches.

The next thing he finds is a doll. It's made out of pink fabric and is lumpily stuffed. It has hair of yellow wool and its face is rendered by black stitching, apart from the scarlet lips. It hangs from a tree by a noose around its neck. Close to it is another doll. This too is pink but it's made of plastic. Its limbs are twisted into impossible positions and this one isn't hanging; it's fixed to the tree by a thin strip of wood nailed across its throat. It has black hair.

Joey looks back at the line he's walked. The villa seems to be encircled by bizarre things suspended from the trees. Are they for protection, he wonders, or are they a line of attack? All the objects are facing away from the house and towards the forest so they must be a defence. Whoever fixed them must intend them to be charms to block evil, a force to resist something coming out of the forest. No, he thinks, that's stupid.

He goes again to the trees and a thought strikes him. He's a town boy and he rarely goes into the country, but one of the things he's noticed when he's been in or near woods in England is the presence of birds; not only their song but the rustlings as they flutter among the branches. Here there's nothing. There's no sound of any sort, neither call nor movement. The forest seems empty of life, and as still as if it's been soundproofed. Yes, that's it, soundproofed. He steps a few paces away from the edge of the wood and he can hear distant noises – a machine of some sort working far away, the bark of a dog. As he moves back towards the vegetation these fade, until by the time he's reached the nearest of the trees they're gone altogether and he can hear nothing. It's like turning down a volume control.

There's another thing too: a chill, a rawness at odds with the heat everywhere else. He shudders and moves away, and it's like stepping from air conditioning into a summer's day. He can see Bruno's point. There really is something weird about the woods. A warning to steer clear of them is pointless, though. Even if you were able to force a way through that tangled thicket you wouldn't want to once you felt the vibe of the place.

He's heading for the house when at the edge of his vision he sees something else, yet another shape swinging from a branch. This makes no more sense than any of the other things. It's a lath of wood. Fixed on each side of it is a clapper, secured by a thong through the lath so that they flap when it's shaken. It reminds him of something from a long time ago. It's a type of rattle or castanet, and he used to love playing with one when he was in first school. He'd sit with the other children in a circle and shake them in time to the music the teacher was playing on the piano. The ones there were smooth and lacquered. This one is homemade. It's been knocked together from bits of scrap and painted red. Hanging from a different cord but close to it is a wooden spoon. It's seen some service because the bowl is stained dark brown from the cooking pot.

He stares at these things, trying to puzzle out what they might mean. He can see that some idiot might place the dolls and the pentacle as good luck charms. And perhaps the dead creatures were strung up there to feed something, or to scare off other animals. But a child's toy? And a cooking implement? What are they supposed to do?

He wants to get away from the woods; they're spooky. He needs a shower and to change his clothes. As he draws near the villa he sees Alex and Elena. Alex is walking about the terrace with two bottles, one of Peroni and another of something else. Elena is coming through the folding doors from the kitchen.

'Hey, Joey. What's up?' Alex calls.

'Nothing. Just been having a look round.'

'Found anything interesting?' says Elena.

Joey doesn't want to tell them yet about what he's seen on the edge of the woods, he needs time to process it himself first, so he says, 'No, nothing.'

'Did you see the studio?' says Alex. 'I looked through the window and it's amazing, top-class gear, but it's locked up. It's a pain – we need to rehearse.'

'Maybe there's a key somewhere,' says Joey.

'No shit, Sherlock,' says Alex. 'The problem is, where?'

Joey wants the conversation over. 'I'm going for a shower,' he says.

'We've taken the two rooms nearest the top of the stairs,' says Elena. 'If I were you I'd go for the one at the far end of the landing. It's got windows on three sides.'

'Oh, right. Thanks. I will.'

'And don't get lost in the en suite,' says Alex. 'The bathrooms are big enough to need a map to find your way around in them.'

Joey takes his backpack from where he'd dumped it in the hall and climbs the stairs. He's almost at the door to his room when an idea strikes him. It's a thought that's so astounding he freezes.

He can understand the pentacle, that's for good luck. But what about the two dead animals, the two dolls, and the castanet and spoon? It's seeing Elena that's planted the notion. One of the dolls has yellow wool for hair, and the hair of the other one is black. Elena is blonde and Mia brunette. What about the other stuff, the castanet and the wooden spoon? Well, castanets are percussion and he's a drummer. And he's training to be a chef, therefore the wooden spoon. So those things might be intended to stand for him. That leaves the two dead animals, a bat devoured from the outside and a rabbit being consumed from within. Are they for Alex and DJ?

Which is which? Alex often seems to put upon DJ. Is he the one being consumed from the outside? And he's sometimes thought there's something deep within Alex that doesn't seem right. Is he the one whose inside is being eaten away?

Could it be that someone has hung in the trees things that are meant to represent the five of them? And the pentacle too. No, it couldn't be. Who here would know enough about the group to do that? And why would they do it?

He's not going to tell the others about the objects he's found, at least not yet, and he's certainly not going to say what he thinks about them. Elena would want to understand them and she'd go on and on. Mia would worry. DJ would think it was some great voodoo game and he'd go and cut down the dead animals to dissect them. Alex would tell him he was being fucking stupid and should grow up.

No, he'll say nothing for now.

11

The drowsy afternoon crawls on. The sun sinks lower and the temperature drops, but only by a little and it's still hot. Elena stands beside Alex on the balcony. She grumbles to him that Mia and DJ have taken the best room because it's cooler than theirs. She doesn't say that she offered Mia first pick. Alex doesn't care. He's in Italy, he's away from his parents, and he has plans.

The view is of the forest. Elena ponders Bruno's warning. Mysterious? Magical? It looks ordinary enough, or does it? Isn't there, when you look closely, something unsettling about its dense darkness? The sense that if once you got in there you might never get out? She shudders. Alex puts his arm around her and she rests her head against his.

'What's the matter?' he says.

'Nothing. I was just looking at the wood and thinking it looks a bit sinister.'

'Really?' Alex studies it. He can't see what she means. 'It's quite a place, though. I mean the whole estate.'

'It's what being a Premiership footballer gets you.'

'Footballer, rock star, hedge fund manager, take your pick,' says Alex.

'Well you've taken yours,' she says. 'You're going to be an oceanographer.' She gives him a peck on the cheek. She likes the choice he's made. It suggests to her a selfless commitment to conservation. She hopes it does to him too.

Alex doesn't reply. She unwinds her arm and goes back into the room.

'I need a shower,' she says. 'I smell like a bear's den.'

'Oh, I've known you worse,' says Alex. She throws a pillow at him and he dodges, laughing.

'I'm going to look around a bit,' he says. 'You shower first. Your need is greater than mine.'

Elena throws another pillow that hits the door as he shuts it behind him. She sinks onto the bed. It's just the right degree of softness. She loves her little room on the top floor of the pub. She's grown up in there, played in there, done her school work in there, met her friends in there, laughed, cried, and had her first, furtive sex in there. This room is different, it's how the wealthy live. Imagine this being your room. Imagine this being what you always have, what you're used to. Imagine this being normal.

She undresses and throws her sweaty clothes in a heap. They'll need washing before she goes home, she can't pack them like they are or they'll foul everything else in her case. There must be a washing machine somewhere in the villa. But she won't need to wear them again so she could just wrap them in a plastic bag. After all, she's brought plenty of other things with her.

The shower is wonderful. She stands for a long time letting the water swill over her. Then she gets out, pats herself with a towel and brushes her long hair, teasing out the tangles. She comes through to the bedroom and rummages in her case. She rejects the one-piece swimsuit she bought when she was with Mia in favour of a bikini. It's one of last year's and it's a tight fit. She's not surprised. Since finishing her exams there's been the awards night, and parties, and drinks with the girls, and drinks with the boys, and drinks with both. Her dad says that he can resist anything except temptation, and she's the same. Mia can spend the whole evening on diet Coke, or make a white wine spritzer last for hours. Not her. And it's not just the drinks, it's the snacking that goes with them. Since learning about the Italy trip she's been on an emergency crash diet she got from a magazine. It was headed, "Time for the New You – How to lose 8lb in a week". You did it by eating nothing but lettuce and cucumber. She managed to stay on it for four days and the scales had shown some improvement, but she's afraid she's undone it all by eating a cartload of junk food on the way there.

She looks at herself in a mirror: full frontal okay, shapely in a generous kind of way; sideways on not so good. She pinches the roll of fat around her middle. What is it they say? If you can pinch an inch you're overweight. She pouts. She can pinch more than that. Oh well, she thinks, it's what comes from being a publican's daughter. Her dad teases her that the boys like something they can get hold of. She turns and examines her back view. Ample, yes, but also curvy. Her grandfather once told her she's got a 'comfortable' bottom. She'd not been sure how he meant it, but the way he said it made it sound like a compliment. She wiggles it.

She takes a long scarf and knots it loosely around her waist, picks up her book and her phone, and goes downstairs.

The kitchen looks to Elena like something from an up-market showroom. The worktops are marble and kitted out with a range of top-class appliances. There's a huge, American-style fridge. She opens it: butter, eggs, cheeses, meats, salads, tomatoes, fresh fruits, juices, sodas, white wine, and a whole shelf of beers. There's enough to keep them for the whole week.

'Are there any keys?' It's Alex, who has just come in. He's poking around on shelves and in drawers.

'No, I don't think so. The place was open when we got here. Why?'

'The studio is across the yard but it's locked, we can't get in.' He stands beside her at the fridge. 'Beer. Magnificent.' He takes a bottle of Peroni and looks for an opener. 'What's in there?' he says, going towards a door in the corner of the kitchen. 'It looks like a pantry.' He goes in, down three steps. 'Hey, look at this,' he says.

The room is lined with stone shelves laden with all manner of things – cans, packets, jars, tubs, boxes. On one of the shelves is a row of tall bottles which contain a clear liquid. The labels show a sketch of the house and the name Grappa di Castelvecchio.

'This must be the stuff Bruno told us about in his note. Look, one of them's been opened.'

Elena takes it, pulls out the stopper and sniffs. It's a sweet, heady smell. She picks up a trace of almonds. She takes a sip and tastes toffee, and herbs. It's obviously potent but it lacks the alcoholic burn of some spirits. 'Mm, it's good. Here, try it.'

Alex takes a sip, then a longer swig. 'Hey, that's good.' He looks at the label and shows Elena a phrase in English: "Not for sale to the public",' he reads. 'Pity. This would go a bomb in your dad's pub.'

Alex always refers to *The Green Man* as her dad's pub, even though it's owned jointly by both her parents. She's sick of pointing this out to him, but she still finds it irritating.

Alex goes back to the kitchen and through to the terrace, the bottle of grappa in one hand and his Peroni in the other. Elena sits on a recliner. She feels the heat stored in the sun-warmed marble. 'Pity there's no pool,' she says.

'I bet there's one at the big house. We might be allowed to use that when Bruno and Tania get here.'

'I hope so. I bet it gets baking on this terrace. Better not go near the house before they arrive, though. Bruno's note was clear about that. We don't want a busload of carabinieri roaring up the hill because they think the place is being broken into.' She points towards the corner of the terrace. 'For now, there's a cold shower over there.'

Alex joins her on the recliner and lies down, his head on her lap. They both close their eyes. Why is it, thinks

Elena, that travelling makes you feel so tired when all you're doing most of the time is sitting still?

'Listen, can you hear it?' says Alex.

'What?'

'Silence,' he says.

She gives him a playful slap on the head. A shadow comes between her and the sun.

'Hi.'

It's DJ, with Mia at his side. DJ's in floppy shorts and a T-shirt. Mia is in a lilac sarong which shows off her athletic body. It looks sexy. Alex's eyes fix on her and Elena can see that he thinks so too. She's without make-up and Elena is struck, not for the first time, at how fresh and unblemished her skin is.

'Where did you two come from?' she says.

'Down those steps,' says Mia, pointing behind her. Elena sees that there's a stone staircase on the outside of the house. 'You can get on to the roof.'

'What's up there?' says Alex.

'Nothing much,' says DJ. 'A satellite dish and a few recliners, that's all. It's too hot to stay there for long.'

'Have you seen Joey?'

'He's gone to his room,' says Elena. 'He likes to keep himself to himself. Do you need him?'

'No. It's just that we've found the studio. Well, DJ did.'

'It's in the building across the yard,' says DJ.

'I know,' says Alex, sitting up, 'but the door's locked.'

'No, it's not,' says DJ. 'I've just been in.'

'Well, it sure as shit was locked when I tried it.'

'Maybe, but it's not now.'

'Somebody must have unlocked it.'

'Duh.'

'Who though? I haven't seen anyone else around.'

'Maybe it was just stuck.'

Alex shakes his head. He'd thought of that and pushed the door hard but it had been firmly fastened.

'It's an amazing place,' says DJ. 'It's got everything we need. There are three keyboards and two full drum kits.'

'That's why I was asking for Joey,' says Mia. 'We thought he might like to see them.'

'You should go check it out,' DJ says to Alex.

Alex doesn't reply. He's peeved that DJ managed to get into the studio and he didn't. He's convinced it had been locked.

DJ notices the bottle on the ground beside the recliner. 'What's that?'

'Bruno's grappa,' says Alex.

DJ picks it up and takes a sip. 'Wow. That's certainly got the secret ingredient,' he says. 'It's hard to place. Sort of herby-minty, kind of sweet but not. Here.' He offers the bottle to Mia but she shakes her head.

'What do you think of your room?' says Elena.

'Amazing. The bed's the size of a tennis court and you need a pilot's licence to work the shower. I think I could learn to like this lifestyle. What did Bruno tell you about the arrangements for the wedding?'

'Not much,' says Alex. 'There'll be a lot of people and I expect some of them will be well-known, but his assistant wouldn't give me any details. She said Bruno would make everything clear when he got here.'

'They probably didn't want you leaking the guest list

to the media,' says DJ. 'People like that expect some privacy.'

'What?' says Alex. 'Celebs? Privacy? That's the last thing they're after. Being seen is what they care about.'

Perhaps, thinks Mia. She's not sure. Everybody wants to be left alone sometimes, don't they?

'Have you thought,' says Alex, 'that there could be somebody at the wedding from the world of music? Somebody who might be interested in *Friendly Fire*?'

'What, you mean to promote the band?' says Elena. 'You're not seeing this gig as leading to some kind of musical breakthrough, are you?'

'I wasn't, well not at first, but since talking to Bruno and his assistant I've been thinking about it.' There's a pause. Then he says, 'Theo and Lita heard us and liked us. And not just a bit but enough to get us to play at their wedding. I know we're not going to find people standing there waving recording contracts at us, but there might be something that could come out of it.'

Elena thinks that Italy, the sun, the whole situation has gone to his head. The band's a hobby, a bit of fun. She enjoys singing, and she likes writing poetry and turning that into lyrics for songs. She likes it when Alex and DJ work on the music that brings her words to life, but that's all. They've put a couple of numbers online for streaming but there's not been much interest. They've never, ever talked seriously about the band trying to make a go of it. And when the few bookings they'd had at the start dried up, nobody minded. They carried on practising in one of the school's music rooms or the basement of Alex's house just for fun. Sometimes they didn't practice at all but spent the evening talking.

'Are you for real?' she says.

'No, but you know, it's possible there'll be people at the wedding who'll go for our music. It could lead to something, couldn't it?'

Elena shakes her head. 'You can be so fucking selfish sometimes,' she says, wearily. She's pleased that Alex looks a little shamefaced. 'Lita liked us, but that's no guarantee that others will. She could be tone-deaf! You play well, DJ plays well, I sing well, Joey's a great drummer, and we write some okay songs, but you know, to be absolutely completely and brutally honest, we're not really that good.'

Alex recoils as if he's been slapped, then he looks wounded, then withdrawn, all in a couple of seconds. DJ and Mia look on, and wonder how it is that Alex can swing so rapidly from supremely irritating to endearing.

12

There's an awkward silence. Alex reaches over to DJ for the bottle and takes a long swig of grappa.

Elena thinks she's probably gone too far and it was unkind to say that the band's not up to much, but on the other hand, Alex needed bringing down to earth. It's easy to dream, she thinks, and dreams are free. But dreams on their own don't get you anywhere. You have to work out the route from where you are now to where the dream comes true; that's the point at which the cost comes in. You have to know the way, of course you do, but you also have to be willing to pay the price of getting there, the price of the dream. Is Alex prepared to pay? She doubts it.

She picks up a magazine she brought from England. She's already read it on the journey but flicking through the pages gives her something to do.

Alex gets up. 'I'm going to check out the studio,' he

says. 'Unless it's suddenly become locked again.' He's still ruffled that DJ was able to inspect it before he could.

'Now the sun's gone I'm starting to feel chilly,' Elena says. 'I'm going to put on something warmer.'

DJ and Mia are left alone. They lie together on one of the recliners and look at the shapes of the trees against the darkening sky.

'Night came on so quickly,' Mia says.

'Yes,' says DJ. 'We get long twilights in Britain but as you go south they're shorter.' He eases his position.

'You okay?' she says.

'Yes. It's just your shoulder's digging into me. You're so blooming skinny. What my gran would call a boney kipper.'

She laughs and pokes him in the stomach.

'Do you think Alex meant it, about the band?' she says. 'Do you think he's really expecting to break through with his music?'

DJ has no idea. He's known Alex since they were boys, and there was a time when he could have told you exactly what he was thinking at any given moment. Now it's different.

'I don't think he knows what he wants,' he says. 'I'm sure he's not hooked on oceanography, that's why he's deferred his place. He only applied for that course in the first place to piss off his folks. A sweet invite from another celeb would go down well.' He laughs quietly. 'Anything so long as it doesn't involve too much work.'

They cuddle. Elena was right, it's cooler, but neither of them can be bothered to go upstairs to fetch more clothing. After a while DJ gets up and goes to the pergola, where he fiddles about behind one of the pillars. Coloured lights threaded in a strand between the vines come on.

'Da daaaa!' he says with a flourish.

'Cool.' It's Joey, who's now wearing a clean white shirt and dark trousers. Mia wonders if he's dressed like that for dinner.

Alex and Elena return.

'Have you seen the stars,' says Elena. 'They're amazing. I can't get over there being so many of them here.'

'There is exactly the same number here as there are at home,' says Alex.

'Smart arse,' says Elena.

'I'm going to sleep out here,' he says. 'Under the stars.'

'You mean under the mosquitoes,' says Elena, rubbing a trio of red marks on her arm.

'What about this food that's been left for us? says Joey. 'I'm starving.'

'Me too,' says DJ.

They go to the kitchen and open the fridge, taking out several cooked meats – slices of chicken and ham, and different sorts of salami. A shelf in the pantry has cheeses – hard and soft, blue, yellow and white. Under a cloth on the table is a bowl of salad, and a plate of sliced tomatoes and mozzarella bathed in olive oil and dusted with oregano. There are hard-boiled eggs, a dish of grapes, a bowl of olives, another of beans, and a tray of carrot batons garnished with tiny onions, like jewels. There are jars of pickles and chutneys, and a fabric bag containing several sorts of bread.

'So this is what Bruno calls "a cold supper",' Elena says.

'Out of this world,' says DJ. 'How many was he expecting? There's enough here for an army.'

'The note Elena read out says that there's a cook coming tomorrow, so it must be just for tonight,' says Mia.

Alex picks out one of the hard-boiled eggs and takes a bite before putting it back in the bowl.

'Hey,' says Elena in angry protest. 'Let's have a few manners here. This isn't just for you, you know.'

Alex wipes his mouth with his hand and looks at her with a boyish grin as if she can't possibly mean it.

'I want to eat properly,' she says. 'I want to sit down with a knife and fork and eat like a person. If you'd rather have a trough you can take it out there on the grass but I want to have a nice meal with my friends.'

'Me too,' says Joey. 'Good food deserves respect.'

It's uncharacteristic for Joey to get involved in something like this and it surprises the others.

Alex's smile fades and he shrugs. 'Okay okay. It was only a fucking egg.' However, he shows he's contrite by picking up two of the plates and following Elena and Mia out to the terrace. There are some candles in jars on the table and matches beside them. Joey lights the candles; the swaying flames and the pergola lights make the table look festive.

'Good,' says Elena. 'Right, there's a lot of work for us if we're going to get through this lot so we'd better make a start.'

They finish ferrying out the food from the kitchen. There's white wine in the cooler and red on a rack, and

DJ brings a bottle of each. Mia gets cutlery and glasses, and Joey plates. Alex mostly watches.

Elena surveys the table. 'Okay, Joey?'

Joey adjusts a couple of the place settings and nods.

Alex takes the head of the table. There's no discussion, he simply goes to that place, sits down and starts to help himself to what's nearest. Mia and DJ exchange a look and take the seats to one side of him. Elena and Joey sit opposite them.

To begin with, nobody speaks. They are all hungry, and too busy filling their plates and eating for conversation. Elena and Alex go for the cold meats. Joey too. Mia chooses beans, olives, and salad. She's trying to be vegan but she crumbles and succumbs to the flaked Parmesan. DJ helps himself to a slice of ciabatta, piles on a thick layer of chicken and salami, squashes another slice on top, and takes a huge bite.

'Okay, Joe,' he says. 'What do you reckon?'

'Huh?'

'The food. How do you rate it?'

'It's very good,' says Joey.

'What do you think we'll get tomorrow night when the cook comes?' says DJ, looking at Elena.

'Who knows,' says Elena. 'If she wants to give us what she might think we're used to she'll go for something simple with chips. Anything with chips goes well in the pub. We do some Italian food, pizzas and spag bol, and you'd be surprised how many people ask for chips with those.'

'I was hoping we might get some traditional Italian dishes,' says Joey.

'Like?' DJ asks.

Joey shrugs. 'I don't know. I've only ever made pizzas, except when I did my trial at *The Golden Bough*. Then I helped one of the chefs do ossobuco.'

'Do what?' It sounds to DJ like something sexual.

'It's veal in a wine sauce, with vegetables. There's cheese sprinkled on the top of it too.'

'I've had that,' says Elena. 'Scrummy.'

Alex reaches from the head of the table and takes one of the wine bottles. He fills everyone's glass to the brim, emptying the bottle, then says, 'Time for a toast.' He raises his glass. 'To Lita and Theo.'

'And to Italy,' says Elena.

'To Italy and us,' says DJ.

They all drink. There's a pause. Then Mia says, 'It's not what I expected.'

'What isn't?' says DJ

'This place. I thought it would be teeming with people getting ready for the wedding.'

'Yes, so did I,' says Joey.

'So where are they? When do you think they'll be coming? I had this idea there'd be lots of preparations going on, and then Theo and Lita arriving in style, maybe even in a helicopter.'

'That could happen yet,' says Alex. 'These folk live in a different world. They don't do things the same way as the rest of us. You wait and see.'

The food goes, and so does the wine. From time to time they refill their plates. Alex sees himself somehow as the host, and whenever a glass has a space he tops it up. The first two bottles are soon gone and Alex tells DJ to fetch more.

'Why me?'

'Because you know where it is.'

'So do you.' DJ is going to argue but he doesn't want to spoil the mood so he goes.

'It's okay,' Alex says crossly, catching Elena's look. 'We were told to help ourselves.' His speech is sounding slurred.

'If you're going to do anything at all tomorrow you'd better slow down,' she says.

'Hark at Grandma,' he says. She glares at him. 'Anyway, what is there to do?'

'Get ready for the gig? Our great opportunity?' Her tone is heavy with sarcasm.

'Oh. Right. Yes.' Alex pushes his glass away, as if renouncing alcohol for good. DJ, Elena and Joey sip from theirs. Mia is drinking hardly anything.

'Pudding,' says Alex. The others are puzzled; is it a request? an order? a suggestion? They wait for more. 'Didn't anybody notice? There's tiramisu in the fridge.'

'That may not be for now,' says Elena.

'Bruno said, what was it? "Make as it were your house". Well if this was my house and there was tiramisu in the fridge I'd have some.' He gets up and makes his way unsteadily towards the kitchen, using the door frame to correct a wobble as he goes in.

'There's fruit, too,' Joey says to Mia.

They follow Alex, and DJ follows them. Elena stays in her place at the table. When they return, the boys with bowls and Mia with a peach, she has her mobile out.

'Can anyone get a signal?' she says.

'No,' says DJ. 'There's no coverage out here. It may be better if you move somewhere else.'

'It's the same all over the house,' says Joey. 'I walked right round it and a way down the track to see if I could connect and there's nothing. Not a single bar.'

'Shit,' says Elena. 'I promised my mum I'd text her when I got here, to say I was all right.'

'Me too,' says Mia. She thinks for a moment. 'It's weird. There's a fantastic kitchen, movie star bathrooms, and amazing accommodation, but there's no way of keeping in touch with the outside world. Has anyone seen a TV? Or a radio?'

'No,' says Joey. 'I thought there'd be TVs in the bedrooms, but mine doesn't have one.'

'Nor ours,' says Elena.

Mia shakes her head. 'A satellite dish on the roof but no TVs anywhere.'

'My phone picks up a wifi signal,' says Joey, 'but it needs a password.'

'Forget it,' says Alex, who's been to the kitchen again. This time he has a bottle of grappa and five shot glasses. 'When we see Bruno we'll get it sorted. For now, let's enjoy what these kind people have left for us.' He fills the glasses, spilling some of the spirit on the table, and pushes one to each of them. 'What's cheers in Italian?' he asks Elena.

'"Salute" means cheers. Or I've heard them say "cent' anni", which is "may you live for a hundred years". They use both. And "chin chin".'

'Salute,' says Alex. 'And chin chin.' He drains his glass

in one. So does DJ. Elena takes a mouthful of hers. Mia and Joey hesitate. 'Come on,' says Alex. 'Just one more toast.'

Joey sips his and Mia does the same.

'To the band,' says DJ.

'To *Friendly Fire*,' says Alex.

They all drink again. Alex, DJ and Elena refill. Mia and Joey aren't keeping up and this doesn't suit Alex. 'What's wrong with you two?' he says. 'You're on holiday. You don't have to do anything tomorrow. Get some of the happy juice down you.'

'Leave them be,' says Elena. 'They don't have to knock it back just because you've decided to get rat-arsed.'

'Who are you?' Alex mumbles. His speech is becoming less clear with each glass he empties. 'The Salvation fucking Army?' Then he immediately softens. 'I just want them to have a good time,' he says.

''Course you do,' says Elena. She takes his hand. 'So do I. But let them please themselves. They don't have to go mad on the booze to enjoy themselves.'

'It's their loss,' says Alex, and sighs.

There's a new sound. Joey hears it first. 'What's that?' There's something in his voice that hushes the others.

'I don't hear anything,' says Elena.

'Listen. It's coming from the forest.'

They all turn towards the trees and strain to catch what Joey means. At first, they can hear nothing; then it comes again.

'It's a dog,' says Alex.

'It's not like any dog I've heard,' says Joey, 'and it's getting nearer.'

It's a disturbing noise, the baleful howl of a creature in pain.

'Ugh. It's creepy,' says Mia. 'Like something's being tortured.'

'I don't like it,' says Elena.

'Whatever it is, it doesn't sound happy,' says Alex. 'And there's another one with it.'

The first baying has been joined by more. Then there's a third, and a fourth, a quartet of despair pervading the forest.

Elena shivers, she can't stop herself. 'Are they dogs? How many are there?'

Alex gets up and goes to the edge of the terrace.

'Come back,' calls Elena. 'You don't know what's out there.'

Alex peers out into the night. Elena goes to him. He can be impetuous when he's been drinking and she's worried he might do something stupid. She anchors her arm to his. The others join them and the five friends stand in a ragged line, taut and edgy.

'It's wolves,' says DJ.

'It can't be,' says Mia. 'They're extinct.'

'No, they're not,' says Elena. 'There are still wolves in Italy.'

The animals are even louder now, and there are yet more of them. They sound as if they have formed an arc across the front of the villa.

'I'm scared,' says Mia, moving closer to DJ.

'Me too,' says Joey. 'Let's go in.'

'Bruno's note warned us,' says Elena. 'He said to keep away from the woods.'

'Good advice. I think we should get the hell away,' says DJ. 'Go inside and lock ourselves in.'

The howls become more frantic. Elena's heart is thumping. Mia is trembling. Joey is ready to run. DJ stares at the fringe of trees. He grabs Mia's arm and backs away. Then, just as the howling reaches a climax and it seems that the woods are about to erupt in a tumble of black shapes, the commotion ceases. There's silence.

'What's happened? Have they gone?' says Mia.

'It sounds like it,' says Joey.

They all wait. There's no sound.

'Thank God for that,' says Elena. 'I was ready to wet myself.'

They huddle on the corner of the terrace and listen to the receding cries. DJ is between Elena and Mia, one arm around each of them. Alex is a little way off, peering towards where the noises have come from. Joey is close to Mia. He wants her to know that he would protect her, from wolves or anything else. He can't say it but he thinks it and he hopes she will somehow feel it.

'I hope that doesn't happen every night,' says Elena.

'Or during the night,' says Mia. 'It's one of the scariest sounds I've ever heard. Right out of a horror movie. Did anybody see anything?'

Nobody had. Despite there being some light from the moon it was too dark to make out any shapes among the trees. There's no sound at all now. The night is still and calm, as if nothing happened. Slowly, they begin to relax.

'Gimme that grappa,' says Alex. He goes back to the table and the others follow. He's very unsteady on his feet.

'I'll tell you something. I'm locking the door of our room tonight,' says Elena.

'Why bother?' says Mia. 'You'll already have a wolf in there.'

'Very funny,' says Alex. 'Wolf? Do guys really get called that still? You sound like my grandma.' He fills the empty glasses.

'I see what Bruno meant in that note,' says Elena. 'There's no way you'll get me anywhere near those woods now.'

They sit in silence, thinking over the past few minutes. Alex is staring at his glass. Elena and Mia are still buzzing from what they feel was too close an encounter. Joey is remembering the mutilated carcasses in the trees and wonders if they have any connection with the wolves. Should he tell the others about them?

DJ speaks first. 'What happened?' he says.

Elena looks baffled. 'You mean just now?'

'Yes.'

'We were visited by a fucking wolf pack, that's what.'

'Did you see them?'

'No, but I heard them.' She looks around the table. What's DJ getting at? 'What's the problem? Why are you asking?'

DJ hesitates a moment, then says, 'That howling. It didn't sound like wolves to me, not actual ones.'

Alex drains his glass and bangs it down on the table. 'Oh yeah? And how many "actual" wolves have you heard, Sir David?' His speech is even more slurred. Consonants seem particularly tricky.

'I haven't heard any at all in real life, but the ones in movies and on the TV sound different.'

'Well, perhaps this lot didn't pass the audition.'

DJ shrugs and shakes his head. For him, there was something not right about the sudden, invisible incursion, but Alex is too drunk to talk about it seriously.

Alex digs in his pocket and brings out a small foil parcel and places it on the table. 'Fuck the wolves. It's time to move on,' he says. The foil contains pills, each about the size of a little fingernail. 'Time to celebrate.'

'Celebrate what?' says DJ.

Alex waves his arm. Elena just manages to save the grappa bottle. 'Celebrate us. Celebrate life, celebrate being here. Celebrate not being eaten alive by wolves.'

Elena examines the pills. 'What are they?' she says. They're pink, and stamped on each one is a cross with a loop on the top. She knows what it is from a visit to a Tutankhamun exhibition. It's called an ankh, and for the ancient Egyptians it was a symbol of eternal life. She doesn't think Alex's pills are promising that.

'They're Sphynx,' says Alex.

'What do they do?'

Alex frowns, as though dealing with a tiresome child. 'What do you think they do? They're a ticket to happy land. They take you on a trip.'

'We're already on a trip,' says Elena. 'We're in Italy.'

'I mean a mind trip,' says Alex.

'I've had enough excitement for one night. A pack of wolves is enough for me.'

Joey has been back to the kitchen and returns with a plate. 'I think these are for us.'

'What are they?' says Mia.

'Petit fours. They're like little cakes. We serve them at *The Golden Bough*.'

DJ examines the plate. There are five of them, small cubes covered in fondant, each with a tiny decoration. 'One each,' he says. 'Look good to me.' He picks one, Elena takes another, and so does Alex. Mia refuses. 'Ellie can have mine,' she says.

'No way,' says Alex. He reaches for the final cake but before he can get it Elena seizes it and pops it in her mouth. She chews it slowly and gives him a smile of pained triumph.

'Oh well,' he says. 'You go your way, I'll go mine.' He sticks out his tongue, places a Sphynx on it, and swallows.

13

Elena and DJ manoeuvre Alex upstairs and steer him towards the bed. It's a struggle because he's a dead weight and they're pretty far gone themselves.

'That's great,' says Elena as they let go and he flops onto the mattress. 'Thanks.'

'He really is in a state,' says DJ. 'I've not seen him like this in a while. Watch out he doesn't throw up. Better turn him.'

They roll Alex over so that he's on his front.

'Sleeping beauty, eh?' says DJ studying him. 'You'll be okay?' he says to Elena.

'Yes. Thanks, DJ.'

'Well give us a shout if you've got a problem.' DJ stands in the doorway and looks back at Alex. 'Man, he's gone. I hope you weren't looking forward to a night of passion. It must be the combination of booze and whatever those pills are.'

'What about you? Are you all right?' Elena herself feels odd; her head is fuzzy and her stomach is uneasy.

'I'm fine. I didn't drink as much as Alex.'

'Nobody did. Mia hardly had anything at all.'

'She rarely does. Great girl to take out for an evening.'

'Pity she can't drive,' says Elena.

'Too right.'

DJ leaves. Elena goes to the balcony and looks out. The moon is well up now, a huge lemon plate high above the trees. She glances at the terrace below. Somebody's turned out the party lights on the pergola – Joey? – and the marble tiles are pale in the moonlight. She returns to the room and checks on Alex. His face is clammy but he hasn't vomited. Not yet. She strips off her clothes and lies on the bed, grateful that it's big enough for her to be able to leave him plenty of space.

Alex's rhythmic breathing has a hypnotic effect. Her eyes feel heavy. Sleep settles on her but not completely. She floats below the surface of consciousness, not awake but aware that she's not asleep either. She's thirsty, a sensation that builds until her throat feels like it's burning. She needs to get herself some water but she can't. And she can't sleep either because Alex has started to snore and the noise is insistent. It's not steady, but a medley of staccato grunts and snuffles.

She rolls onto her back and stares at the ceiling. Her thirst is worse. It's a demand that she can't ignore. She sits up, swings her legs off the bed and waits for a moment, elbows on her knees and her head in her hands. The room is spinning. Too much grappa, she thinks. It didn't seem very potent at the time – there wasn't the savage kick you get from high-proof spirits – but it must have been stronger than she thought. Why did I do it? she asks herself. Alcohol is poison. Why did I drink poison?

She goes to the bathroom, sits on one of the stools, turns on the tap and lets it run while she fills a tumbler, drains it, and then fills it again. She splashes water on her face. She needs more liquid, but something with a taste. Juice or soda. That means a trip to the kitchen. She stands up slowly and waits for her head to get used to the idea. When she feels ready she goes back into the bedroom. Alex is still out. The snoring has stopped; now with each outward breath he's making a little whimpering sound, which is in its way endearing. She's naked and the night is surprisingly cool, the marble floor chilly under her feet. The T-shirt and pants she took off earlier are screwed up on the floor beside the bed. She untangles them and puts them on.

She goes out to the landing and down the stairs. There's a light in the hallway but no sign of anyone about. The door to the terrace has been left open and a horde of moths has flown in. They're battering themselves against the lampshade in futile attempts to get to the sweet source of the radiance.

She gets a can of Orangina from the fridge and goes out to the terrace. The night is oppressively still. Was it only a few hours ago that they stood on this very spot listening to a pack of wolves? If that's what they were. DJ didn't seem to think so but he never said what else they could have been.

She steps off the terrace onto the grass. There's no sound of wolves or anything else, but she is nervous that there might be other things that bite or sting. She's sure she's read somewhere that there are scorpions in Italy. And snakes? And spiders? No, please not spiders. She thinks the dance called the tarantella is from Italy, and that it has something to do with being bitten by a poisonous spider. She could go back for her trainers, but even as she thinks that it no longer seems important.

She takes a few steps away from the house and looks up at the moon. It's bright, flushing the tops of the trees with silver. No wonder the ancients thought it a goddess: Selene, daughter of the Titans. Her English class looked at some poems about the moon and some lines come back to her now.

> *By thy pale beams I solitary rove,*
> *Serenely sweet you gild the silent*
> *grove,*
> *My friend, my goddess, and my guide.*

No harm can come to her under the gaze of such a benevolent watcher. Can it?

On the edge of her vision, the light in the hall goes out. Somebody else must be awake but she's not interested. She doesn't want to talk to anyone.

A dog barks, far far away. There's a screech. An owl? Some other nocturnal hunter? Closer she hears the whine of a mosquito. She flaps in the direction the noise is coming from and it fades. The screech comes again, from deep within the woods. She takes a few steps across the grass. The grass is slightly damp. She thinks about scorpions again: it's probably best to keep moving.

She's aware that she's closer to the edge of the forest than she wants to be. She starts to turn back, then sees something suspended from a branch. It's a child's doll. Some kid staying at the villa must have forgotten it and left it on the grass, and somebody else has put it in a tree. Why here? Why not take it to the house? And why like that, with a cord around its neck as if it's being hanged? She reaches up and pulls. The doll comes down easily. It's made of stuffed fabric. The moonlight neutralises the colours but she can still see that the hair is pale wool. The rosebud mouth and the round eyes make it look goofy, but also appealing. She feels drawn to it. She'll keep it. After all, the kid who lost it must be long gone. She'll take it home and sit it on the shelf in her bedroom. She'll give it a name.

It's as she's thinking this that someone calls her. It's not her actual name but the shortening that her family and friends use, Ellie, and it doesn't come from the house but from the woods. There it is again, clearer now, and twice: Ellie. Ellie. Or is it? It might just be some animal cry. She waits. Then whoever, whatever is summoning her repeats the call, and this time there is no doubt: 'Ellie. Come. Help.'

It sounds human. Female. Her heartbeat speeds up. She can't be sure of the direction but it seems to be dead ahead of her in the trees, and not very far away. Ellie, repeated three times, punctuated by sobs. Someone's in trouble, someone needs her and is shouting to her and crying.

Quickly she glances around. All thoughts of wolves are gone. To her left, there's a path through the trees. It twists so she can't see where it goes, but it looks passable even though it's narrow, and it's going in the right direction.

'Hi,' she calls. 'Is anyone there?'

There's no answer. She pushes her way into the undergrowth, squeezing between trees and scratchy bushes. She hears the voice again, much much closer. 'Ellie. Ellie. Ellie.' It sounds familiar. Her mother? Her gran? Don't be silly, it can't be.

'Hello. Where are you?' she answers. 'I'm here. I'm coming.' The sound of her voice goes nowhere, muffled by the woods. It's like shouting into a blanket. She presses further along the path. Spiky things dig into her feet but she's forgotten about scorpions and snakes and spiders now. She must get to whoever it is that needs her.

It comes again. 'Ellie. Save me.'

'Yes, yes,' she replies. 'I will. Where are you?'

'Here. I am here.'

She looks towards where she thinks the sound is coming from and sees a red-orange splash flickering through the trees. It's a fire. Oh my God, a fire! The forest's tinder dry. A fire will be a disaster. The sane thing is to run, to get away as fast as she can, but the fire and the calls are all one. Someone who knows her is in danger and the fire is part of it; she can't flee one without abandoning the other.

'Hello. I'm coming,' she cries. 'Where are you?'

The flame is only a few metres ahead. Then it vanishes, snuffed out like a blown candle.

With the fire gone, she has no sense of direction. She turns towards where she thinks the house is and takes a few steps. The moon doesn't penetrate the trees and it's pitch dark. She's lost the path. She tries to go forward but her legs are like lead. She turns to go back but the way is blocked by brambles. She has no idea how she got into the forest, or the direction of the way out, or where the calls came from. She revolves helplessly in an effort to locate some waymarker but she can see nothing.

Then it happens. She's seized from behind. Talons dig into her arms. Her eyes are covered. The claws that grip her are tight as a vice. She feels a rough push in her back and she lurches forward. She can't see where she's going and her foot scrapes a rock, stubs on a root. Thorns rake her shins. She's thrust against a tree and her head bangs the trunk. Something is wrapped around her waist and pulled till she cries out. It digs into her flesh and she struggles to wriggle free, but she's bound to the timber and can do nothing.

The pressure eases, but only a little. There's heavy breathing close to her ear.

'You have the doll,' she hears. It's not the voice from before, the one that called her name. This voice is deep, guttural, and coarse. It's accusing, and with the accusation is a threat.

She finds her voice. 'I'm sorry,' she croaks. 'Is the doll yours?' She holds it out in front of her but it's not taken.

She's terrified. Fear chokes her throat; she wants to scream but she can't, no sound will come. Her legs are now like marshmallow and it's only the rope around her middle that's holding her up. Who has caught her in this way? What are they going to do to her?

She hears a grunting noise and there's a foul stench,

acrid and buttery. It's like a mix of urine and sour milk. She's smelt it before: it's goat, strong enough to make her retch. From nowhere the idea of rape explodes in her head. Is that what's going to happen to her? The smell is worse, closer, and she can feel something press against her. She senses hands, and steels herself for when they probe under her clothing, but they don't. They loop something over her head and around her throat. It's a rope.

'Ellie asked you to help her. You agreed. Now you must take her place. Now it is you who must hang from the tree.'

'But I'm Ellie,' she croaks.

'No. The doll is Ellie.'

The noose tightens and she can feel it poised to swing her into the air. She's shaking so much she can barely stand. Her head falls forward and she can see shapes under the edge of the blindfold. They're hooves, and as they shuffle closer she sees a pair of hairy thighs, the haunches of a goat, and an animal phallus. There's the tip, then the rest, a meaty, wrinkled tube swinging obscenely between the creature's legs. It's huge. Its menace terrifies her.

There's more than one goat-man. She can hear a herd of them, an ungulate beat and a chorus of bleats that sound also human. She writhes and tries to free herself but the bonds are fast and won't give, and the more she twists the tighter they get. The noose is squeezing her throat and stopping her breathing. The chanting grows louder and the feet she can see begin a clumsy, stumbling dance, at first on the spot and then edging to the side to be replaced by others as the circle rotates around her.

'Now you must hang,' the voice croaks. 'It is your turn.'

She gasps, struggling for air. The fear of death comes upon her. Is this how art ends? She struggles again, and at last finds her voice. 'Help me,' she shouts, as loud as she can. 'Don't. Please help me. Please. Please.' She starts to sob. The rope heaves. There's a jerk and something rocks her. She feels her body squeezed. She draws all her remaining strength into a terrible scream filled with anguish and fear.

'What is it? What's the matter?' DJ is holding her and peering into her face. She's on her back. She's on the bed. She's drenched in sweat and quivering uncontrollably.

'Oh, my God.' She flings her arms around DJ, and clutches him as tight as she can.

'What is it?' That's Alex, propping himself up.

'She's had a nightmare.'

Mia is there too. 'Is she okay?' she says.

'My god,' says DJ. 'I thought someone was killing her.'

'She's really scared,' says Mia. 'Look how she's shaking.' She sits beside Elena and takes her hand. 'You poor thing. You're trembling like a kitten. There, there. You're all right now. It was just a bad dream, that's all.'

Alex turns to DJ. 'Hey, flick that switch, will you?'

Light fills the room and Elena shuts her eyes against the glare.

'Do you want to talk about it?' Mia says. 'When I have a nightmare telling somebody about it helps clear it out of my head.'

Elena wants to tell them what she saw and felt, but she doesn't think she can. She's not sure enough of what it was to describe it. Did she go downstairs? Did she walk towards the woods? When did she stop doing that and start dreaming? If she was in the woods, how did she get back here?

'What have you done to your legs?' says Mia.

Elena looks down at her shins. There's a lattice of scratches all over them. The images of her nightmare jostle around her: the woods, the thorns, the doll, the cries, the grip, the blindfold, the noose, the dance. And, most terrifying of all, the goat-man.

'It's like you've been dragged through brambles,' says DJ.

'And your arm,' says Mia.

Above her elbow there are four red blotches. She looks at the other one. It's the same. They are like the marks made by huge claws.

STAGE 2 – TRANSITION

14

Alex is on a recliner on the terrace. His eyes are closed but he's not asleep. He still has the dregs of a headache from the night before. Elena is upstairs.

'I wonder how much of this belongs to him?' It's Joey, who's appeared from the house and is standing on the edge of the terrace looking out at the forest.

Alex is irritated by the interruption. 'How much of what belongs to who?' Joey is against the sun and Alex has to squint to look at him. The bright light makes his head worse.

'This footballer guy. How much of what we can see here is his?'

'The "footballer guy" is called Theo Vasilias. You're living in the man's house, and what's more he's paid for you to be here, and he's feeding you while you stay. You might at least learn his name.' Alex's tone shows his exasperation. Joey makes a big thing of his lack of interest in all sports. Alex thinks his ignorance is fake, an inverted form of showing off. '

'Yeah, whatever,' says Joey. He likes winding Alex up and is pleased with the response, but he doesn't show it.

Alex sighs and sits up. 'To answer your question, I've got no idea. This house is his, obviously, and the other one. I don't know how big the estate is. There may be other places around here that belong to him, as well.'

'We passed a fancy entrance on the way up here,' says Joey. 'I don't know if you saw it, a mile or so down the track?'

Alex remembers a large pair of elaborate gates supported on stone pillars topped with carvings of lions. 'I saw them,' he says. There's a pause, then, 'Hey, move over will you? I can't see you without looking into the sun.'

'Oh, sorry.' Joey shuffles to the side. 'What are you doing?'

'Well, I was trying to chill out before you turned up, catch up a bit. Elena had a rough night.'

'What's wrong? Isn't she well?'

'She's okay. She had some bad dreams though.'

'Oh.' Joey is interested.

'Yeah, she woke me up yelling as if a dozen devils were after her. DJ and Mia heard it too. I'm surprised you didn't.'

'I sleep like a baby,' says Joey. 'Once I'm gone I'm gone.'

'And all without the help of alcohol. Or Sphynx.'

Joey grunts. 'I don't really do that kind of stuff,' he says.

'You should,' says Alex. 'Help you relax.'

Joey shakes his head. 'It's not my scene.' He looks around again. 'So, how much do you reckon it's all worth? This house, and the other.'

Alex doesn't want a conversation but it's a question that intrigues him. 'I'm not sure. I don't know anything about property values in Italy. Tuscany's popular. A lot of English people buy out here. And Germans. Castelvecchio's got plenty to offer. It could make money as a hotel. I think maybe up to a couple of million for this place? Four or five for the big house? It's hard to say without seeing it and without knowing what goes with it. Why, are you thinking of making Theo an offer?'

Joey snorts. Then he says, 'Do you think it's fair?'

Alex sighs. Why does Joey never explain properly what he means? 'Do I think what's fair?'

'Do you think it's fair that one man owns all this? Not just one house but two, worth more than most people will see in their whole lives?'

Alex doesn't answer straight away. His father has built his own business. He started as an accountant with very little and now he employs fifty people in three offices. Last year he bought an investment company, Croesus Wealth Management. They have a big house, his mother doesn't need to work, and he and his sister have their own cars, bought new on their eighteenth birthdays. He knows that he's luckier than the other four.

'It's not simple,' he says. 'On the face of it, okay, I admit it's hard to defend a set-up where one person has a hundred times more than another. But I think on the

137

whole people get what they deserve, and what the world determines is right.'

'Do you really think that?' says Joey. 'What about DJ? His dad's a doctor and his mum's head of a primary school. They won't get paid anywhere near what this Theo guy gets, yet he's saving lives and she's educating kids. Isn't that more important than kicking a ball about?'

'They're different things. You call what Theo does "kicking a ball about". When you put it like that it sounds nothing, but there aren't many people who can kick a ball about as well as Theo can. Thousands of people go to watch him, and a lot more see him on TV, all over the world. He represents his country in a sport that means a lot to a lot of people.'

Joey isn't convinced. 'I'm not saying he should get the same as my mum gets for working in the care home. Just that he doesn't need as much as they give him.'

'What people need and what they get are different, and they always will be. Even communism hasn't managed to solve that one. As for Theo, you've got to take into account the situation he's in. He has to be dedicated to being at peak fitness all the time. Every time he goes out onto the field he runs the risk of picking up an injury that could end his career, just like that. And even if he stays fit, in just a few years his playing days will be over. Finished. The Blackbirds think that's worth a lot of money.'

'Okay,' says Joey. 'Nothing personal here, but what about your dad? Isn't his job all about helping people to get out of paying their taxes? He doesn't entertain people or make them better. He just helps the rich stay rich, and perhaps get even richer.'

Alex resents this from Joey. It's all very well for him to be saying it's not personal, but it is. It's out of order. He tries not to let his pique show. 'My dad's firm does people's taxes and company accounts and makes sure that everything's proper and fair. He checks that people don't pay more tax than they have to, but he also makes sure they pay what they should. And Croesus Wealth doesn't just deal with rich wankers. A lot of its clients are people who only have a little bit, nest eggs, pensions and savings that they've built up over years. They trust him to look after their money, to keep safe what they've worked for, and maybe help them to add a bit to it. That's worth something isn't it?'

Joey says nothing. Alex makes his dad's business sound like a public service, but he's seen the adverts. *Touch Gold with Croesus*. They create the impression that if you hand over your money to them they'll add a lot to it. It's only in the small print where it says that you might not get back everything you give them. To Joey, it sounds no different from the gambling his father did. 'All I'm saying,' he says, 'is that if people like this footballer...'

'Theo Vasilias.'

'...yes, okay, if people like Theo Vasilias had less, there might be more for the rest of us.'

Alex shakes his head. He doesn't want to be having this conversation, he'd rather be napping in the sun, resting his head, but he can't let it go. Joey is being a hypocrite and needs to be told so. 'You're going to work at *The Golden Bough*, right?'

'Yes.'

'And it's your dream job, something you're looking forward to.'

'Yes, it is.'

'*The Golden Bough* is a posh restaurant. It's got some Michelin stars and is very expensive. Who do you think goes there? Certainly not families like yours and Mia's? Our family has only been there a few times, on special occasions. The people who eat there regularly are very well off. And these are the people you are going to cook for. If rich people didn't go there you wouldn't have a job.'

'I suppose not,' says Joey. 'But it still doesn't make it right that some people have everything and others nothing.'

'Maybe not, but you'll be okay. Do your training at *The Golden Bough* and then open your own place, and you'll soon be raking it in. Sounds like a plan to me. We can't all have the same. Life's not like that. There'll always be haves and have-nots. You just have to make sure you're one of the haves.'

Joey gets up. He can see some of what Alex says but he can't bring himself to agree. The leftovers at *The Golden Bough* go in a waste bin. When he does have his own restaurant he'll make sure they go to the homeless and the hungry, and that there's always something left over for those who can't afford to pay to eat there. He gets up.

'I'm going to get some coffee,' he says.

Alex knows he hasn't won. He's had arguments like this with Joey before, in classes and outside them. Joey doesn't give up – it's a break in hostilities, that's all – and

Alex feels angry and resentful. People make their own luck, and they get what they can where they can, and when. If some people don't get as much as others it's because they don't take the chances that come their way. Joey's dad was a waster. He gave up working, and when he wasn't in the pub he was in the betting shop. Then he walked out and left Joey, his mum and his sister on their own. Being poor is a lifestyle choice, and those who make that choice have no right to go on at those who've made a different one. 'If you don't like it, Joey,' he says to himself, 'then change it.' The ironic thing is that if Joey does get to be a top chef he'll earn a lot more than Alex would if he were to go on to study oceans and the climate. What would he be saying about "fairness" then?

It also angers him that Joey makes a lot of assumptions about Alex's home, but Alex's father keeps a tight hold on the purse strings. Money doesn't flow like water in the Brandish household, no way. Yes, he gets an allowance but it's only just enough to cover what it costs him to run his car, and if he needs more he has to find ways to earn it. His parents were against the idea of him taking a year off. His dad was quick to say that when he left school his allowance would stop and anything he needed would have to come out of his university fund, and in any case, that's only on offer if he actually goes to university. Well, fuck that. This next year is going to be special. It's going to set Alex up. And he has a feeling that it's starting with this trip.

Joey must drink his coffee somewhere else because he doesn't return. Alex lies in the sun. He turns over so he's face down, and feels the warmth on his back. He drifts into sleep.

He's woken by Elena rubbing lotion on him. 'That's nice,' he says.

'Good job I came along,' she says. 'Your shoulders are getting quite red. Maybe you should move out of the sun.'

She sits beside him on the recliner and he rolls over. Then he sees her face. She looks strained, her hair is all over the place and there are dark rings around her eyes. 'Are you okay,' he says. 'You look rough.'

'Why thank you, kind sir,' she says. 'I feel fucking rough. You don't look so hot yourself.'

Alex rubs his eyes. He won't admit to his hangover, he never does, but she knows he has one.

'I've been trying to sleep,' she says, 'but every time I shut my eyes I see things from my dream. It was so real.' She shudders, and rubs her ankles and shins, where there are bruises and scratches. She nods towards the woods. 'My legs weren't like this when I went to bed. Do you think it's possible that I really went into those woods last night? Was I sleepwalking?'

'It's a thought,' he says. 'I suppose you might have been. But I'm sure one of the things about sleepwalking is that people don't remember it, whereas you can remember your nightmare.'

'Yes, I can. Every single depraved second of it.'

'So it seems more likely you were in bed the whole time.'

'Then how did I get these?' She points to the angry marks.

Alex shrugs. 'It could be that you somehow did it

yourself, with your fingernails? You know, while you were in the dream?'

She looks at her bitten nails. Hardly likely, she thinks, but she says nothing.

There's a pause. There is something she needs to say to him. She doesn't want to, but she must. It's why she came down from their room, why she's sought him out. While she was upstairs she saw his wallet. It was on the table at his side of the bed. She didn't want to pry but curiosity got the better of her. She looked in it. She's not sure how to broach this so she jumps straight in. 'When I'm not thinking about my dream I'm thinking about Mia's money. I'm worried about her.'

'Why? She's not mentioned it again. I don't think she's that bothered.'

'Don't you? I do. So does DJ.'

'Really?' Alex feels irritated. People keep talking to him and he wishes they'd leave him alone and let him have some peace.

'He brought it up. He says she tries to pretend it's nothing, but she's really upset. She feels stupid for bringing so much with her.' There's a pause. 'How much did you bring?'

He answers quickly. 'Not a lot. Just a few euros. You know.'

She does know. When she saw Alex's wallet there were more than three hundred euros in there. Would he, might he have stolen from Mia? Can she believe that of him? Sadly she thinks that perhaps she can.

15

Elena doesn't know what to do. She knows that although his family is wealthy Alex himself is not as well off as he pretends, and that forces him into deception. Often when it's his turn to buy a round or to chip into something they're doing together there'll be a reason why he can't. He's forgotten his wallet. Or he's just filled up his car and he's skint till he can get to a cash machine. Or one of his mates was short and he's just subbed him. It's always something. She's suggested that he get a job. Her parents could find him occasional work in the pub, but Alex says he hasn't the time. She suspects that the real reason is he thinks it's beneath him.

She's in the kitchen and she runs herself a glass of ice-cold water from the fridge dispenser. It tastes wonderful. She swills it and feels the chill coursing down her throat. She gets herself another. She thinks she's probably become dehydrated and that's why she has a headache. Although it could be last night's grappa.

She carries her glass into the sitting room. It's a

moment before her eyes become accustomed to the dimmer light so she doesn't immediately notice Mia. Then she sees her at the far end of the room, holding an open book.

'Have you seen this?' she says.

'Seen what?'

'This book.' Mia holds it towards her.

The book is a slim hardback and looks old. The front and spine are blank and she turns to the title page: *Forbes Lexicon of Dreams*. The line underneath the title tells her it's by The Reverend Samuel Forbes, MA (Oxon), issued by a publisher she's never heard of in London in MDCCCLXXXVIII. She scratches around in her memory of Roman numerals to work out that means 1888.

'Don't you think it's odd?' says Mia.

'I don't know. Is it?'

'Yes. Don't you see? It's in English.'

Elena doesn't see. There were publications in English on the bookstall at Florence Station. Material in English doesn't seem at all hard to find in this part of Italy. 'So?'

Mia explains. 'I was looking for something to read and so I came in here to see if there was anything on the shelves. I was out of luck because all the books are in Italian, apart from a few in German. Then I saw this. It's in English, and as far as I can see it's the only book in the whole library that is.'

Elena shrugs. 'Theo's an Italian and this is his house. It's not surprising that his books are in his own language. And maybe not that many English people stay here. I expect a previous English visitor left it.'

'You think? Feel it. This isn't the sort of thing you take

146

on holiday. It's not light reading, it's a heavyweight hardback. What's more, it's the subject.'

'Yes, dreams,' she says. 'Now that *is* interesting.' Perhaps the book might shine some light on the horrors she experienced during the night. She puts the book on one of the side tables and turns the pages while Mia watches. There's an introduction, then a dictionary section with topics in alphabetical order, each with a paragraph or so of explanation: Abandonment, Abdication, Abduction. She turns over some more pages. Dagger, Disease, Doctor, Doll.

> "For a gentleman to dream of a doll is an indication that his affections are wandering and that he seeks female companionship. For him to dream of a male doll suggests trouble with a servant. For a lady to dream of a doll indicates that she feels a threat to her womanhood, or that her current relationship is no longer satisfactory to her."

Is that what the goofy doll with stringy hair meant? Does she feel sexually threatened? Who by? Was her nightmare connected with what she is coming to realise are cooling feelings towards Alex?

'What does the introduction say?' she asks.

'I've only read a bit of it,' says Mia. 'It seems to be saying that how we react to what we see, hear and feel during sleep is as valid an insight into character as how we behave when we're awake. There's a whole section on nightmares. The book says that they have more impact on us than our other dreams and they often have more meaning too. It says that everyone dreams every night –

well we know that don't we – but usually we only remember the dream we're having at the moment we wake up. It says that nightmares are so vivid that they often wake us, and that's why we remember the bad dreams more than the good ones.'

'Mine certainly woke me up, and I certainly remember it. I wish I could forget it. Does he say anything else?'

'Yes, quite a lot but I haven't had time to read it all yet.' She folds her arms and looks steadily at Elena. 'When did you last have a nightmare?'

Elena can't remember. 'I don't know. Quite a while ago, I think.'

'So you don't have them often.'

'No. I went through a spell when I was a kid when I had a lot, but not now. Why are you asking?'

'Because it seems strange, don't you think? You have a bad dream, your first for a long time, and now here's a book that says a lot about dreams, and it's the only one in English out of the...' she looks around '...what, a thousand books in here? And there's something else. When I found this book it wasn't on the shelves with all the others. If it had been I probably wouldn't have noticed it. No, it had been left open on the table, as if somebody had just been reading it and left it there. Now, don't you think that's funny?'

She does. It connects with some thoughts that she was beginning to form herself but they'd seemed too extraordinary to mention. Yesterday when Alex tried the studio door it had been locked. He was convinced it had been, and that there was no mistake. Then DJ went there and found the studio door open. Somebody must have come and unlocked it, but they hadn't seen anyone. Last night they heard wolves, very close, in woods that Bruno said were mysterious. There'd been a funny feeling too, as if some force was operating around them. She'd been telling herself that it was nothing, that she was overreacting. Now there's this book.

'I came in here yesterday,' she says, 'when I was looking around, not long after we got here. I'm sure there weren't any books on the table then. I would have seen them if there had been.'

'I came in here too,' says Mia. 'There was nothing.' She's watching Elena closely. 'Are you thinking what I'm thinking?' she says.

'I don't know. What are you thinking?'

'I'm thinking that someone put this book on the table on purpose, just so one of us would find it.'

16

It's later in the day. Alex closes the bedroom door. He does it gently because he doesn't want to wake Elena. He wants her to sleep for her own benefit, but more than that he wants to avoid another stressful and fraught reliving of her dream. She's been through it with him at least half a dozen times, and with every retelling she seems to become more upset.

He goes quickly down the stairs, across the terrace and out towards the woods. He's determined to end this nonsense. Elena's had a bad dream, but that's all it was. He's had them himself, but when you wake up they go; that is if you let them. Elena isn't letting hers go, she's wallowing in it, going over and over again what she thinks happened. At first she believed it was all a dream. Then she saw the scratches on her leg and decided some of it must have been real. Now she's convinced that the whole thing was real. It's garbage and he's going to put a stop to it, but he needs ammunition.

He gets to the edge of the grass and walks along the

boundary of the trees. He's looking for evidence that someone's been there, but he knows there won't be any. Elena says she dropped the doll that was in her dream but there's no sign of one, so that can't be real. Most telling is that there's no way that he can see to get into the woods at all. Elena talks about going along a path, but there isn't one. The forest is ancient, the trees and bushes woven together over hundreds of years. Low branches would stop you from walking through. He bends down. You might be able to crawl on all fours between the trunks but there's a lot of stuff on the forest floor – twigs, thorny branches, stones. You'd rip your knees to shreds if you tried to get through that lot. There's no way Elena went that way. He can't account for the scratches on her legs, but they would have been much worse if she'd really been in the wood.

He turns away and goes back to the villa. Elena is deluded. It's all down to this crazy stuff from Bruno about the woods being magical and mysterious, and then on top of that the grappa. Maybe she shouldn't have had so much of it, but for Christ's sake she's a big girl; she ought to know what she's doing. Could it be some psychological thing she's going through? This is not the time or the place to be cultivating a breakdown. His father maintains that mental health is something you control yourself and Alex thinks he agrees. She needs to pull herself together.

There's nobody on the terrace. If Mia had been there he could have asked her about it. She was on the Psychology A level course and they must have covered dreams; she might have some idea of what's going on in Elena's head.

He goes along the side of the house in the direction of the studio. As soon as he pushes open the outer door he hears Joey. There are two drum kits in there, behind plastic screens on a dais at the far end. Joey is at the larger one, an eight-piece with a brace of kick drums and he seems to be trying to strike all of them at once.

He stops when he sees Alex. 'Shit, I need three feet,' he says.

'Two proper ones would be a good start,' says Alex.

'Ha. Ha. Ha,' is Joey's reply.

There are a pair of keyboards set up in the middle of the room, a Yamaha and a Roland. Alex has a Yamaha at home, a couple of models down from this one. He sits on the stool and switches it on. He has a tune in his head and he wants to do some work on it. He begins to play, and Joey starts drumming again. Joey isn't used to playing two kick drums and is finding it hard to manage them both and a hi-hat at the same time. The on-off of the rhythm and the missed beats when he loses it are distracting. Alex turns up the gain on the Yamaha as far as it will go, but he still can't concentrate against the racket.

'Hey, Joey,' he shouts. 'Knock it off for a spell, will you? I'm trying to work on something here.'

Joey looks hurt, but he stops drumming and begins to investigate the way the snare is fixed. It's set at the wrong angle for him to get a decent rim shot. Alex continues trying to extend his melody. After a few minutes Joey leaves and Alex is alone in the coffin quiet.

When Alex heard that there was a place where they could practice he thought it might be a kind of shed with, if they were lucky, an amp and an old reel-to-reel tape deck. It's not. State-of-the-art would not be overselling it.

The building is long and rectangular. It must once have been a barn but it's now insulated and thoroughly soundproofed. Even more impressive is what it contains: it has everything needed to make a professional recording. As well as the drums and keyboards there are isolation booths for vocalists, and spread around the room chairs and stools for other performers. There's an assortment of mics and stands in one corner. In another, there's an enormous gong, suspended in a frame as tall as DJ. Cables snake the floor. It's easy to imagine some supergroup recording here. Whoever the "Italian rock star" who built it was, he – or maybe she – must have been doing spectacularly well.

To the left of the main door is the control room. Alex has already tried the door so he knows it's locked. A pity. You can see through the window computers, a huge mixing desk, and monitor speakers. It would be good if they could get to use those. Perhaps the door to the control room will open as mysteriously as the one to the studio had.

He plays his composition again. Without the distraction of Joey's drumming it comes more easily. He works on the refrain and then begins on a bridge to the hook. It sounds okay but it needs more colour, so he adds some triplets. Yes, that works. He smiles to himself, sits back, and cracks his knuckles.

'Well, what do you think?' It's DJ, who pauses in the doorway and looks around the room. 'Have we died and gone to heaven?' He's carrying both his guitar cases.

'Not bad, is it?' Alex agrees.

'It's amazing,' says DJ. 'Who needs Abbey Road?' He puts down the guitars, goes to the control room and tries the door.

'It's locked,' says Alex.

'Pity. It looks like a great setup in there. Hey, if we can get in we'll be able to record some of our songs, maybe for an EP.'

He organises a couple of stools and gets out a guitar, his electric one. He plugs in one of the cables coiled on the floor and tries a chord. He adjusts the amp and sweeps his plectrum across the strings. He retunes, and strums some more.

'Okay, what shall we play?' he says.

'Why don't we do the same set we did at the awards?' says Alex. 'That's the stuff Theo and Lita heard and liked. All of it will suit the occasion.'

'Yeah. Except for *Saturday Girl*. I don't think Lita will think a song about being dumped is a good thing to play at her wedding.'

Alex laughs. 'No. We could swap it for something else. I've been working on some words Elena wrote on the way over. It's called *You For Me For Ever*.' He catches DJ's expression. 'Yeah, I know, it sounds cheesy, but it is for a wedding.'

He plays the tune he's been working on and sings Elena's words.

DJ waits until Alex has finished, then says, 'I like that, I think it will work. No offence, mate, but we do need Elena to sing it.'

Alex knows that vocals aren't his strong point. 'Yeah,

it's a girl's song anyway. She's getting some rest but she's been there a while. I'll go get her.'

'Get Joey too. It's time we did some proper rehearsals.'

Alex leaves. DJ gets out his other guitar, the acoustic, and fiddles around, playing a few chords and tweaking the tuning pegs.

He's absorbed for a few minutes. Then he notices Alex's backpack on the floor beside the keyboards, and an idea begins to form. He puts down his instrument, goes over to the backpack, and stands looking down at it. He hasn't been able to get out of his head what Mia said to him about Alex and her purse. He can't believe that Alex would do what she thinks. On the other hand, Mia is probably the most level person he's ever met, and she wouldn't make an accusation like that without first giving it a lot of thought. This is a chance to settle it. Alex keeps his wallet in his backpack, in an inside pocket. Just a quick look. If there are less than a hundred and fifty euros in there, as Alex claims, then Mia must be wrong.

The flap of the backpack is loose. He squats, peels it away, and looks inside. There's a T-shirt, screwed up not folded. He takes it out so he can see what else there is. A graphic novel, *Legions of Thor*. He remembers seeing Alex reading it on the journey. He takes that out too. Next, there's a notebook, most of the pages scrappily marked up with lines of letters, the notation Alex uses for their songs. There's a photo in the notebook. DJ thinks that's unusual at a time when most people have all their pictures on their phones, but when he sees it he can understand why Alex might want to keep a print of this one. It's Elena. She's lying on a bed and the picture's been taken from her feet. One knee is drawn up and her head is on a pillow so she's looking directly at the camera. She's completely naked. She has a tattoo that looks like a twist of flowers on her lower belly, below her bikini line. DJ hadn't known about that, but then why would he? He gazes at the photo, then puts it back and pushes the notebook aside. He continues rummaging.

It doesn't occur to him to consider the rights and wrongs of invading his friend's property, or the wisdom of it. The search has become an end in itself. He finds Alex's phone, a pair of socks, and some tissues balled into a wad. And then he goes cold. Underneath the tissues is a small, pink purse. Pink, heart-shaped, made of leather, with a leaf logo embossed in green. It's Mia's. Unmistakably. It's the one she brought with her from England. It must be hers, he's never seen another one like it. It's the purse that contained her euros, the one that was stolen in Domodossola. He undoes the zip. It's empty. He's frozen for a moment while he tries to make sense of what he's found and its implications.

'Elena will be down in a bit and I can't find Joey...' Alex is speaking as he comes through the studio door. His voice tails off as he sees DJ. Then he realises what's going on. 'What the fuck? That's my stuff. What are you doing?' His voice rises in pitch and volume. 'WHAT THE FUCK ARE YOU DOING?'

Alex is furious. DJ's guitar is on the stool. He grabs it and swings. DJ tries to dodge but the guitar glances off his shoulder and cracks him across the side of his head. He takes a step back. Alex comes at him again, aiming a punch. DJ sees it coming and turns away but it smacks his ear. Now DJ is angry. He lashes out at Alex and connects with his nose. Alex yells and grabs DJ by the shirt. The two grapple with each other, one of them trips and they both fall to the floor, rolling on the guitar, struggling among toppling music stands and tumbling furniture.

Suddenly there's a crash like the end of the world. It's ear-splitting and body shaking and it shocks the two fighters so much that they roll apart. Alex gets up, one hand clasped to his face. He grabs the tissues and dabs his nose. The wad comes away scarlet. DJ sits on the floor holding the side of his head where the guitar struck him. The instrument lies near him, its fretboard broken and its body crushed. Both his and Alex's shirts are splattered with blood.

'What the hell do you think you're doing? Stop it! Stop it now!' It's Elena. She's standing by the gong, holding the beater, and she looks furious. 'For Christ's sake!'

DJ gets up and scrabbles for the pink purse. He holds it out towards Elena. 'Alex had it. It's Mia's purse. And it's empty.'

'What?' Elena comes towards him. Both of them look at Alex.

'Yes it is, but it's...' he starts, then he changes his mind. 'What? You think I took it?'

'What does it look like?' says DJ.

'Fuck off. I don't have to explain to you,' says Alex, moving towards the door. He's still holding the tissues to his face.

Elena blocks his way. 'Yes you do,' she says.

Alex thinks for a moment and dabs his cheeks, which are smeared with crimson. 'All right then. It is Mia's. At least I'm pretty sure it is.'

'I'm absolutely sure it is,' says DJ. 'How come you've got it?'

'I found it on the station, when we came out of the waiting room where we'd been dossing, where it was nicked. Mia and you,' he nods towards Elena, 'were ahead with DJ and Joey was behind you. I was last and I saw it. It was under a bench, like it had been kicked there. It looked like Mia's so I picked it up. I was going to give it to her but I saw it was open and there was nothing in it so I stuck it in my pocket.'

'Why didn't you say anything?' says Elena.

'I was going to, but then I thought, What's the point?'

'The point is, it's the purse her dad gave her,' says DJ.

'Yeah, but it was empty, Besides, I had an idea. I thought I'd put some money in it, a hundred and fifty euros, what she lost. I've got plenty of cash with me, my whole month's allowance.' He holds his hand up, anticipating the objection. 'I know I said I hadn't brought much, but that was because I didn't want it to look as if I was showing off.'

That would be a first, DJ thinks, but he says nothing. To him the story sounds thin but he wants to believe it. Elena says, 'How were you planning to give it to her?'

Alex looks down. 'I don't know. I mean, I couldn't just walk up to her and hand it over, could I? And the longer I left it the harder it got. That's why I've not done anything about it yet.' He looks at DJ. 'I thought of asking you if you could somehow smuggle it in with Mia's other stuff, so she could maybe come across it and think it was just that she'd misplaced it.'

'But you didn't,' says DJ.

'No.' Alex looks at the floor again. He gingerly feels his nose; it's stopped bleeding but it's tender. 'How's your head?'

'It hurts. How's your nose?'

'Okay, I think.' He pats it with the tissues. They're a sodden mess, and useless. 'You shouldn't have been going through my stuff.'

DJ considers. Does he believe Alex's story? It sounds far-fetched but it's also in a way believable. Finding the purse and keeping it to himself is just the sort of thing Alex would do. Getting it back to Mia with money in it? Possible. The main thing, though, is that Alex has been his friend for a long time, and even though they're not now as close as they used to be he's still a good mate. 'No, I shouldn't have been doing that,' he says. 'I don't know why I did. I'm sorry.'

'You should have asked me.'

'Yes, I should.'

'You won't say anything to Mia.'

Is that a question or is it an instruction? DJ doesn't know. 'No. Okay,' he says.

'I'll make sure she gets her purse back before we go home.'

'Right.'

DJ catches Elena's eye. Does she believe Alex? He's not sure that she does.

17

Joey leaves the studio and goes back to the house. He's hoping that Mia might be on the terrace but there's no sign of her. He gets himself a cold Coke from the kitchen and takes it outside, where he stands on the edge of the marble tiles and looks towards the woods.

He's pissed off with Alex. He was in the studio first, and he started on the drums before Alex arrived. It's a fantastic kit and he was enjoying getting to grips with it, then his lordship came in, sat down at the keyboards and told him to shut up, as if he owned the place. Or as if he had some right to take over. But that's Alex. He always assumes he's the boss. Like last night, when he took the seat at the head of the table. Not that Joey wanted to be there, heaven forbid, but there was no discussion. Alex just did it.

Anyway, Alex doesn't rate drumming. He thinks it's no more than laying down a beat on a kick drum with occasional fills on the snare and a cymbal strike every couple of bars. When Joey tries to be more creative Alex grumbles that he's being too flashy and distracting from the words, or the tune, or what the rest of the band is doing.

The Coke can is empty and he screws it up in one hand. He wants to throw it, to hurl it in a great parabola into the trees, but he knows that would be gross so he leaves it on the table.

Joey has always found Alex difficult because he looks down on him. It's not just that his own family is skint and Alex's is loaded, there are other things too. He's got a way of making Joey feel that whatever he's doing is not quite right, that whenever he opens his mouth what comes out of it is stupid, and that nothing he does is good enough. He talks down to him like he was a kid. That's one reason why when everyone's together Joey doesn't say much. All the others are going to university but he isn't. He's going to be a chef, and although that's a long and hard training it's obvious Alex doesn't think it compares with doing a degree. He wasn't even impressed when Joey got the job at *The Golden Bough*. 'They must have been desperate!' he said when he heard the news. He said it as if it was a joke but Joey knows he meant it. DJ and Elena aren't as bad but sometimes he gets the same feeling from them too. The only one who seems to think he's as good as the others is Mia.

He's liked her from the moment she joined the school. He, DJ and Elena were in the sixth form common room when the 'new girl' walked in. Joey was immediately smitten. Elena started talking to her and so did DJ, but he couldn't think of anything interesting to say. The first time he saw her out of school was a few days later. He was walking home and she was running along the opposite pavement. She didn't notice him and he stood still, watching her easy strides and her ponytail snapping from side to side. He crossed the road and followed her, staying twenty or thirty metres behind. He could keep up with her on the level, but when she turned into a road that went uphill she left him behind.

A few of the houses in the terraces that lined the street had been "improved", with upvc double glazing, leaded windows, and loft conversions. More of them hadn't, and they showed peeling paintwork, rotting timbers, and overflowing bins. One he passed had an old mattress in the front garden, the fabric mildewed and stained. A dead plastic trike lay beside it.

He watched the receding figure of Mia drawing farther ahead. The houses higher up the hill were better cared for, and near the top he saw her turn into a gateway. He carried on until he reached what must be her house, compact and neat, with a tidy front yard. Now he knew where she lived.

The street is only a few minutes walk from his own home. Several times over the next couple of weeks he found reasons to walk past Mia's house. At least twice he hung around the general store on the opposite corner hoping he might see her coming in or going out, or maybe glimpse her at a window. Then one day he got home from school to find his mother watching the TV. It was a discussion programme, and a woman was describing how the same man regularly passed her house and she often saw him loitering outside. She said that the man was stalking her and she felt threatened.

Joey was horrified. Is that what he was doing to Mia? Stalking her? He meant no harm, he just wanted to see her, but he resolved in that instant to stop it.

For several weeks he was so embarrassed she might have seen him that he avoided her. That was until Elena had asked him one day, 'Why don't you like Mia?' Is that what it looked like? Is that what Mia herself thought, that he didn't like her? Or perhaps she thought nothing. Perhaps she didn't even notice him. And even if she did, perhaps she didn't care. But how could he put it right? What should he do or say? He's never been good with girls. It's an impossible situation and it makes him miserable.

He looks up and something catches his eye. A little way off a man in green overalls is watering the grass. It occurs to Joey that apart from his four companions this is the first human being he's seen in over twenty-four hours. 'It must be like being on a desert island,' he murmurs to himself. The gardener waves and calls something. The only two words of Italian that Joey knows are "grazie" and "si". He tries both, 'Si, grazie.' The man smiles and waves, so it must be all right.

Joey watches the watering from the edge of the terrace, looking towards the woods which start no more than fifty metres away. The gardener finishes, coils up his hose, loads it onto a buggy and leaves, up the hill in the direction of the big house. Joey waits until he's out of sight and then walks towards the trees. The grass is damp and soon his trainers are soaked.

He wants to check on what he saw yesterday in the trees. Elena's dream troubles him. It was a nightmare; people get those and that would be okay, but for the doll. The one she described, a pink rag doll with yellow hair and an embroidered face, was like the one he found. She can't have seen the one in the trees before her dream because he's sure that if she had she would have mentioned it. So why would she dream of one the same? Yesterday he'd concluded that the things he'd seen somehow represented the five of them, the yellow-haired doll being Elena. He'd found it suspended by the neck, and then Elena dreams about being hung. That's more than a coincidence. If he can find the doll again he'll get it down from the tree, take it to her, and ask her if that was the one in her dream. And he'll tell them all about the other things too.

He stops at the edge of the grass and looks up and down. He can remember roughly where the rag doll was and there's nothing there. There's no sign of the other doll, the plastic one, either, or the animals, or the other objects. He feels a momentary quiver, a faint tremor like a tiny earthquake. Is he crazy? Or was he crazy yesterday? Did he really see them? He knows he did. Why hadn't he taken pictures on his phone so he could be sure?

He walks beside the trees. There's nothing in the branches and nothing on the ground where they might have fallen. They were there yesterday and they're not there today. None of them. That means somebody must have removed them. Was it the gardener he saw just now? There was a container on his buggy and they could have been in that. But why shift them? Why go to all the trouble of hanging them up there – you'd need a stepladder for some of them – only to take them down?

There's another question too. If they were meant to ward off evil, does that mean that the evil has gone? Or that protection from it has been withdrawn?

18

'It's a good job it was my acoustic,' says DJ. 'If it had been my Strat you would have knocked my brains out.'

'Such as they are,' says Alex.

The five of them are together at the table on the terrace. Alex is again at the head, just like the previous evening.

'There's no need to sound so cheerful about it,' says DJ. He's feeling better than when Alex first clouted him but he still has a headache and the side of his face is sore.

They're eating the meal that Gianna, the cook, has prepared for them. She appeared towards the end of the afternoon just as promised in Bruno's note. They don't know where she came from. One minute the kitchen was empty and the next she was there. She's in her middle age, slightly built, and stooped, which Joey assumes must be the result of a lifetime of working in kitchens, bending over pots and chopping boards. Her dark hair, longish and tied back, shows flecks of grey. She has flat shoes, trodden down at the heels. She smiled at them uncertainly when she arrived and then set to work straight away chopping, frying and boiling. Joey watched her for a time, eager to see what she was doing and pick up some tips, but he sensed this was making her feel uncomfortable so he came away.

'She probably thinks you're checking up on her,' Elena says.

The food – pasta in a spicy sauce with a salad of fresh tomatoes, peppers, cucumber, olives, and basil – is delicious. The pasta is like Joey has never tasted before, very different from the dried variety he's had in England. Gianna has prepared two versions of the sauce, and it takes them some time to understand her when she mimes that one of them contains meat and the other doesn't.

'Vegetariana,' she says, pointing to Mia, the only vegetarian among them.

DJ thinks that's odd. How does she know? Did Alex tell Bruno that one of them was vegetarian? And if he did, how does this woman know which of them it is? But he's too interested in the food to raise it.

They're all hungry and the plates and bowls are soon empty and scraped clean.

Gianna clears away the dishes. Then she holds open the freezer door and indicates several large tubs of ice cream, with the action of a conjuror revealing the climax of a trick. None of them can manage to eat anything more, at least not yet, and they shake their heads. Gianna smiles and bows.

'I think Gianna is what you might call "a treasure",' says Alex.

'I wish we had her at the pub,' says Elena.

She signals that she's leaving and they make lavish gestures to express their thanks – smiling, rubbing their stomachs, gently clapping, putting their palms together. She looks at them quizzically and a little nervously, and backs out.

'She probably thinks we're English nut jobs,' DJ says.

'Well she's right about that,' says Elena. 'At least as far as two of us are concerned.' She looks at Alex.

'Tell Joey and me what happened,' says Mia. 'Did you head butt the studio door?'

She's already asked DJ once about his swollen face but he brushed off her enquiries. Now, a cold compress, a couple of hours and several glasses of red wine later, he's feeling more mellow.

'It was an accident,' he says. 'Stupid. Alex was swinging my guitar around, doing a kind of rock and roll thing, and he caught me with it. I saw it coming and ducked so it mainly hit my shoulder, but it got the side of my head too.'

It isn't a story he and Alex have concocted, it's something he has come up with on his own. He's been thinking about how to account to Mia and Joey for what happened. He hopes Elena won't say anything about what she saw.

'Should you be drinking if you've had a bang on the head?' says Mia.

'That is the very best time to drink,' says DJ, and laughs. 'It numbs the pain.'

'Any time is the best time to drink,' says Alex, and refills his glass and DJ's. Elena's relieved to see that the two of them seem to have got over what happened in the studio.

'Is your guitar bust?' says Joey.

'Oh yeah,' says DJ. 'Totally. The body's fucked and the fretboard's broken off.'

'Can it be mended?'

'No way. It's a cheap one anyway. I think it's time to thank it and wave it bye-bye.'

'We need to give it a proper send-off,' says Elena. 'A formal farewell to celebrate its achievements.'

'What achievements are those?' says Alex. 'That it sometimes managed to be played in tune?'

'Watch it,' says DJ.

'A funeral,' says Joey enthusiastically. 'We should have a ceremonial burning. There's a fire pit on the edge of the terrace. We could do it there, like cremating a warrior.'

'Why not?' says DJ. 'It's no good for anything else and I'm certainly not taking it back to England. I'll fetch the corpse.' He gets up and goes towards the studio.

'And I'll set up the libation,' says Alex. He goes into the house and returns with two bottles of grappa from the shelf in the pantry. Already the stock looks reduced. Did they really drink two of them on their first night? 'It should be raki for a proper offering to the gods,' he says, 'but I guess this will do. Make some space.'

Alex charges their glasses with generous slugs of grappa. Uncharacteristically, Mia doesn't protest but allows hers to be filled too. She sips, and winces.

'Hey, that's good,' says Elena. 'It tastes different from

last night. Stronger.'

'Maybe they've put the bottles on the shelf in order of potency, so that it started with weak stuff and gets more powerful as we work our way along the line,' says Alex. 'So we can get used to it. Kind of build up immunity.'

'I don't think I'm immune enough yet,' says Elena and chinks her glass against Mia's. They both drink.

'Anybody got a light?' It's DJ with the stricken guitar. It's a poor, battered thing, dangling wretchedly from his hand. He drops it, takes his grappa and drains the glass in one go.

'Hey,' says Alex, 'that was for the libation.'

'Then pour me some more and I'll libate that,' says DJ.

DJ sits on a bench and quickly removes the guitar's strings. 'No need to waste these,' he says. He coils each one carefully and wraps it so it can't unravel. When all the strings are off, Elena moves to his side. She's holding her lighter.

'How will we start it? The fire, I mean,' says Joey.

'There are some old newspapers in one of the kitchen drawers,' says Mia. She goes to fetch them.

Elena stands on the corner of the terrace, still clutching the lighter. She looks great in the light spilling from the pergola; tall, powerful, an Amazon queen. DJ looks at her and has a sudden vision of the tattoo of flowers. He can't remember it being there during the short period they went out together, but come to think of it they only once got into a situation where he might have seen it. He wonders how many other people know about it.

Mia crumples the sheets of newspaper and stuffs them through the sound holes of the guitar and Joey helps her. 'Not too tight,' she says.

Alex goes around the glasses filling them again and drifts over to Elena on the edge of the terrace. Beside her is a shallow bowl carved into the rock of the hillside.

'I assume that is a fire pit,' he says. 'It looks to me more like a font.'

'As if you've ever been in a church,' says Elena. 'How would you know what a font looks like?'

'Well, it's fire-pit now,' he says, as Joey and Mia join them with the guitar.

'Better watch it,' Joey says. 'The forest is bone dry, we don't want to start a fire.'

'It wouldn't be Castelvecchio,' says Alex. 'More Castelscorchio,' He laughs. So do the rest of them, but not as much.

'Good job there's no wind,' says Mia.

'Speak for yourself,' says Alex, laughing again. This time no one joins in. He pours yet more grappa. His, DJ's and Elena's glasses are always empty. Mia is drinking more than on the previous evening, but she and Joey are nowhere near keeping up.

DJ's headache from the blow with the guitar has now been replaced by a fuzzy euphoria. He places the broken instrument reverentially in the fire pit. Mia lays the last of the newspaper around it and piles twigs on top.

Alex stands and begins a pseudo-dignified rendition of the Dead March. 'Dum dum-de-dum, dumdum dumdum dumdum dum. I think you should dance,' he says to Mia. 'Something wild and pagan, like that

Stravinsky guy did. And it needs to involve taking your clothes off.'

Elena picks up a clod of earth from the edge of the grass and throws it at him.

'In your dreams,' says Mia, but she does do a pirouette, fluid and graceful as a cat. Joey watches her enrapt.

DJ holds out his hand for the lighter and Elena gives it to him. He kneels, flicks it and puts it to the paper. It catches and he nudges a couple of the twigs onto the nascent, flickering tongue. The flames drool around the guitar like a pack of wolves eyeing up their prey. As they encroach the varnish starts to bubble and they become edged in green.

Alex stands and raises his hand in the air. 'This is a solemn moment,' he says. His speech is slurred. 'Farewell to DJ's faithful friend,' he calls, looking up to the smoke rising into the night in a narrow column, 'You have given much pleasure. Especially to those who weren't in the room when DJ was playing you.'

'Ha ha haaa,' says DJ.

Alex remains in his pose, staring at the sky, one hand aloft and the other holding his glass. DJ tips his glass and empties it onto the fire. There's a fizz and a purple flare.

'Hey, not all of it,' says Alex. 'That stuff's too precious to waste.'

'Good cause,' says DJ. 'There's plenty more, you said.'

The first bottle of grappa that Alex brought out is already empty and he uncorks the second, helps himself and passes it around. Only he and DJ take some. Elena doesn't want to risk another bad dream so she refuses. So do Mia and Joey. They all settle on the sun-warmed tiles and watch the fire. Already it's dying down. Although burnt, the guitar retains its shape, a charcoal ghost of its former self. DJ gets a stick, pokes it, and the brittle shell crumbles.

The happy feelings Alex was experiencing after the alcohol are ebbing and being replaced by dull anxiety. He can't pin it on anything or identify what he might be worrying about but he has an unpleasant sensation of disquiet. He feels in his pocket and brings out a small plastic box. He takes off the lid and offers it to DJ.

'What is it this time?' he says.

'More Sphynx,' says Alex.

'Okay,' says DJ. 'It didn't seem to do much for me last night, but I'll try it again.'

'Don't feel you have to,' says Alex. 'This stuff costs money, you know.'

Elena is watching them. 'Where did you get it?' she says.

'From a bloke who works for my dad. Why?'

'Oh, I don't know,' she says. 'A guy who comes into the pub, one of our regulars, got some pills online and they were way too strong. They almost killed him.'

'These are okay. I've had them from this guy before and taken them loads of times.'

'Have you taken them?' she says to Mia. Her friend shakes her head.

'Miss pure doesn't do drugs,' says Alex. It's not kindly meant.

Mia gives him a cold smile, raises her glass and drains it.

19

Mia lies on the marble floor and gazes at the stars spinning slowly above her. Is it the stars revolving or is it the terrace? Her vision is blurring and she feels out of control. It's the grappa. This is why she doesn't drink. She only had a couple of glasses but it's enough. She feels slightly sick. Dinner on the whole was nice, but there was something not quite right about the dish Gianna had prepared for her, a slightly metallic flavour. She can taste it now.

DJ's face looms out of the haze. 'My head's throbbing,' he says. 'I'm going up. You coming?'

She wants to be left alone but can't put the feeling into words. She flaps her hand as a gesture of dismissal.

'Okay,' says DJ. 'See you later.' His shape disappears.

Voices come and go. They echo as if in some giant building. A cathedral. The cathedral of Castelvecchio. She closes her eyes and the voices recede. She hears one she knows. It's closer, in her ear, in her head. It's Alex.

'Just you and me now,' he says. She doesn't respond.

He lies down beside her, on his back like she is. Have the others all gone? She ought to go herself. She doesn't want to be here alone with Alex. He's lying very close. She'd like him to shift, to leave some space between them. She tries to move herself but she can't. She feels unwell. Why did she drink so much? She never drinks. She doesn't even like the stuff. Her eyelids are too heavy to open. Sleep steals over her and she feels herself sinking.

~

The house is in darkness. She knows her mum has a late shift but Michael must be out too. Heaven knows where Ant is. But what about Lou? The little girl can't have been left in the house all on her own.

Mia lets herself in, turns on the hall light and drops her coat and bag.

'Lou?' she calls.

There's no reply. Michael must have taken her with him, wherever he's gone. Yet somehow the house doesn't feel empty, there's a presence.

'Lou?' she calls again. 'Lou-Lou. Are you there, love?'

She goes into the living room. Nothing. There's no one in the kitchen, either. She runs upstairs to the bedroom that she and Lou share.

Her half-sister is sitting on her bed, squashed in the corner with her knees drawn up. She's covered in her blanket and holding a doll. It's made of pink plastic and has dark hair. Mia hasn't seen it before. Lou is sucking her thumb, which is always a bad sign. Her mother is trying to cure her of the habit and Mia gently eases the hand away and holds it.

'Is that a new dolly?' says Mia. She sits on the bed beside her.

The little girl nods.

'Did mummy give it to you?'

A shake of the head.

'Daddy?'

She nods again.

'What's her name?'

Lou looks at her blankly.

'She has no clothes. Shall we find some for her?'

Lou isn't crying but she looks as though she might have been. Mia is troubled. She feels a dread, a deep disquiet.

'Hey kiddo, what's happening?' she says.

Lou fixes her eyes on Mia but doesn't reply. She rubs the little girl's shoulder.

'Is something wrong? What's the matter?' There's still no answer. 'Something at school? Trouble with one of your friends?'

Lou shakes her head.

'Is mummy cross about something?'

Lou shakes her head. As Mia's questions narrow down the possibilities a dark cloud begins to form.

'Is it Ant?' says Mia.

Again Lou shakes her head.

A tight knot is forming in Mia's stomach. 'Daddy?'

This time Lou doesn't shake her head. She just looks very steadily at Mia. She's not even blinking.

'Lou, was it daddy?'

No answer.

'What did daddy do?'

No answer.

'Did daddy touch you?'

Very slowly Lou nods.

'Where did he touch you?'

There's a long long pause. Then Lou says, in a voice so soft that Mia can hardly hear it, 'My princess place.'

Mia feels sick. 'And did you touch him?'

'He made me.'

It's something Mia has feared ever since Michael arrived but she thought she would be the target, not the little girl. There are so many questions – When did he do it? Has he done it before? How many times? – but she can't grill the child.

She imagines herself in Lou's place, a large hand crawling up her leg, rough fingers feeling her. Then the hand takes her small, chubby one and pulls it towards the man's groin. She touches something smooth and hard as a bone. The man grunts and shudders, and he flings her hand away like discarding litter. This has never happened to Mia. She knows it hasn't, but the vision is as vivid as a UHD movie. She recalls a topic they did in Psychology on racial memory, the way thoughts, feelings, and traces of experiences may be transmitted from generation to generation. Is this that thing? Is it some atavistic horror deep in the female collective unconscious that emerges when it receives the right stimulus?

'Come here, sweetie,' she says to Lou, and gathers the

child in a cuddle. She gently rocks her, and Lou's thumb returns to her mouth. This time Mia doesn't remove it.

Mia feels sick, but she's also angry. Fucking Michael. What does her mother see in him? Something has to be done. Angelina must be told, then maybe she'll kick him out. And Ant too. He's almost as bad, with his jeers and his smutty wisecracks. But her mother won't dump Michael, she knows that. She's too soft, and maybe more than a little afraid. It will have to be Mia herself who deals with this.

From downstairs comes the sound of the front door opening. It can't be her mother. Angelina's on a late shift and won't be home before midnight. It's either Ant or Michael.

'Stand by your beds,' a voice shouts. 'The boss is back.'

It's Michael. She hears him in the living room, hears him in the kitchen, and then there's a heavy tread on the stairs and her heartbeat quickens.

'Stay there,' she whispers to Lou. She tucks the blanket around the little girl and pushes her into the corner. She stands up and faces the door.

Michael gets to the top of the stairs and comes straight in. He's surprised to see Mia and he smiles. 'Well, two for the price of one,' he says.

Mia has moved away from Lou's bed and has her back to the wall. She's very conscious of what she's wearing, a skinny crop top that leaves most of her midriff exposed. Too late to do anything about that now, she thinks.

Michael glances at Lou, then looks at Mia. He comes towards her and before she can react his forearm jerks upwards and is across her neck, pinning her head against the wall. She tries to get away but he pushes harder, squeezing her throat till she can hardly breathe. She wants to knee him but he's too close. Lou lets out a cry and rolls off the bed.

'Shut up, kid,' Michael snarls.

His face is centimetres from Mia's. She can smell his beery breath, feel his spittle on her lips. 'Don't think much of me, eh? Well, let's see what you think of this.' His free hand rests on her stomach. He makes a circular movement with his fingers, then slides his hand down inside her jeans. Her hips pull back, trying to avoid the touch. 'Come on, you know you want it,' he urges.

Mia's been collecting a gobbet of saliva and she twists her head and spits in Michael's face. Except is it Michael? It looks like Alex. His head jerks away and she pounds his shoulders and his sides, beating with her fists. She screams and screams and screams until a red mist forms.

'For fuck's sake! What the hell?' someone yells.

The mist clears. Mia sees Alex, his face very close.

'Get off me,' she says. 'Get away from me. What do you think you're doing?'

'I'm not doing anything.' He's moved away and there's a gap between them.

Mia's head is spinning. She's confused. 'I was asleep. You got on me while I was asleep.'

'I didn't,' says Alex. 'You were groaning. I thought you were ill. I leant over and you started yelling like I was trying to strangle you.'

She has a recollection of Alex on top of her and his

hands on her. Or was it Alex? 'I think I was dreaming,' she says, faintly.

'Too fucking right you were.'

'What's going on?' It's Elena. She's standing in the doorway.

Alex gets up. 'Ask her. I was asleep and she started screaming in my ear, enough to scare me shitless.'

Mia looks up at him. The tiles under her are cold but that's not why she's trembling. She knows she's been dreaming, but when did the dream stop? Or perhaps it's still going on.

Elena squats beside her. 'Are you okay?'

Mia nods.

'A nightmare, eh?'

Mia gulps, and nods again.

'I know what they're like.' Elena sits on the tiles and snuggles up. 'Ouch!' She's sitting on something hard and spiky. She reaches behind her and pulls it out. 'Where did this come from?'

It's a doll. It's made of pink plastic. It has dark hair.

STAGE 3 - DEEP SLEEP

20

Alex comes down from upstairs wearing the shorts he's been sleeping in. Elena is already on the terrace. She's sunbathing, topless on a recliner. Her body shines with lotion and sweat. Alex feels awful, and gingerly he sits on the lounger next to her. It's partially shaded by the awning and he's relieved to be able to keep his head out of the sun.

'Shit. What happened last night?' he says.

Elena opens her eyes but otherwise doesn't move. 'As I recall it,' she says, 'you got tanked up on wine and grappa and then, just in case there was a living brain cell left in your head, you took Sphynx. Then you moved in on Mia.'

'No way,' he says.

'You know very well you did,' she says coldly. Then a little more emotion shows. 'How can you do that? How can you try to make out with my friend, and while I'm in the same house?'

He puts out his hand to reach her but she dodges it.

'I'm sorry Ellie,' he says. 'I did nothing, honestly. It was all in her head.'

'Yeah, you're such a hunk that all the girls fantasise about being screwed by you.'

'For fuck's sake,' he complains, 'it wasn't me, it was Mia.'

'Oh, I see,' says Elena. 'The woman's to blame, of course.'

'She dreamt it. You know what that's like, how real it can seem.'

The truth is he only has the vaguest idea of what happened. He can remember the others going and it being just Mia and him. Unusually for her, Mia had been drinking. She was warm and she smelt good. They were close, he thinks he might even have been holding her hand. He remembers looking up at the stars and he remembers Mia snoring, soft as a mouse and him thinking how cute it was. Then everything goes blank until he's aware that he's on top of her. She must have done something for him to be like that, he wouldn't have moved in on her without encouragement. He's never had a problem getting what he wants from a girl and the suggestion that he was forcing himself on Mia is an insult.

He tries a joke. 'Hey, if God didn't mean me to get off with different girls he shouldn't have made them so sexy.'

Elena doesn't laugh. 'Arsehole,' she says.

There's a long silence. Elena's still on her back. She's wearing sunglasses so it's hard for Alex to see her eyes. He lies on his side, looking at the way her long hair drapes over her shoulder and the curve of her breast.

'I feel foul,' he says.

'Serves you right.' Despite that judgement, she reaches down beside her recliner and picks up a glass which she holds out to him. 'Here, drink this.'

Alex sips. The liquid is warm, the temperature of old tea, but it quenches what he realises was an unpleasant thirst and he drains it.

'I'm truly sorry,' he says. 'I really am. To be honest, I don't know what happened. I was smashed. I don't think I did anything, but if I did, I'm sorry.'

Elena rolls onto her side and faces him. 'Well, Mia certainly thinks you did something. She can't have led you on. She was asleep for Christ's sake. She had a bad dream, and then she woke up to find your hand in her pants.'

He can't remember doing that but still he mumbles, 'Sorry.'

She gives him a long, hard look. 'There's one thing I want you to know. Do that again, play around with somebody else under my nose and I'll walk away. But first I'll kick you in the balls. Hard.'

There's another pause. Then he says, 'What have you said to Mia?'

'I haven't said anything to her, other than to share my opinion that you can be a complete shit.'

Neither of them speaks. There's something that's been on Alex's mind and here's an opportunity to resolve it.

'In a few months you'll be in St Andrews, right?'

Elena's not sure that she's going to let him move on to

a fresh topic yet, but she's curious and decides she will. 'Yes,' she says.

'Yeah, well, that means I'll be at home and you'll be four hundred miles away. I mean, suppose you meet someone else, another guy – or guys – you fancy.'

Elena can see where this is going. 'Yes, I'm supposing.'

'Well, I want you to know that if you want to go out with somebody else, that's all right.'

Elena can scarcely believe what she's hearing. 'Oh, that's all right, is it? Well, a big fucking thank you for the dispensation.'

This isn't going quite the way Alex had intended so he tries to clarify. 'Don't get me wrong. I want us to go on seeing each other during vacations, and of course I'll come up to St Andrew's sometimes, but I want you to know that I'm not claiming any hold over you.'

She looks at him in disbelief and shakes her head. 'Listen, it's right that we talk about these things, but I don't need your permission to live my life. You can get off with whoever you like when I'm not around. I don't care who you screw or how often. I'm mad about what you did with Mia...'

'I didn't do anything...'

'...okay, whatever you say, I'm mad about that because firstly, she's my friend, and secondly, you were trying it on when I was only a few feet away. How would you feel if I started snogging, oh, Ethan Murray when you were in the same room?' She chooses Ethan because he's without a doubt the best-looking boy in the 6th Form, one Elena has fancied herself, and she knows that Alex sees him as a rival. 'It's one thing being with somebody else when we're a long way apart. It's different if one of us is fooling around right in front of the other. We've not made any pledges. It's not as if we're married, God forbid, but there are things that it's not right to do.'

Alex doesn't respond at first. He's got part of what he wanted: Elena's view that if he becomes involved with other girls while she's away she'll still see him when she's home. He was also hoping that she would say that he can do as he likes but she will save herself for him. He's disappointed that she didn't. He thinks he'll have to return to that later. For now, it's best to move on.

'Where's DJ?' he says.

'Not seen him.'

'Does he know about last night?'

Elena shrugs. 'I haven't told him. Mia might have, but I doubt it.'

Alex is relieved. DJ owes him one for the crack on the head and he doesn't want him to have any reason for payback. 'Joey?' he says.

'Joey was already in bed and knows nothing about it.'

'Where is he now?'

'Gone for a run.'

'A run? In this heat? He must be mad.'

'Or perhaps it's to do with him not drinking or taking drugs, and wanting to keep fit?'

'Jesus, listen to grandma,' says Alex. 'You were pretty far gone yourself.'

Elena doesn't answer that. She holds out a tube of suntan cream and rolls over. Alex sighs inwardly; he's forgiven. He kneels on the tiles beside her recliner, squeezes a blob of the lotion onto his palm and starts to apply it to her shoulders. He eases her hair aside and smooths the cream down her spine.

'Mm, that's good,' she says.

'Yeah, well I was thinking that maybe during my year off I could earn some dough by becoming a masseur.' He continues to work in the lotion. 'Rubbing the backs of sexy chicks for money. Hey, why bother with uni at all?'

Elena rolls over. She tilts her head forward and her eyes half close. They kiss. 'You can be a dick sometimes,' she says. 'I don't know why I put up with you.'

'It must be my charm.'

It's quiet on the terrace. From somewhere a long way off comes the buzz of a chainsaw. There's the occasional drone of an insect or a snatch of birdsong. Apart from that, nothing. Elena's phone and earbuds are beside her.

'What were you listening to?' Alex asks.

'Just a compilation I put together. I don't have much music on my phone. I must have played this a dozen times and I'm sick of it. I don't even have any of our stuff. Speaking of which, when are Bruno and Tanya coming?'

Alex has been wondering the same thing. He thought they might hear something yesterday but there was no message. He hopes nothing has happened to upset the arrangements.

'I'm as wise as you are,' he says. 'I thought Bruno's assistant said that he and Tania would be here when we arrived but the note he left said they wouldn't get here for a day or two. I suppose they might come today.'

'It doesn't leave them long to get everything ready for the wedding.'

'Perhaps it's all done, all set up in the big house so that they simply have to walk in.'

Elena is doubtful. 'I don't know. You'd think there'd be some staff around, wouldn't you? People bringing things in? If you were going to the house you'd have to pass here but we've not seen anyone.'

In truth, Alex has no idea what to expect. He's always known that his life is more comfortable than the lives of his friends, but the glimpse he's had of Theo and Lita, and of Bruno, tells him that these people are in a different league altogether. Alex's family flies business class, but Theo has a private jet. Alex's family has a big house in town and another in the country, but Theo has houses and apartments all over the world. Alex's family employs a foreign maid and a part-time gardener. These people are used to having a whole team of others to do their bidding. So how do rich people organise something like a wedding? It could be that this is normal, that later on in the day, or tomorrow, a fleet of vans will arrive and set up a complete banquet, all in a few hours.

'If we want to know about the wedding we could look online,' says Elena. 'There's bound to be some gossip about it.'

'There's no phone signal. Remember?'

'Shit, of course. There's the landline, though. We could phone home and ask.'

'Dead. No dialling tone, nothing. I think one of the satellite dishes on the roof is wifi, but even if it is we don't know the password. And we can't ask Gianna.'

'So we're stuck.'

'Yup,' says Alex. 'At the back of beyond, with no way to

communicate with anyone else and no transport to get us out of here. If it wasn't such a great place and we weren't being looked after so well it might be scary.'

'What might be scary?' This is DJ, who's coming out from the house. He's wearing only shorts and his hair is wet. Elena checks him out. He looks good, muscular, although he does carry some weight that isn't muscle. She tells him what they've been talking about.

'So basically,' he says, looking at Alex, 'you know fuck all about what's going on. I thought you were supposed to be in charge of this thing.'

Alex is indignant. 'I was. I am. I was the one who worked with Bruno's assistant to sort out the travel. Half a bloody day on the phone, that took. I even got them to fork out for your girlfriend. Where were you when I was doing that?' He sticks his little finger in his ear and twists it in an exaggerated gesture as if trying to clear a blockage. 'Oh, I'm sorry, all those loud offers of help you made have deafened me.'

'It wasn't me that Bruno talked to,' says DJ. 'It was you he arranged it with because, as you've told us loads of times, he assumed you were the band leader. Everything we know about this we've got from you and you've kept it all pretty much to yourself. You're even keeping our tickets, like you were in charge of a school party.'

Alex feels anger bubble. 'You can have your fucking ticket.' Before DJ can reply he gets up and walks off.

The problem with a dramatic gesture is you need to have a convincing follow-up. Without that, you look stupid. Quite recently Alex stormed out after a row with his father, only to have to go back because he'd forgotten his phone. His father laughed at him, mockingly, not kindly. He has no plan for where to go next so he heads for the studio.

He sits at the Yamaha and turns it on. LEDs glow and a screen jumps to life. From the menu he selects 'standard piano' and 'pop'. He cracks his knuckles and tries a few chords. He adds a soft drum beat and begins to improvise, making spiky, jagged chords that fit his mood.

Mia made a big fuss about last night. More fuss than the incident deserves, he thinks. One interpretation is that it's camouflage and she's trying to conceal the fact that actually, she's keen on him. That might be worth following up. And Mia will be in Loughborough, and that's a hell of a lot nearer than St Andrews.

21

Alex has been at the keyboard for a few minutes when the door opens and DJ comes in. He's carrying a couple of beers. It's an olive branch and Alex takes the one that DJ offers. The bottle is cold, beaded with condensation that drips to the floor.

Alex looks at his watch. 'Beer at this hour,' he says. 'That's rock and roll.'

'Any hour's good for beer,' says DJ. They both drink. 'Were you playing that song we were working on yesterday?'

'Yes. I've been working on the hook a bit.'

'It's not bad.' Alex is surprised. From DJ that is praise indeed. It must be another peace offering. 'Do you have the words here?'

'Yes.' Alex turns again to the keys and replays the song.

DJ comes behind him and puts a hand on his shoulder. 'Hey, I'm sorry bro,' he says. 'About back there. I let myself get wound up. I mean it's great here, but I need to know what we're doing. We don't want some dudes suddenly turning up and expecting us to play right away. We need to know when we're wanted, and we've got to rehearse. We've hardly played since the school gig and we made some mistakes then. This wedding's more important and we have to be the best we can be.

'Yeah, right,' says Alex. 'Everything does seem to have gone quiet, for sure. But I'm betting Bruno will be here soon. Till then we wait.'

'It doesn't look like we have much choice. Don't me wrong, I appreciate what you've done to get this trip on the road. We all do. I'm sorry I fired off at you.'

'Accepted,' says Alex. DJ apologising is rare, and apologising twice is unheard of. 'You've got a point, though. I'll give everybody their tickets so it doesn't look like I'm trying to control everything. Yeah, and I'm sorry too, about your head and the guitar. How is it?'

'The guitar? It's ashes, man.'

Alex gives him a playful push. 'No, I mean your head.'

DJ runs his hand down the side of his face. It's still sore, but it was the flat back of the guitar that caught him so it was more of a slap than a blow. There's no bruise but there's still a bit of redness and swelling. He takes a pull of his beer. 'It's okay,' he says. 'Anyway, I deserved it.'

'Forget it? Make a new start, eh?'

'A new start,' says DJ. They fist bump, clink bottles and drink. DJ runs a hand across his mouth. 'Have you thought about what you're going to do with Mia's purse?'

'No,' says Alex, 'I've no idea.' He belches. 'I should have given it to her right away, as soon as I found it. It's a bit late now. What would you do?'

'Nothing. I wouldn't do anything. What could you do? You're spot on when you say that giving it to her empty would just rub salt in the wound. And you're right, too, that you can't give it back with a hundred and fifty euros in it because there's no convincing story you could come up with to explain why you have her purse with her money and why you've not said anything till now. I know her dad gave it to her so in that way it's special, but she'll get over it. I'd lose it. Dump it somewhere. She thinks it's gone, so let it go.'

Alex knows DJ is right. He needs to get rid of the purse, and he needs to do it quickly. 'I should have burnt it along with your guitar,' he says.

'That would have been difficult. But there are loads of places to hide it. I suggest you go a few yards into the trees and bury it under a stone.'

'I might do that. I'll have to be careful though, because,' and he puts on a quavering voice, 'there's magic in them there woods.'

DJ laughs. 'You'll need to watch out for the wolves, too. I'm glad they didn't come back last night.'

There's one more thing Alex needs to settle: does DJ know anything about Mia's dream?

'How's Mia?' he says, realising as the words come out that the change of subject is rather abrupt.

'Okay,' says DJ. 'Why? Shouldn't she be?'

'I haven't seen her this morning, that's all.'

'No. She's still in bed. She's catching up on sleep. She had a bad night.'

Alex waits. Is this it? Has she told DJ that the girls

think he played a part in her bad night? 'Oh,' he says, 'sorry about that. Is she sick?'

'No, she's not sick. It was nightmares. Well, just one, really.'

'Like Elena's?'

'No. It was scary all right, but it wasn't like Elena's. Hers was about her stepdad.'

Alex waits but DJ has nothing further to say. It looks like Mia has told him no more. 'Elena had a nightmare on our first night, Mia on our second. What is it about this place and bad dreams?' he says.

'Well, Mia had been drinking. She's usually stone-cold sober. I expect it was that.'

'She definitely seemed to be developing a taste for the grappa,' says Alex. 'Better watch her tonight or there'll be none left for the rest of us.'

DJ pulls out a carton of cigarettes and offers one to Alex.

'Are we allowed to smoke in here?'

'Don't see why not,' DJ says. 'Anyway, who's here to stop us?' Alex takes one. DJ picks up his guitar and plugs it into an amp. He sits on one of the stools and picks the strings. 'Let's work on that song some more. Run it by me again.'

Alex opens the notebook where Elena has written her poem and starts to play, putting the words to the tune he's composed.

> *We lived together on the shore*
> *I knew I couldn't love you more*
> *Can't we be like we were before?*

We walked together by the sea
The moon, the stars, and you and me
So many things I couldn't see.

DJ picks up the melody quickly and joins in well before the end of the second verse. Alex goes into an eight-bar chorus – there are no words for that yet so he just la-las it – and then into verse three. By the time he finishes, DJ is playing along. At the end they look at each other, each of them pleased with himself.

'Hey, this is good,' says DJ. 'Elena's words are a bit cheesy but it's great for a wedding, and your tune's great too, a real earworm.'

Alex says nothing but he's delighted with DJ's approval. They try the song again, DJ adding some riffs of his own and Alex polishing the accompaniment as it bridges from verse to chorus and back again.

At the end of the third run-through DJ says, 'It's sounding good but the words and the music fight a bit, don't you think? It's about the ache of love, the pain of being apart, but it sounds too bright. Have you thought of putting it down a semitone?'

They try the transposition. The song is now in a minor key and is more haunting and better. DJ smiles at Alex and they do a high-five.

'Now the control room's open we can use the gear to record it,' DJ suggests. 'Then when we get home we can put it online.'

'Control room open?'

'Yeah.' DJ goes to the door and pushes it wide. 'See? Everything a self-respecting rock star might need.'

Alex looks in behind him. 'Wow. Is that cool? Do you think we can work this stuff?'

'Yeah. It's way beyond the gear at school but the principles are the same. I checked it out earlier and it doesn't look too hard.'

'How did you manage to unlock the door?'

'I didn't. I came in before and there it was, wide open.'

Alex is silent. So is DJ. They are both thinking the same thing, both wondering who unlocked the room and whether it was the same person who dealt with the door to the studio yesterday.

'Gianna?' says Alex.

DJ shrugs. 'Could be. Or maybe there's some sort of caretaker. Somebody keeping an eye on the place. That wouldn't be surprising.'

'Funny we've not seen anybody, though.'

'Maybe that's the sort of service Theo likes. People do things for you but they're invisible.'

'Maybe.'

They go back to the instruments to practice the song again. Alex is pleased with what they've achieved. Elena's words and his tune, and DJ's suggestions have been constructive and they've improved it. Real teamwork.

'We need Joey to work on the drum part,' says DJ.

'I'm not sure. It doesn't need big drumming. I think maybe just brushes, don't you?'

DJ agrees. The song is soft and emotional; the problem with Joey is that he likes to make a lot of noise. Drumming is for him more than just providing a beat, it's about putting on a show. When he's not playing he's quiet and unassuming, nothing like the stereotype of a rock and roll drummer, but when he starts to play he becomes a different animal – noisy, flashy and flamboyant. It's as if the drums are a shield and once he gets behind them he takes on a different personality, one at odds with the usually meek and mild Joey.

They're both quiet for a spell, working on their instruments. Then Alex says, 'I wonder whose turn it will be tonight.'

'Whose turn for what?'

'To have a weird dream. We've been in Italy for two nights and both the girls have had nightmares. Tonight it may be you.'

'Or Joey.' DJ snorts a laugh. 'Anyway, I've had my nightmare.'

Alex takes him seriously. 'You have? When? You didn't say.'

'It was just now,' says DJ. 'You singing.'

Alex shows him the finger.

22

Joey is watching Elena and Mia. They are side by side at the kitchen worktop and they're looking at a book together. He doesn't know what it is, and he doesn't care; it's the girls who are absorbing his interest.

They are friends but they're not at all alike. Elena is funny, bright, interesting, and fun to be with. She's a big girl, tall and well-built. She used to be fatter when she was younger, when he first knew her lower down the school. She's lost some weight since then, what his mum calls "puppy fat", but even now nobody would call her slender. She carries it well because she's tall, taller than Alex even in her sandals. Her best feature is her hair. It's long, luscious and natural blonde, although it has a mind of its own and can be unruly. Her face is open and friendly, with blue eyes and a full mouth. But at rest her face can look sullen, as if she has a sulk on. It's what his mum would call a "mardy cow" face. If you were to sum her up you would say she's sexy, but you wouldn't call her beautiful.

Mia, on the other hand, is beautiful; to Joey's mind amazingly so. Not only is she shorter than Elena but everything else is scaled down too, in perfect proportion. Her waist is slender, her legs and her arms sculpted. Yes, that's the word, he thinks, because she is sculpted, like the statue of some fantastic goddess. Her face is a perfect oval, with large brown eyes, arched brows and naturally long lashes. Her dark hair is cut in a neat fringe and usually tied in a ponytail. Her movements are smooth and graceful. Whereas Elena lolls gawkily on the counter as if holding herself up is a challenge, Mia's posture is poised and balanced, a dancer's.

Joey is well aware that he's not an expert on girls. He'd like to have a girlfriend but he doesn't know how to turn knowing a girl casually into something more. He finds it hard to work out what to say, and by the time he's done so the opportunity to say it has always passed. Studying Elena and Mia as he is doing now, Joey reaches a conclusion about girls and women. He's always thought that sex appeal and beauty are the same things, but they're not.

Elena is wearing a white t-shirt with the Levis logo. With that, she has shorts made from sawn-off jeans. They are cut high on her thighs, so high that the curve of her buttocks is in full view. White pockets protrude and hang down her legs like a pair of ears, which Joey thinks looks ridiculous. Her head is bent and her hair falls forward around her face in an untidy jumble.

Mia, at her side, is in a black halter top and running

shorts. Her legs are smooth and strong, and she's barefoot. Her back is firm and straight, the back of a gymnast. The slight angle of her head shows off the perfect planes of her face and the smooth curve of her neck. She has a purple scarf tied around her throat, which is there to hide a bruise that Joey noticed earlier.

And there you have it. Mia is a nymph, the sort of girl you can't take your eyes off. But for Joey beauty equals distance, and unattainability. Mia is so perfect he can't think of any reason why she might be remotely interested in someone like him. On the other hand, Elena isn't beautiful, but she is appealing. She invites ogling. She's a girl to visit a boy in his sultry dreams. But Mia is the one for him. If he is to know her better he must find a way to make himself more interesting to her. And he must find a way to talk to her. But where? And when? And how? And what about DJ?

~

Elena picks up the scent of Mia's perfume. It's probably one she found in her room. It has freshness, with just a hint of sophistication. It seems absolutely right for her, an expression of her personality.

She's always liked Mia and has enjoyed being her guide and friend, welcoming her when she first joined the school, showing her how everything worked, and introducing her to people. She can remember feeling quite jealous when she hooked up with DJ and started spending time with him. Hers and Alex's sex life is an open secret. Alex spends nights at her place and she occasionally, but much less frequently, stays at his home. All her friends including Mia know that. They all know, too, that she's on the pill. But Mia has never talked to her about her relationship with DJ. She assumes they have sex but it's never cropped up. She didn't know what she expected, but it came as a surprise when they were exploring the villa and Mia took it for granted that she and DJ would share a bed.

Since last night Elena has been fantasising about Mia having sex. The idea of her and DJ together, Mia's lissom limbs clenched around her lover, is a vision she's found distinctly arousing. Several girls at school are known to be gay. Some of them brag about it. More than once another girl has moved on her but it's mostly been light-hearted and ambiguous, and nothing has ever come of it. She has never been tempted. Not until now.

She drops her arm around Mia's waist.

23

They all have lunch at different times, snacking when they're hungry. Mia cuts open an avocado, removes the stone, scoops out the flesh, crushes it and spreads it on a ciabatta. Alex and DJ come over from the studio for what is actually breakfast for them both. DJ cuts several slices of the ciabatta, toasts them and spreads them with Marmite he's brought from home. 'I don't expect you can get it in Italy,' he'd said when the others laughed at him about it.

Alex ambles around like a grumpy bear and can't find anything he fancies. He goes to the big, chrome coffee machine, scratches his head and looks around for Elena. They have one that looks like this in her dad's pub so she'll know how to work it, but she went upstairs and hasn't come back yet.

'There must be some instructions for this thing,' he says.

'Well if there are they'll be in Italian,' says Joey.

Alex scowls at him. He stands in front of the machine

and turns a knob. Nothing happens. 'Working it can't be that hard,' he says. 'One of Casia's mates is a trained barista and she's as thick as they come. I give up.' He finds the instant coffee and boils a kettle.

DJ shakes his head. 'A coffee machine that costs as much as a small car and you can't figure out how to use it.'

'Okay, smart arse, you do it.'

'I don't want any coffee.'

They drift off, DJ and Alex to the studio again, Mia to her room.

Joey sits at the table in the shade of the vine-clad pergola. Heat builds. Grating cicadas orchestrate the afternoon. After a while, Mia returns. Joey pretends not to notice her. He's drawing something, concentrating on the page. His eyes are only a few inches from the paper. He holds a clutch of coloured markers and his hair flops forward, hiding his face. Then he looks up at her, brushes his hair back, and to his surprise and joy she smiles. He has to look away and he bends again to his task.

Mia doesn't want to talk and she's pleased that none of the others is there. She sits on the side of the table opposite Joey, a little way along. She can't see the detail of what he's drawing but there are a lot of bright colours. She tries to read her book but she can't concentrate on it. She still feels shaken by her dream and by what Alex did – what was it he did? – but she doesn't want any more questions and she doesn't want to see anyone else. If there has to be one of the other four here Joey is her choice.

She reads a few sentences but then loses the thread

and has to start again. After a while she becomes conscious that Joey is looking at her, staring quite openly. On his face is an expression that she's not seen before. It's part appraisal, part enquiry, part challenge, and part... desire? Really? Yes, she's sure of it. She feels a quiver in her stomach, and that surprises her too.

'What?" she says.

'What?'

'That's what I said. What? You're staring at me.'

She immediately regrets speaking to him so sharply. Joey looks abashed and she thinks he blushes, but his face is in the shade and it's hard to tell.

'I didn't mean to,' he mumbles. 'I was thinking.' Mia waits to see if he'll elaborate, but he doesn't. Instead, he asks her a question. 'What are you reading?'

Mia glances at the cover of her book, as if to check. Then she holds it up so he can see it. He reads the title aloud. '*Many Rivers - some currents in western thought.*' He says the words slowly and deliberately as if he finds them difficult. 'Looks heavy,' he says.

'Not really,' she says. 'It's quite readable, and very interesting.'

'What's it about?'

Mia waits a beat. This is Joey initiating a conversation. It's something she's not known him to do before, at least not with her.

'Well,' she says, 'it's what it says on the cover. It's an account of major intellectual movements. There are the big religions, obviously, and then things like Classicism, Romanticism, Modernism, Communism, and Humanism. It deals with change, how and why one movement dies and another takes its place. The bit I'm reading at the moment is talking about entropy.'

Joey nods. 'I know about that,' he says. 'We did it in science. It's to do with energy, and how you can never use all of it and some is always wasted. It's why perpetual motion isn't possible.'

'Yes,' she says. She's impressed. Joey doesn't have the reputation of being a scholar but clearly some things from the classroom have stuck. 'What you're describing is the second law of thermodynamics, which says that when energy changes from one form to another entropy increases. So entropy here means waste.'

'Yeah, I remember,' says Joey, becoming more animated. 'We did an experiment. We melted ice in a bowl of water and wrote down the changes in the temperature, and then we compared them with something.' Joey looks sheepish. 'But I can't remember what.'

Mia nods. 'Melting ice is a good illustration of entropy. When water's frozen the individual molecules are fixed and ordered. That's why ice is hard. Apply energy to it and it melts and the molecules become free to move about and are disordered.'

'Yes,' says Joey, excited. 'That's why you can swish your hand through a bowl of water but not through a block of ice.'

'Yes. And if you heat the water to make steam, the molecules then move freely through space. More energy, more disorder.'

'I can't remember where the waste comes in,' Joey says.

'It's to do with the cooling and heating, the conversions from liquid water to ice or to steam. With each change some energy is lost.'

'Yes, right, that's it,' says Joey.

He seems interested so Mia carries on. 'The man who wrote this book talks a lot about entropy. He says that it comes from a Greek word that means transformation.' Mia flicks through the pages till she finds the section she's looking for. 'He says that in the middle ages, philosophers used the term to explain the tendency of things to go wrong.' She reads, *'Entropy describes the natural state of the world, in which everything ultimately disintegrates, the status quo sub luna.'*

'The what?' Joey looks puzzled.

'It means the way things are on Earth.'

'Couldn't he just have said that?'

'He probably thinks he did.'

'Okay. What else?'

Mia picks up the book again. 'He says *Everything is subject to entropy, a product of which is chaos, and chaos continually increases.* It's like if you put one mouldy apple in a bowl of good apples, the good ones won't make the mouldy apple better. Instead, the mouldy one will turn the good ones bad and ruin all your fruit. Nothing stays as fresh as it was when it was new, or first made, or just picked. Everything perishes.'

'So the whole world is falling apart. Sounds gloomy,' says Joey.

'Yes, it is. Decay is the norm. And it gets worse. The author applies it to people and organisations. He says it's why a single group can never stay on top. A country might dominate for a time but sooner or later its power will go. It happened to Ancient Egypt, Greece, Rome, and Great Britain, and it will happen to the USA. China's on the up, he says, and will eventually rise to the top. It'll be there for a time and then its power too will decline and there'll be the chance for another country to replace it. It's the same in sport. A team may top the table for a season or two, but they can't stay there forever and in the end, they'll sink.'

'Change and decay in all around I see.'

'What?'

'It's from a hymn we used to have when I was a kid and my mum sent me to Sunday school.'

'Well, it's right. As the guy who wrote the book says, nothing lasts and in time everything fails or wears out.'

'Cheerful bloke,' says Joey. 'I wonder if he gets invited to a lot of parties.'

Mia laughs. 'Maybe not,' she says, 'but it's true. If you want an example closer to home, look at us.'

'What do you mean?'

'When I first came to our school Elena kind of adopted me. We became really good friends and we used to spend all our spare time together. We had no secrets, we'd tell each other everything. But we've drifted apart and now we're not as close. Alex and DJ are the same. They used to be best mates but now they argue a lot. Yesterday they even had a fight.'

'A fight?'

'Yes. You don't believe that story about Alex swinging DJ's guitar and clobbering him by accident, do you? He did it on purpose.'

'You really think so?'

'I know so.'

'Why?'

'It's obvious, isn't it? To start with it's a lame story. And then did you see them at dinner? At first, they could hardly look at each other.' She doesn't pass on what Elena told her about going into the studio and finding the two of them rolling on the floor.

Joey mulls this over for a moment. Then he says, 'I get on all right with both of them.'

'That's because you get on with everybody. And you don't argue with them, you don't try to push them. In fact, you let them push you.'

Joey nods. He supposes she's right. 'What about you and DJ?'

'What do you mean? What about me and DJ?'

He wants to know if they are still as close as they were. It's something he has to settle to try to manage his feelings for her. 'You're going to Loughborough in September and DJ is going to Bath. They're a long way apart. Will you still see him?'

Mia doesn't answer straight away. She likes DJ and they've always got on. Things have been easy at school where they've been together every day, and she'll certainly get on a bus or train to visit him in Bath. But how often will she do that? And how many times? 'I don't know,' she says. 'Perhaps he won't want to see me.'

'I would,' says Joey. He looks away quickly, and now he really does blush.

Mia is surprised. It's the first time she's heard Joey say anything like that, to her or to anyone else. It was unsubtle, but it was also touching. She's not sure how to respond. She tries a diversion to spare his embarrassment, and hers. 'What are you drawing?' she says.

Joey looks at the notebook in front of him, and then holds it up for her to see. The picture he's made is brightly coloured, dramatic, and powerful. He's drawn an eagle in full flight. Its wings are spread and its head thrusts forward, bursting through the air. Its eye is yellow, beady and cruel. That's not the most striking thing, though. It's the creature's claws, or rather what it carries in them. They are locked around a human figure. The drawing is skilfully done, but the image of the torso dangling from the bird's talons and dripping blood is gruesome.

'It's for my tattoo,' Joey says.

'A tattoo? You're going to have that tattooed on you?'

'Yup.' He smiles at her.

'Really? Where?'

'Here.' He points to a space on his arm between his elbow and shoulder. Mia says nothing. 'You don't like it, do you?' he says.

'It's not a question of liking it,' says Mia. 'You've drawn it well, it's very clever. I'd forgotten you were good at art.' She looks at the picture again. Joe's rendition is bursting with detail, from the creature's fearsome talons to its ferocious beak. Every feather is painstakingly executed. The scale of the human is of course out of proportion, either that or the eagle is extraordinarily large, but that aside it's totally lifelike and it explodes with energy. 'I think it's terrific, but it's a bit...' she can't find the right

214

word, then she does, '...extreme, isn't it? I mean for a tattoo. For something you're going to carry on your body for the rest of your life?'

Joey doesn't answer her question directly. Instead, he says, 'It's what I'm going to do when I get my first pay. Half will go on this, and the other half I'll give to my mum.'

Mia has nothing against tattoos but she's surprised Joey has decided to spend his first proper wage on that. 'Do you mind me asking why?'

'It's because it's a complete waste of money.'

Mia laughs. 'To be honest, that's exactly what I was thinking.'

Joey shakes his head. 'That's why I want to do it. It's something that will always be mine. It can't be stolen, or sold. I can't give it away. Nobody can take it off me. I'll have it until they put me in a box. And when it's done I'll go visit my dad and it'll piss him right off. He'll look at it and think how much beer he could have bought with what it cost me.'

'You could put the money in a bank account,' she says.

'Yeah, I could,' says Joey, 'but that wouldn't be the same.' He puts his marker down and thinks, trying to put what he wants to say into the right words. 'There's never been any spare cash in our house. There's only ever been enough for essentials, and sometimes not even for those. Since my dad walked out, and before, we've never had money to throw around. I don't need this tattoo. It will be a luxury, something I don't have to buy. It's useless, but it's got a message. Whatever happens to me in the future it will always say that there was a time when Joey

Braithwait had money to throw about. I'll think that every time I see it, and other people will too. I'm not a show-off like Alex, but I'm not a nobody either.'

'I know you're not,' says Mia.

She understands. She doesn't need to be told what it's like to come from a home where money is tight and you can't always trust people who should be looking out for you. She also has recent experience of being the victim of a thief. She reaches across the table and covers Joey's hand with hers. He looks surprised. For a moment he does nothing. Then, abruptly and roughly, he squeezes her fingers, and he blushes again.

There is so much more that Joey wants to say to Mia. He wants to tell her that he's always liked her, right from the moment she first arrived at their school. He wants to tell her that she's smart. And funny. And beautiful. He wants to tell her that her smile can brighten his day, and a few moments of her attention sweeten his blackest hours.

He wants to say all these things. But it would be embarrassing to say some of them and he doesn't know how to say the others, so he says nothing.

24

The remainder of the day drifts along. DJ, Elena and Alex spend some time in the studio. Later Joey joins them. The session goes well and they decide that tomorrow they're going to try to record a couple of songs on the equipment in the control room. Alex spends some time in there figuring out how things work. Joey goes to his room. Mia drifts in and out. She's finding it hard to settle to anything. She tries some yoga on the terrace. It helps a bit, but she still finds her attention returning to her dream.

Even without air conditioning the house manages to stay cool, but outside it's very hot. Everyone feels it and there are regular trips to the fridge where the stock of cold drinks is going down fast. In the late afternoon, Gianna arrives and begins her work in the kitchen. The smells of her cooking, the aromas of garlic and onions, drift out to the terrace.

There's no agreed time for dinner and over about an hour the company assembles in ones and twos. As each of them arrives at the dining table they automatically go to the seat they had the previous two nights. DJ gets there before Alex and it crosses his mind to take the place at the head of the table. However, he thinks that's pathetic. If sitting in that spot matters so much to Alex then let him knock himself out, and pity his small mind. And if he didn't choose it on purpose, if he just sat there without thinking, where's the issue?

They wait for their starters, moving on from cold lemonade – which they all chose first after a caution from Elena that attacking wine or beer with the thirsts they had would be a bad idea – to what seems to be an endless supply of red wine. DJ, Alex and Elena smoke.

There's a silence that they all find uneasy. Each of them is thinking the same thing. Elena is the first to voice it.

'I don't mind telling you,' she says. 'This - is - weird. It's our third night here, and the only other human being we've seen is Gianna.'

'I saw a guy doing the garden,' says Joey.

'When?'

'Yesterday.'

'Did you see him today?'

'No.'

'That's what I mean. The place is deserted, but in a few days five hundred people are supposed to be coming here for a wedding reception. I thought we might see somebody today, or there might be a message from Bruno, but no. Zilch. Nothing. We have no visitors, no way of getting in touch with anybody else and no transport. It's like we're prisoners. We can't leave.'

'Do you want to leave?' says Alex. 'We have everything we could want, fantastic accommodation, great food, all kinds of drink and plenty of it, an amazing studio where we can rehearse and record. I certainly don't want to go.'

'Nor me,' says DJ.

'That's not what I mean,' says Elena. 'I don't want to leave either, at least not yet. But it's different if you can't, if you don't have a choice.'

'I know what Ellie means,' says Mia. 'I feel it too. It's like we're under house arrest.'

There's silence. Then Alex says, 'So what do we do?'

'Good question,' says Elena. 'We might start by taking a look at the big house, Castelvecchio itself.'

'But Bruno said don't go there,' says Joey.

'Yes,' says DJ, 'and he also told Alex that he'd be here when we arrived. And then he wrote us a note to say that he'd be here in a couple of days. Neither of those things has happened, we've not seen him and we've heard nothing from him. I think that gives us some leeway.'

'You can't say he's not looking after us,' says Elena. 'We may be prisoners but the prison is paradise.'

'Taking a look at the house is a good idea,' says DJ. 'That must be where Gianna hangs out.'

'Why do you say that?' says Alex.

'It's obvious she has no transport. It's so quiet here that if she came by car or scooter we'd hear her from miles away. She must get here on foot, which means she comes from nearby, and that must be the big house.'

'Not necessarily,' says Elena. 'There may be some properties beyond it, on the other side of it. We don't know because we've not been there. Bruno warning us off exploring makes me think he's trying to keep us here, and there must be a reason for that.'

'That sounds creepy,' says Mia.

'There could be some people in the big house and we've just not seen them,' says Alex.

'Right,' says DJ. 'There must be somebody about. The studio door was locked and then mysteriously it was open. And the door of the control room too, the same.'

'Perhaps we are not alone after all,' says Alex. He ta-ras the X-Files music. 'The truth is out there,' he intones.

'Well if there is anyone in the house they must be able to get around in the dark,' says Mia. 'You can see it from our room and there are never any lights on.'

The rest of them think for a minute. Then Elena says, 'How do we do that? How do we explore a place we've been told to keep away from?'

'I think that's up to our "organiser" here,' says DJ. He puts an ironic emphasis on organiser. 'I think Alex should make it his mission to go to the big house tomorrow and see if he can find out what the fuck's going on.'

'I think it should be the girls,' says Alex. 'Elena's Italian will be useful if there's no one who speaks English, and if anyone grumbles at them for being there they can say they didn't know they were not supposed to.'

'I see,' says Elena icily, 'stupid women pleading ignorance. Good idea.'

Alex ignores her sarcasm and tips the remains of the wine bottle into his glass. As if by magic Gianna appears with another and begins to prepare the table.

Once more the food is excellent. Tomato gazpacho

followed by veal cutlets, and a big bowl of figs and tiny, sweet oranges to finish. Gianna has again prepared a vegetarian dish for Mia, and she brings her main course separately.

'Melanzane alla parmigiana,' she says. She sets it down before her with a flourish and returns to the kitchen.

'Eggplant with parmesan cheese,' says Elena.

'What's it like?' says DJ, wrinkling his nose.

'Delicious,' says Mia, taking a forkful. 'Want some?'

'Yuk,' says Alex. 'No, thank you.'

'I wasn't asking you,' says Mia. She takes another mouthful, then glances at Joey, who sits opposite her. 'What's up, Joey? You're frowning.'

'Did you hear Gianna?'

'Yeah, I heard her but I couldn't understand her,' says Alex. 'What's your point?'

'Bruno's note said she's deaf.'

'True. That doesn't mean she can't talk.'

'No, I know that. But she didn't sound like a deaf person. My auntie's deaf, and even if you didn't know that you could tell it just by listening to her speak. She doesn't sound like you or me. The way she pronounces things is kind of distorted.'

Alex is sceptical. 'She was speaking Italian. You have no idea how she should sound. You can't tell.'

Joey is insistent. 'Yes, you can. It's nothing to do with the words, it's how she says them. Deaf people can't hear other people talk and they can't hear themselves properly, so their tone is different.'

'Perhaps she's not been deaf for long,' says Mia.

'No,' says Elena, 'I think Joey's got something. I'm not an expert in Italian but I've heard enough of it to know what it should sound like. Gianna's speech seems perfectly normal to me.'

There's a long silence. Then DJ voices what they're all thinking. 'What if Gianna isn't deaf at all? What if she can hear as well as the rest of us?'

'And what if, as well as that, she can speak English?' Elena adds, quietly.

'So why would Bruno say she's deaf if she's not?' says Mia. Then the logic of it strikes her. 'He said that so we'd not be afraid to talk openly in front of her.'

'So she could spy on us,' says DJ. 'Holy shit!'

'Don't be daft,' says Alex. 'What do we have to say that anybody else could be interested in, least of all Bruno? Besides, there are cameras in the shared rooms. There's even one out here.' He points to a cctv camera on the edge of the pergola. It's pointing directly at the table where they sit. 'If Bruno wanted to spy on us he could do it with those.'

'I'm going to find out if she's deaf,' says DJ. Abruptly he gets up from the table and goes into the kitchen. Gianna is at the sink with the tap running. 'Is there some grappa, per favore?' He speaks loudly and suddenly, hoping he might catch her unaware. There's no response from Gianna, who remains with her back to him. As he moves towards the pantry to help himself she turns from the sink, drying her hands on her apron, sees him and starts. He goes out to the table and tells the others what happened.

'How do you know she wasn't putting it on?' says Elena.

'It was obvious she wasn't. She didn't know I was there. She turned, saw me, and it startled her.'

'I'm not surprised,' says Alex. 'Seeing you would startle anyone.'

'Very funny,' says DJ. 'I don't think she was acting.'

'Well, there's one way to find out.'

'How?'

'We wait till she's busy, then one of us creeps up behind her and makes a sudden noise, bursts a bag or claps their hands or something. If she hears it she won't be able to hide her reaction. It's a reflex. Either she'll jump because she's surprised, or she won't react at all.'

'It might settle it one way or the other,' Elena admits, 'but if the poor woman really is deaf she'll be freaked out. She'll think we're attacking her.'

'I've got an idea. Whose is that notebook?' says Alex, pointing to the far end of the table.

'It's mine,' says Mia.

'Can I borrow it for a minute? And the pen?'

She passes them to him. He opens the notebook to a clean page and pushes it in front of Elena. 'Here, write something in Italian.'

Elena frowns at him. 'What do you want me to write?'

'It doesn't matter. Anything. Write, "Where is the nearest telephone".'

'Why?'

'Just do it. Please.'

She does, and gives the book back to Alex. He holds it open and waits. They all sit quietly, eager to see what he intends. Before long Gianna comes out of the kitchen to collect the last few things on the table. As she approaches Alex stands up and holds the notebook open in front of her. 'Per favor,' he says.

Gianna looks at Alex's face, at the notebook, back at his face, and at the others. She shakes her head, smiles weakly, shrugs, and says something in a quiet voice. Then she turns and goes back to the kitchen.

'What did she say, Ellie?' says Alex.

'I think she said she can't read. *Ma non so leggere.*'

'Shit.'

'What was that all about?' says DJ.

'I had an idea. I thought maybe Gianna can't hear us, but perhaps we could communicate with her through notes, and ask her when Bruno and the others will be here.'

There's another silence. It was a good idea, but it seems that they can't get through to Gianna that way either. They are in the dark.

25

Several of them are yawning but no one wants to go to bed, so the grappa is drained, the glasses are refilled, and the conversation drifts. There are long periods when no one says anything and they look into the darkness or at the insects swirling around the pergola lights.

'I wonder where we'll all be this time next summer,' Mia says.

'Three of us will have finished our first year at uni,' says Elena, 'and Joey will be head chef at *The Golden Bough*.'

'In my dreams,' says Joey. 'They might have slung me out by then. I'm on six months trial.'

'We're in the same boat, Joey,' says Mia. 'DJ's place and mine at uni depend on our exam results.'

'Ask me what I'll be doing for the next year,' says Alex.

'You'll be a gentleman of leisure,' says Elena. 'Mr Idle, taking a year off.'

'You're one to talk. What are you doing? English. You

can speak that already. Why do you need to go to university to learn something you can already do?'

Elena knows he's joking but it doesn't stop her from taking the bait. 'It's literature, dumbo, but you wouldn't know that, being as how you can't read.'

'You're going to spend three years sitting around reading?' Alex says with affected incredulity. 'Three years on your arse? It'll be even bigger than it is now!'

Elena shrieks and throws an olive at him. She misses and he throws one at her. She sighs. 'Yes, English at St Andrews. What am I going to do with a degree in English?'

'You can always teach,' says DJ.

'Yeah, I suppose.' Elena laughs. 'What is it my dad says? Those who can do it do it, those who can't do it teach it.'

'And those who can't teach it become accountants,' says Alex. 'I've heard it.'

Elena is thoughtful. 'What I really want to do is write.'

'I thought you already could,' says Alex.

'Oh you are so funny. Pardon me while I fall off my chair laughing. What I mean is write books. Novels.'

'Have you written any yet?' says DJ.

'No. I've started a couple but not got further than the first few chapters.'

'If you write a novel, I'll read it,' says DJ.

'That'll be a first,' says Mia.

'No, seriously I will.'

'So will I,' says Mia, 'of course.'

'I will too,' says Joey.

Alex says nothing.

'Well thank you,' says Elena. 'My first readers already lined up. Mind you until I do manage to write something and get it published I think it really will be teaching for me.'

'What *are* you going to do next year?' Mia says to Alex.

It's the first time she has spoken directly to him since the previous night and he takes it as a good sign. 'I fancy doing some travelling,' he says. 'I've an uncle in Canada who owns an import-export business and I thought I'd go over and see him for a bit. He might give me some work. He's in Vancouver, right over on the west coast and I could go from there down into the USA. I've never been to California and I'd like to see Big Sur. Then I'll spend some time staying with my sister, Casia, and her friend in London.'

'Sounds like you'll be busy,' Mia says.

'Yeah. I'm looking forward to it.'

He would if he thought it might happen. The truth is he has no firm plans. What he does know is that he doesn't want to do a degree. The problem is that he doesn't have the money to do anything else. He must find a way to get some cash.

The conversation ebbs and flows. Elena is worried that she hasn't managed to get a message to her parents. Mia is too. She wants to talk to her mum and she wants to be sure Lou is all right. She doesn't think Michael has done anything to her, or that he will, but since her nightmare the possibility has been constantly on her mind. Alex keeps glancing at the security camera, the single eye that peers down on them from beside the pergola. It's niggling him. In the end, he leaves the table and picks up a pair of his shorts from one of the recliners on the terrace. It takes him a couple of lobs to get them over the offending object but he manages it and the camera is covered. Then he turns and gives it a huge V-sign. The others watch, amused.

'What happens if when Mia and I go up to the house tomorrow there's no one there?' says Elena. 'We'll be no further forward.'

'So?' says Alex.

'So we leave. I'm prepared to give it one more day. Then if nothing happens I want to go home.'

'I think we should stay,' says Alex. 'Besides, we agreed we'd play. It's like we have a contract.'

'Some contract,' says Elena.

'Anyway,' says Alex, 'how are you planning to leave? You've no transport.'

'See what I mean about us being prisoners?'

There's a pause. Mia stands up and stretches. 'I'm whacked,' she says. 'I'm going to bed. Nothing like a day doing nothing to wear you out.' Then to DJ, 'Are you coming?'

'No, I'll hang out here for a bit,' he says.

'I'm going too,' says Elena. 'If I stay here I'll just keep on drinking and I don't want to risk having any more dreams.'

'No way,' says Mia.

The two girls go into the house, leaving DJ and Alex. DJ refills their glasses.

'Where's Joey?' says DJ. They've only just noticed he's missing.

'Probably gone for a pee,' says Alex. 'He's been drinking Coke all night.'

Joey's Coke glass is on the table, half full. Alex feels in his pocket and brings out a twist of paper. He looks around to check that Joey's not on his way back, tips pink powder from the paper into the glass, and stirs it with a fork handle.

DJ is horrified. 'What are you doing?' he says. 'That's not Sphynx, is it?'

'Yeah. I ground up one of the pills.'

DJ can't believe it. 'He doesn't do drugs. You know that.'

'It's only a bit,' says Alex, 'not even a whole one. It will do him good, help him unwind.'

'But it's not what he wants.'

'It's what he needs.' Then, as DJ still stares at him he adds, 'Name me one famous drummer who's not taken drugs at some time in his life. It goes with the territory. Besides, he might enjoy it.'

'If he comes back.' DJ is hoping he doesn't. He decides the best thing is to take Joey's glass away or knock it over. He's about to do that when Joey returns.

'Better?' says Alex.

'Yeah,' says Joey. 'I just needed a minute.'

'What's the problem?' says DJ. 'You've been going around looking like a wet week in Blackpool.'

Joey shrugs. It doesn't at first look as though he's going to answer but then he says, 'I wish I could get a mobile signal.'

'Your mum?' says DJ.

'Yeah, partly, but mainly it's work.'

'*The Golden Bough*?'

'Mm. They weren't too happy about letting me go when I'm meant to be starting my job. It's one of their busiest times. I said I'd check in with them after a couple of days.'

Alex shakes his head. 'You've been there for five minutes and they can't manage without you. The girls are going up to the big house tomorrow. If there's anybody there we'll ask for a wifi password. Then you can call them. Okay?'

Joey looks more relaxed and nods. 'Okay. Thanks.'

'Good,' says Alex. 'So cheer up.' He raises his glass. 'Drink to our futures,' he says.

DJ sees what's happening but he's too befuddled by alcohol to do anything about it. Before he can react Joey picks up his Coke, chinks it with Alex, and they both drain their glasses.

26

Joey can't sleep. He feels odd. His mind is in turmoil, hitting one thought and glancing off it to another and then to another, like an endless snooker break. Usually, he has no problem sleeping. Even when things are bad at home it's rare for problems to keep him awake. Tonight is different; something is wrong.

He can't get comfortable. His head hurts and so does his stomach. It's a recurrent, clenching gripe which eases when he changes position but after a few minutes the torment returns. Can it be what he's eaten? The food all seemed fresh and good, and it tasted great. He was on soft drinks all day and at the meal. Perhaps that's the trouble; he should have had some of the grappa. Alex and DJ live on it, and Elena downs her share.

His thoughts go to Mia, as they so often do. He sees in his mind's eye the image of her when she came out to the terrace. Her eyes had been made up, her skin smooth, her dark hair shining. She'd looked so perfect he'd been nervous about saying anything to her, and he was pleased with himself that he'd plucked up the courage to speak. And it had been a proper conversation. Mia treats him in a way the others don't.

It's not just that Mia's so great. He feels drawn to her because of their backgrounds. The other three are well off, Alex's family spectacularly so; in contrast, for him and Mia things are very often tight. That's what makes the theft of her purse especially bad. Losing a hundred and fifty euros is a big deal for her, just as it would be for him.

What happened while they were in that waiting room? He was next to her and her bag was on the seat between them. He slept a bit but he was awake a lot too. At one stage Alex left the room. DJ too. As far as he knows Elena and Mia didn't stir. He wasn't aware of anyone coming in. If they had he would have known.

'Are you sure?'

The words come from Alex, who's sitting at a table facing him in a large room. It has a high ceiling with elaborate, pendant lamps, panelled walls and tall windows. It's dark and rich. Something tells Joey it's *The Golden Bough*, although it looks nothing like it.

'I asked if you're sure that nobody came in.'

Joey's standing up. There's no chair and so he has to remain like that, although his legs are tired and he wants to sit down. He thinks about walking off but when he looks around he can't see any way out, the room has no doors.

'Yes,' he says.

'In that case, it must be you that took Mia's money.'

Alex now has a dog, a black bull mastiff which is staring at him. It's slobbering, and growling quietly. 'It has to be you.'

Joey is horrified. 'No, I wouldn't.'

'How much money do you have?' Alex is now wearing a suit, and his hair is slicked down like Steve Sutton's.

'I haven't got any money.'

'Empty your pockets.' Alex slaps the table.

Joey goes to the table and is surprised to find when he puts his hands in his pockets that they're stuffed with money. He pulls out a handful of notes; it's far more than he brought with him, far more than he should have.

'There you are,' says Alex. He's triumphant. Alex thumbs through the notes. 'One hundred and fifty euros. I knew you had it.' The dog growls louder.

Joey panics. He has no idea how the money got there. His legs go weak and he's afraid he's going to fall. He wants to sit. Why is there no chair?

'That's not mine,' he says. 'Somebody must have planted it on me.' His voice sounds to be coming from a long way off. There's no strength in it. He doesn't think they can hear him but he can't make it any louder. 'I didn't. It wasn't me. How can you think that?' he says.

'I'm looking at the evidence,' says Alex. There are a lot more people at the table now, which is much bigger than it was. Alex turns to them. 'It's just as I suspected,' he says.

'What shall we do with him?' It's not Alex any more, it's the manager of *The Golden Bough*. He's a thin, pale-faced man and Joey knows he doesn't like him, confirmed by what he says next. 'We should never have taken him on. I was always against it. The boy's no good. What shall we do with him?'

'Get him out there.' It's his father now, who is standing at a door that has appeared and is open. Through it Joey can see a wide lawn, and rain. 'Get out there and dig your mother up,' his father says. 'Do it now, before she suffocates.' He points to the grass.

Joey goes through the doorway and he's on the lawn of the villa. In the centre is a mound of freshly dug soil, the width and length of a body. The rain is turning the earth into sludge. He knows his mother is there. She's under the ground and unless he can get her out she'll suffocate, choke to death, her mouth and nose full of mud. Tears flood his eyes so he can't see properly. He rushes to the mound and begins to scrape at it with his bare hands. It's soft and easy to dig, but however fast he goes, however much soil he moves, the mound doesn't get any smaller.

'Here, use this,' the manager shouts. He hurls a tool at him. It's a large wooden spoon, the bowl stained from the cooking pot, or perhaps from the earth. 'Get digging. And hurry, you little shit.'

'Yes, hurry,' yells Alex, who's come back again. 'Do you want your mother to die?'

A crowd surrounds him. It's made up of people from school, teachers as well as students. He can see Gina Meredith, and Steve Sutton, and Charlie Dodds. Everyone is jeering and shouting. Then he sees that he's not the only one digging. There are other mounds, with other people scrabbling at them. There's DJ at one, Alex at another, and Elena at a third. It seems to be a race.

They're getting on much faster than he is. They have spades and he thinks how unfair that is. He jabs at the earth with his spoon but it's no good, so he scrabbles with his fingers. The soil is now so wet that everything he moves slides back into the hole.

The manager stands behind him. He takes off his belt and swings it at him. Joey dodges. 'I knew you were no good the moment I saw you. You're a waste of time.'

'You're late,' another voice yells. 'The gig was over an hour ago.'

'Get on with it,' someone else screams. 'If you don't get to her soon you'll be too late, she'll be gone.'

He digs and digs, on his knees, scooping out handful after handful of earth, clawing with his fingers. He's crying. The rain runs down his cheeks and drips off his chin.

'I'm coming,' he shouts. 'Hold on, mum. Don't go. I'm coming.'

He digs furiously, faster, but now someone is stopping him. They have his wrists. They're holding him, trying to pin him down. He struggles. 'Let me go you bastards. She's going to die.'

Arms envelop him and he's dragged away from the mound. He tries to resist but he has no strength. Then at once he feels release, as if a weight that's been pressing down on him has been lifted off. Someone is holding him. It's a girl. Her face is next to his, her hair brushes his cheek. She rocks him gently. It's Mia.

'Hey, Joey' she says softly, soothingly. 'You're all right. You're all right. Take it easy.' The rocking continues, with soft, cooing sounds.

'What's the trouble?' That sounds like Elena.

'He's been sleepwalking. I heard him from our room and found him down here trying to dig the ground with this.'

Mia has the wooden spoon. They're on the grass beside the terrace. There's a shallow hole in front of him, as if a dog has been scratching. His fingers hurt. His fingernails are rammed with dirt and his finger ends are bleeding.

'We'd better get those washed,' says Mia, taking his fingers gently in her hands, 'before you pick up any bugs.'

DJ is there too. He helps him to his feet. Joey feels shaky and has to be supported as he moves towards the house.

'Are you okay?' says Elena, putting an arm around him from the other side.

'I think you were dreaming,' Mia says.

Joey nods. He must have been, but it seemed so real.

'A nightmare?'

Joey nods again.

'Welcome to the club,' says Elena. 'What is it about this place and dreams?'

27

Elena has been in bed for a couple of hours since they cleaned up Joey and got him to his room but she can't sleep. Joey's dream has made her think of her own. Every time she gets to the brink of dropping off she wakes herself up because she's afraid of another fantasy vision. It's as if there's some alarm inside her head that throws a switch to stop her unconscious mind from being swept again into the terrifying world of their nightmares. Of Mia's nightmare. Of Joey's. He hasn't said much about what happened in his dream, she thinks he's too upset to describe it in detail.

She goes downstairs. It's much hotter than it has been on the previous two nights. There's no breeze and the air feels humid. She's wearing a silk camisole that sticks to her skin and feels clammy. She'd put it on with French knickers for Alex but he'd been too drunk to be interested. He'd come in, fallen on the bed and gone immediately to sleep. She pulls the camisole over her head and lets it fall to the ground. She stands still, revelling in the feeling of the air brushing her skin. She drops the knickers, stretches, turns, and sees the glow of a cigarette. Shocked, she moves to cover herself, even though it's pitch dark. The smoke has a pungent smell. It can't be Alex, she's left him snoring in the bedroom, and Joey doesn't smoke.

'DJ?'

'Sure,' comes a soft voice from the blackness.

The cigarette glows again. She can just see a towel on the recliner beside her and she snatches it up and wraps it around her.

'Don't cover up on my account,' he says. His eyes must be working better in the dark than hers because she still can't see anything. 'You can't sleep either?'

'No. Too hot. You'd think somewhere like this would have air-con, wouldn't you?'

'No way. It's a trillion years old. There was no air-con when this was built and to install it now would ruin the place. Want a drag?' The glowing cigarette waves about in the air. Elena is trying to cut down on her smoking, but the offer's tempting. 'Come over here and park your arse.'

'Charming,' she says, but she laughs and joins him, pulling the towel around her.

DJ is sitting on the marble stones at the edge of the terrace, with his legs dangling over a short drop to the grass below. She lowers herself beside him. The marble tiles are cooler than she expected and she adjusts the end of the towel beneath her legs. They're only a few meters from where Joey was scraping the grass, not far from where she dreamt she broke into the woods. Absently her hand goes to her neck, to where she felt the rope. Her eyes are getting used to the darkness and she's starting to be able to make things out in the starlight.

DJ hands her the cigarette. The blackness is so intense that the glow as she draws on it is dazzling. The smoke tastes sour and makes her cough.

'Yuk,' she says, handing the thing back. 'What is it?'

'Foul, isn't it?,' says DJ, cheerfully. 'It's from a packet I bought in Bern, on the station. It's all I've got left. I've run out of everything else.'

'My God, are they Swiss? You'd think an up-together country like that would be able to come up with something better than this.' Elena wonders about going upstairs to get her own cigarettes, but she's happy being here with DJ. 'Anyway, what are you doing? Looking out for the fairies?'

'The fairies?'

'Or the goat-men.'

'Oh yeah, your dream. No, I don't fancy seeing any of those.'

'Bruno said that the forest is magical. I thought you might be sprite spotting.'

'Interesting,' says DJ. 'I'm not so sure about sprites, but if a sexy wood nymph came flitting out from the trees that would be different.'

'Dryad.'

He doesn't understand. 'Come again.'

'A wood nymph is called a dryad.'

'Ah, I see,' he says. 'And what's a water nymph called? A wetad.'

He laughs. It's a joke Elena has heard before but she

joins in. They're both whispering. None of the bedrooms they're using is on this side of the house so it's unlikely they'll wake the others, but they've both decided independently that they don't want anyone else to join them.

Elena's perspiration has done what it was supposed to, it's evaporated and cooled her body. She pulls the towel around herself more tightly. DJ puts his hand on her shoulder. 'You feel chilly,' he says. His fingers are firm, and they stay there a little longer than was really needed. She finds the touch exciting. 'Hang on there,' he says. He gets up and goes into the house.

Half a minute later he returns. He has a blanket, which he tucks around her shoulders. He also has what looks like a grappa bottle. 'There you go,' he says. He sits beside her, a little closer than before, and hands her the grappa. 'This will warm you up too.' There are no glasses. She takes a sip from the bottle, and feels the chemical bite of the spirit. It tastes stronger than it did before. She returns it to him and he drinks too.

'That's two out of three things needed to raise your body temperature,' he says.

'Oh, thank you. What's the third?'

'Me,' he says. He hooks his arm around her waist and pulls her towards him. He doesn't turn his face to hers, there's no suggestion of kissing; they simply sit there, shoulders touching, heads side by side, facing the forest. She feels the warmth coming from him.

Elena remembers when things used to be different from the way they are now. They'd been in the same group since first going to secondary school and had slowly grown close. They shared each other's packed lunches. 'What have you got today?' would be the regular question when they sat down in the dining hall and investigated what they'd been given. 'Swap you an egg for a mini-roll.' After that they'd do homework together in a corner of the library. One time she was waiting at the bus stop and three boys came along. She knew them slightly and had run-ins with them before, but that day they were more aggressive than usual. They started on her at once, calling her a fat cow and pulling at her clothing. They got rougher and she was starting to feel scared when DJ appeared like a knight in shining armour. Although there were three of them and only one of him, he was big even in those days and they ran away, shouting impotently once they were out of range. DJ's standing rose even further in her eyes, and the incident propelled their relationship to a new level.

They were never a couple in the usual sense, in the way that some of their contemporaries were. They were more like two straight friends of the same gender. They rarely demonstrated any affection for each other. They never had sex, although on one occasion they got close. It was an afternoon early in the summer holiday before they went into the 6th Form. Like almost everyone in their year group, they'd recently become sixteen and there were many jokes among them about now being able to 'do it' legally. DJ had come to the pub. It was closed and Elena's parents had gone on their monthly trip to the cash and carry. Both of them knew that they'd have the place to themselves for a couple of hours. They went up to Elena's room and lay down on her bed, and started kissing. They had been doing that more of late, and it was usually initiated by DJ. For Elena it didn't feel right, especially when he used his tongue, but she liked DJ and thought she ought to enjoy it, so she carried on. She'd been wearing a skirt and a loose-fitting top. DJ had fondled her breasts through her bra, and then she'd felt his hand come up between her legs. It had been a jolt, a shock that ran through her. It wasn't right. Not this, not now, not with him. She wriggled away and stood up, pulling her top down and smoothing her skirt.

'What's up?' he'd said. 'I'm not very good at this. Did I do something wrong?'

She could remember how hurt he'd sounded. She'd been unable to explain how she felt. DJ was kind, thoughtful, good looking; a lot of the other girls thought he was very and they didn't believe her when she insisted that their relationship was purely platonic. Now she was embarrassed. Here was she, Elena Barnes, a grade-A English student, and she couldn't explain why she didn't want to do what he so obviously wanted.

He'd gone home soon after that, and things from then on had been different. They still saw each other, but not as often as before. Then the new term started and Mia arrived. Mia. DJ was drawn to her like a moth to a flame. Elena had thought she ought to be jealous, but she wasn't because she found herself receiving a lot of attention from Alex.

DJ's hand moves and she feels his fingers in the middle of her back, stroking the ends of her hair. It's nice.

'What are you thinking about?' he says.

'I was thinking about you and Alex kicking the shit out of each other in the studio yesterday.'

'Oh.' His hand stills and she feels his body tense. 'It was nothing, just a daft misunderstanding. It was my fault really. I shouldn't have been looking through his stuff.'

Each wants to ask the other if they believe Alex's story about Mia's purse but, perhaps avoiding what they think might be the answer, neither does. Instead Elena says, 'Can you remember how things used to be for all of us? All together for so long, and now we're moving on.'

'Are you nervous about it?'

'No, not really. Curious I suppose. I'd like to have a magic time machine and be able to go forward a year or so and see how things work out. Just to satisfy myself that everything's all right, and then come back.'

'I'll make one for you,' he says. 'You can probably do the parts on a 3D printer.'

She laughs softly. 'Are you? Nervous about the future?'

'A bit,' he says. 'Mind you I have reason to be. It's okay for you, your place doesn't depend on your exam results. Mine does. I need two As and a B.'

'You'll get those, of course you will.'

He shrugs. 'I don't know. One of the papers was really tough and I think I may have screwed up.'

'Nonsense,' she says, 'you'll be fine.' She winds her arm around him. His T-shirt has ridden up and her palm contacts his bare skin. She senses him keeping very still. Her fingers move slowly over his back. He feels solid and dependable. 'Will you carry on seeing Mia, when you've both gone to uni?' she whispers.

There's a pause before he answers. 'I don't know,' he says. 'We've talked about that. Loughborough's a long way from Bath and it won't be easy to meet during term time. We've decided that we're going to stay in touch and see how things work out. Sort of play it by ear, I suppose. What about you and Alex?'

'Same. It makes sense given what's happening.'

There's another pause. Then DJ says, 'One thing I do know. I want to carry on seeing you.'

It's not what she was expecting. She feels a rush of warmth and her heartbeat quickens. Before she can decide what it means, or whether it means anything at all, his face turns towards her. His lips are parted. There's a moment while everything is on hold, like a car poised on the brink of a roller coaster drop. Then they're kissing. It's quick, deep and hungry, as if they're both trying to feed off each other, to get as much of each other as they can while they can. She pulls him onto her. The flags are cold and the blanket's in an uncomfortable ridge beneath her. DJ's mouth is on hers, his tongue flickering around hers. His hands are on her, washing over her. His thighs are between her legs. He slips down his shorts. She feels his fingers working her. He pushes hard, squeezing her against the tiles. The stone is solid beneath her and what he's doing hurts. She cries out and beats his back with her fists. DJ mistakes it for ecstasy and pumps harder. She thinks she might split open like a nut, her shell broken and her soft kernel exposed. Blood rises and rushes in her ears. She hears herself shriek. Then he groans, shudders, and his body goes limp. So does hers. It's done.

DJ rolls off her and leaves her on her back, sweaty and bruised. She wonders what she's done. Who started it? What might it mean? Her mind slips out of focus and she finds herself thinking not of Alex, but of Mia.

STAGE 4 – RAPID EYE MOVEMENT

28

Mia thinks she's first up because she's heard no sound from any of the other rooms. She's surprised to find that she's not. Joey is sitting at the kitchen table, half-eaten scrambled egg and a nibbled slice of toast on the plate in front of him.

'Hey,' he says.

'Hey yourself.'

'How are you feeling?' she says.

'I'm fine. A bit of a headache but otherwise I'm okay.'

'No more bad dreams?'

'No.'

'Good.' She fills the kettle.

'Thanks for last night,' he says. 'For taking care of me.'

'You're welcome,' she says. 'You were in a state. It must have been a really scary dream. Do you want to talk about it?' He shakes his head. She doesn't mind. When he wants to tell her more he will.

'I know now what you and Ellie went through. It's

shit. I hope DJ and Alex are ready, because it'll be one of them next.'

Yes, thinks Mia, it probably will. Their dreams seem to be following some strange pattern. 'How are your fingers?'

Joey looks at his fingertips. There are plasters on the first three of his right hand and the first two of his left. 'They're a bit sore. It's a good job I don't play the guitar. Did you put the plasters on?'

'No. Elena did.' She notices that Joey's backpack is on the floor beside his chair. 'What's that for? Going somewhere?' It's not a serious question and she doesn't expect the answer she gets.

'Home.'

She's astonished. 'What? Why?'

Joey looks uncomfortable. 'I just need to,' he says.

'Because of your dream?'

'A bit. Partly. I can't explain. I just have to get away from here.'

She knows how he feels. They're all of them beginning to think about leaving. All except Alex.

'You can't go home,' she says. 'You haven't done the gig yet. And besides, how will you get there?'

He reaches into his pocket and takes out an envelope. 'I've got my train tickets, we all have.'

Mia is nonplussed. Is he serious? 'But how will you get to a station?'

'I'll walk down the track till I reach the main road and then I'll hitch a lift to Florence.'

'Walk to the main road? It's miles. It must be five at least.'

Joey shrugs. 'It's all downhill.'

'And what about the gig?'

'What gig?' he says. 'I don't see any sign of a gig, do you? Anyway, they don't need me. For the set they're planning they just need a steady beat, not a proper drummer. Alex can synth that on the keyboards.' He pushes his plate aside, stands up, and swings the backpack onto his shoulders.'

He's serious, thinks Mia, he really is serious. What's happened to chase him away? Was it last night? If he goes now, on his own, will he be able to manage?

'How do you plan to get a lift?'

It seems to Joey a pointless question. 'I'll hitch. I'll stand at the side of the road and thumb. Somebody's bound to stop.'

Maybe, thinks Mia, but when? They hadn't seen anybody hitching when they'd been on the way from Florence. He could be waiting for ages. There's another problem too. 'You don't speak any Italian. How will you tell the driver where you want to go?'

'I'll just say Florence. After that, it will be sign language and grunts. Anyway, a lot of people over here seem to speak English.'

Perhaps some people speak some English, thinks Mia, but a lot don't. 'If you tell an Italian driver you want to go to Florence they might not understand you. They don't call it that. Its name in Italian is Firenze.'

There's so much more she wants to ask him. Does he know how to find the station? What will he do if his lift gets him as far as the suburbs and drops him there? And of course, the constant issue for the hitchhiker, although usually more of a concern for girls than boys, is the possibility of running into somebody who means them harm.

While they've been talking Mia has been busy. She hands Joey a paper bag. 'Here, take this with you,' she says.

'What is it?'

'Sandwiches. You're going to be hungry before you get to Firenze. It's only cheese I'm afraid, I can't find anything else.'

Joey is moved. 'Cheese is great. Thanks.'

'And take some of these Cokes,' she says. 'There's no point having to go in somewhere to buy things if we've got them here.' She helps him stow some cans in his backpack. She offers four but he takes one out because of the weight. 'Do you have any money?' she asks.

'Some. Enough.' He takes two steps forward, leans forward, and kisses her on the cheek. It's awkward because his feet are a pace from hers and he has to lean over, as if he's afraid of any other part of their bodies touching.

Mia follows him to the doorway and watches him trudge down the hill. She can still feel the spot where his lips brushed her cheek. He doesn't look back, or wave. Eventually, he goes around the bend in the track and disappears. It's a long walk to the road, she thinks, and then he has to hope for a lift. Joey is the youngest of the five of them and the least travelled. He seems a baby compared with Alex or DJ. She's worried about how he'll manage to get all the way to England on his own. She prays he'll be all right.

She returns to the kitchen, bins Joey's uneaten food and puts his plate, knife, and fork in the dishwasher. Then she makes herself a mug of tea and sits in the kitchen doorway, watching the sun throw cloud patterns on the far hills.

Elena comes in. Her hair is tangled and her face is puffy.

'Another bad night?' says Mia.

'I didn't get much sleep,' she says.

Mia nods. 'Me too. It was hard to go off after Joey's dream.'

'What on earth was it about?'

'He won't go into the details, but from what he's said so far he was dreaming that his mother had been buried alive and he had to dig her up before she suffocated.'

'Jesus,' says Elena, frowning. 'That's awful.' She goes to the coffee machine and starts to work on it. Then she turns to face Mia. 'That's three of us who've had bad dreams. I don't just mean run-of-the-mill nightmares, but something really really nasty. Something so super scary that it hangs around with you for a long time after you've come out of it. I can still feel that rope around my neck. I can still smell the goat men.' She comes back to the table with her mug.

'When you think about it,' says Mia, 'it's as if this whole thing is a dream. We're here in this great place but we're cut off from everything, and the things that happen here don't seem real. I wouldn't be surprised to see a unicorn come galloping up the road.'

Elena too is puzzled. 'Perhaps we'll make some sense of it all when we go up to the house.'

'I hope so, although I don't expect we'll find out anything about our dreams.'

Elena looks around her. 'It could simply be this place,' she says. 'There's something funny about it. We've all felt it. We were warned to avoid the woods but you wouldn't want to go near them anyway. They feel peculiar. The trees are like witches surrounding the house, casting a spell on whatever goes on here.'

Mia shudders. The two girls are silent for a moment. Then Mia says, 'Joey's gone.'

'Gone? Gone where?' Elena glances in the direction of the big house. 'Up there?'

'No, home. He's gone home.'

Elena is so surprised she almost drops her coffee. 'Home? When? Why? I mean, how? He can't.'

'Well, he has. When I came in here he was already up, with his stuff packed and all set to go. He finished his breakfast and he went.'

'You mean he just cleared off?'

'Yes. He said he was going to walk down to the main road and then hitch to Florence.'

Elena is incredulous. 'Walk to the main road? It's miles!'

'Yes, I told him that. He said it would be fine because it's all downhill.'

'How will he get a lift? He can't speak Italian.'

'He'll be okay. I told him to ask for Firenze, not Florence. Once he's on the train it will be easy.'

'You think? Have you seen the route Bruno's assistant has booked? Talk about round the houses. It's worse than getting here.'

Mia is surprised. 'No, it's straightforward. Our tickets say one train to Torino and then another straight on to Paris and the Eurostar.'

'What, really? Alex's and mine take us on a coach to Antibes first, and then we have to get two trains to Paris. The bus takes hours and the trains don't run every day, so we have to plan carefully when we go. '

'That's crazy. Why do we have different routes? I wonder which one Joey's got.'

'It does seem strange,' says Elena. 'There must be a reason why Bruno's arranged different itineraries for us. Doesn't he realise we want to travel together?'

'Maybe Alex knows,' says Mia.

'Maybe Alex knows what?'

This is DJ, who's just come in. He glances at Elena and looks away again. Mia can't read the body language but there's something between them. Have they fallen out?

DJ's response to the news that Joey has left is the same as Elena's, with the same questions: When? Where? How? Why?

'Shit!' he says as he digests the impact. 'That means we don't have a drummer. I'd better let Alex know.' He leaves, clearly flustered.

'We can't even call Joey to check he's okay,' says Elena, looking at her useless mobile phone. 'It's incredible. A millionaire's pad like this and there's no mobile signal.'

'Maybe the very rich have servants to take their messages for them,' Mia says. She's not entirely joking.

DJ returns with Alex. He's businesslike, and cross. 'He

could have told us he was meaning to leave. Selfish little tosser. What are we going to do now?'

'When you were talking about it back in England you said we could manage without a drummer,' Elena reminds him. 'You said that you could synthesise a backing beat on the keyboards.'

'Yes, but I was trying to put the best face on it in case he didn't make it. To come here, piss around for a bit and then clear off without doing the gig, it's...' He runs out of words. 'We'll look useless without a proper drummer,' he grumbles. 'We'll look like bloody amateurs.'

'We *are* amateurs,' says Elena.

Alex glares at her. 'Anyway, I know why he's done it, why he's run out.'

The three of them look at him. Mia and Elena glance at each other, puzzled.

'I think it's those fascists at *The Golden Bough*,' says DJ. 'They tried to stop him coming here in the first place. Maybe he got word that they want him.' He stands up straight, points towards the road, and assumes a commanding voice. 'Return to your post, Joseph Meads, or you're out on your ear.'

'Don't be daft,' says Alex. 'How could he have heard from them? They sent a carrier pigeon? No, I know why he's gone.'

'Why?' says Mia.

Alex gets something from his pocket and slaps it on the table.

'That's my purse!' says Mia. She grabs it, looks inside, and tips it. Nothing falls out. 'Where did you get it?'

'I found it on the station at Domodossola. I saw it on

the floor outside the waiting room when we were going for the train. I was planning to give it to you but I was waiting till we got back to England because I didn't want it to keep reminding you that you'd been robbed.'

'And it was empty when you found it?'

'Yes.'

'What's this got to do with Joey leaving?' says Elena. She has a sense of foreboding.

'It stands to reason, doesn't it? It was Joey who took Mia's euros.'

They can't believe it.

'You must be mad,' says Elena.

'Never,' says Mia.

'He's our mate,' says DJ. He finds it easier to think of Alex taking the money than Joey.

'Which of the four of us is hardest up? Who needed money the most?' says Alex. 'Not you, DJ. Not you, Ellie. Not me. That leaves Joey, and we all know he's skint. The reason why he wasn't going to come in the first place was that he couldn't afford it.'

Elena, Mia and DJ are stupefied. They look at Alex in total disbelief.

'I'm not saying he planned it,' Alex says. 'But he was dossing next to you, Mia, and your bag was between the two of you. All he had to do was reach into it while you were asleep.'

DJ and Mia are silent. DJ is surprised that Alex can remember exactly where Mia's bag was. He can't.

'Look,' says Alex, 'I know you might find it hard to believe, but think about it. Motive and opportunity, isn't that what the police say? And who else could it have been?'

'There was that homeless guy who was hanging around,' says Mia.

'The waiting room door was shut,' says Alex, 'I shut it. If he'd come in one of us would have heard him.'

Mia can't handle the idea that it might have been Joey who stole from her. She begins to cry.

29

Elena looks at her reflection in the mirror and frowns. There are too many puzzles. Alex's assertion that it was Joey who stole Mia's purse is inconceivable. She knows Joey doesn't have any money, he never has had any, but he's always seemed to her to be totally honest, obsessively so. She can remember him once finding a £5 note at school and handing it in because he was concerned it might be somebody's lunch money. He's now got a promising job that ought to lead to lots of opportunities. Why choose this moment to steal from a friend? It's not as if they need any cash here, there's nothing to spend it on. The main thing, though, is that he wouldn't steal from Mia because he's nuts about her. It's obvious. She's seen the way he looks at her, the way he always manages to sit near her at mealtimes, on the terrace, on the train.

How long have the five of them been at the villa? It feels like ages but it's only three nights. Yet such a lot has happened, things that she could not have predicted. It's not just the dreams, it's the way they're reacting to each other. Attractions and relationships seem to be in flux. Last night she and DJ had sex on the terrace, in the dark, while everyone else was asleep. Exactly how it happened is a bit of a blur, but it wasn't a date, she didn't go downstairs planning it; she didn't even know DJ was there. In contrast, she has a strong suspicion that Alex set up what happened between him and Mia, and that he's had her in his sights for some time. On the other hand, Mia's interest seems to be moving away from DJ and towards Joey.

Then there's her and Alex. There was a time when she thought they'd be together always. Way back when they were first an item she inscribed their names in a heart in her diary and they sent each other soppy cards. She wrote poems for him. That's changed. Every day now he shows another aspect of his character that she finds unattractive. On some days she's not even sure she even likes him any more. It's a slow fade that every day seems to get quicker.

Like most mornings nowadays she has a hangover. Suddenly she hears her grandmother's voice: 'You'll never keep your complexion if you drink like that!' She leans towards the mirror and examines her face. No wrinkles. Yet. But she is only nineteen. What will she look like in ten years? In twenty? Not for the first time she tells herself that she must at least slow down, if not stop. Her head aches and she takes a couple of paracetamols. Then she goes down to her favourite lounger on the terrace.

She's been trying to make headway with a book. It's one from the reading list she's been sent by St Andrews and she wants to get into it but she can't concentrate. It's too hot. The noise from the insects is hypnotic. Every time she begins a paragraph her eyes swim and the print blurs. She closes her eyes and watches red and yellow blobs swirl. She dozes.

She's woken by a shake as DJ sits heavily on the end of her lounger.

'Hey,' he says.

She blinks up at him. He's against the light and she fumbles for her sunglasses.

'What are we going to do?' he says in a soft voice.

'Do we have to do anything?'

'Yes, I think we do.'

'Okay. I thought I'd read for a bit but I can't settle to it, so I think I might go to the studio to try a few of our numbers.'

DJ looks irritated. 'I don't mean that. I mean what are we going to do about us?'

'Us? You mean you and me? What is there to do?'

DJ glances around to check that no one else is about and they have the terrace to themselves. 'Last night,' he says. 'What we did. It must change things.'

Elena thinks she might rather forget it. 'I don't see why it should.'

DJ adopts the tone he would use if he were trying to explain something difficult to a slow-witted child. 'Mia is my girlfriend. She is also your best friend. Alex is my best friend and you are his girlfriend. Last night we, you and me, had sex. Kind of complicated, eh?'

'It was a baking night,' she says, 'and we were both tanked up. We'd been disturbed by Joey dreaming and after that neither of us could sleep. It was pure chance we met on the terrace. We had another drink, talked for a bit, and, well, you know. Now unless you're going to tell me you've fallen head over heels in love with me, or unless I come back to you in a few weeks to tell you that I've missed my period, that's all there was to it. You're not in love with me, are you?'

DJ doesn't answer.

Elena is relieved. 'I thought not,' she says.

DJ looks glum. 'That's how you see it.'

'Yes. Don't you?'

He sighs and puts his head in his hands. She swings her legs off the recliner and shuffles next to him. 'Hey,' she says. 'What's up?'

'Nothing,' he says.

'Come on,' she says. 'What is it?' She puts an arm around his shoulder. 'It can't be this business with Joey.'

There's a long pause before he speaks. 'It's not Joey, it's us. Can you remember when we were in Y10? And Y11? You and me, we were always together.'

'Yes,' says Elena, 'and it was great, but we were just mates. We were never boyfriend and girlfriend.'

'We might have been, except you moved in on Alex.'

'Hang on,' says Elena. 'I didn't "move in" on him. We just started talking, that's all. Anyway, it was you who set it off. You got smitten by Mia. As soon as she appeared you couldn't keep away. You were trailing around after her like a puppy.'

DJ looks at her and smiles drily. 'It wasn't like that,' he says. 'It was self-defence. You were drifting off. I thought it might make you jealous and bring you back.'

Elena doesn't believe him. 'Bollocks,' she says. 'Is that the only reason you've been going out with Mia? For two years?' She's going to add sarcastically that of course it's nothing to do with Mia being really nice and good company and mega-fit and great looking, but she doesn't. She drops her arm from DJ's shoulder. She doesn't want this conversation. She doesn't want to go where it appears to be heading.

'Look,' she says, 'nothing about the four of us is permanent. We've talked about this. In a few weeks we're all going our separate ways. We'll be miles apart, in different places where there'll be thousands of other people of our age. We'll be there for the next few years. Do you think there's maybe, perhaps, the teeniest tiniest remotest chance that we might just possibly meet someone that we get on with as well as you and Mia, me and Alex, you and me? Perhaps even better?'

'So you're saying we've got no future together.'

'I'm saying I don't know, but our lives are going to change a lot and it's best to be prepared for that.'

What happened in the night means more to DJ than she thought. She wants to forget it, but for him seems to be a big deal. It's an interesting role reversal, she thinks. In her experience, it's often the girl who's inclined to treat impromptu sexual encounters seriously while for the boy it's just a casual nothing.

The next thing he says surprises her. 'I might not be going to Bath,' he says.

'Why not? Surely you're not thinking about taking a year off, like Alex.'

'No, it's my grades. I think I fucked up the second Maths paper.'

Elena squeezes his shoulder. 'You'll be fine, I'm sure. We can all of us think after an exam how we might have done better. Anyway, what's the worst that can happen? You go somewhere else instead.'

'That could be even further away from everybody.'

It strikes Elena that what DJ is experiencing is a sort of premature homesickness, a nostalgic wish for things to carry on as they always have been, probably brought on by the uncertainty facing them all. It's odd. DJ has been talking for the whole year about how great it will be to be rid of school and to move on. Now the time is here it's as though he's wishing it wasn't.

'You'll be fine,' she says. 'It's just that hanging around for results is an anxious time. I remember what it was like waiting to hear how we'd got on in our GCSEs, and these exams are more important.'

They sit for a while in silence. DJ gnaws at a fingernail. 'Anyway, last night was good,' he says.

'Yeah. For me too,' she says. It wasn't really, but he needs to hear that. She kisses him on the cheek. 'And if we get another hot night and neither of us can sleep, who knows?' She gives him a friendly dig to show she's not serious, and he smiles. 'I thought when you asked what we were going to do you might have been talking about the gig. Has Alex said any more to you about it?

DJ shakes his head. 'No.'

'This morning he told me he thinks that the gig will be on Saturday.'

'What's today?'

'Thursday. So in two days. "One hundred per cent," he said. God knows how he claims to know. There are no messages, and he certainly didn't say that when we asked him yesterday. I was wondering if he's said anything to you.'

'No, nothing. It's great here, though, isn't it? What's the point of rushing back? I'd rather be here than get bored at home. Why don't we just lay back and enjoy it?'

Elena doesn't respond right away but looks towards the forest. Even under the bright sun, it seems sinister. Every patch of woodland she's ever visited has had gaps between the trees, windows through the branches that give glimpses of other spaces beyond and invite you in. Not this one. It's ominous and dark. This wood wants to keep you out. It was over there, just a few metres from where she now sits, that she dreamt she was scratched, tied, taunted and almost strangled. If, that is, it was a dream. But if it wasn't a dream, what was it? She shudders.

A nearby cicada ramps up a rasping invitation to mate. Go for it, little guy, she thinks. If you believe that'll make her come hopping over to your tree, good luck.

'Okay,' she says. 'I don't suppose any of us feels that desperate to get away.'

'Except Joey.'

'Yes, except him. I don't know why he's gone but I don't buy Alex's explanation. I don't believe for a second he took Mia's money. It makes no sense. Suppose he did, why would he leave now when it might arouse suspicion? I think it's something else that's made him take off.' She sighs. 'I know there are people who would lay out a lot of money to be in a place like this, and it seems ungrateful to feel restless and want to go. If we could communicate with Gianna we might get something from her, but the only link we have with Bruno is a woman who's deaf. Has it been done deliberately to shut us out and stop us from asking questions?' She has a sensation of helplessness, and she doesn't enjoy the feeling. She likes to know where she is and vagueness makes her uneasy, it always has. 'Bruno should have talked to me, not to Alex,' she says. 'I would have made sure everything was clear and we all understood the arrangements.'

'Come on,' says DJ. He gets to his feet and holds out a hand to help her up. 'Let's go rehearse our songs. At least we can do that.'

30

Elena and Mia walk beneath the trees that line the track, making use of the shade. The sky is deep blue. A few thin clouds smudge the horizon but the rest is clear. Elena wears dark glasses but still squints into the light. She has a headache. How much did she drink last night? She seems to spend most of her days either vaguely drunk or with a hangover. She won't be able to go on like this at St Andrews. She must get a grip

'Trouble in Toyland?' says Mia.

Elena had called at the studio to say they were going and she found a row in full swing. DJ and Alex had been arguing. Things hadn't come to blows this time but it had looked to be getting close. She's been telling Mia about it.

'Yes, and it's getting worse,' she says. 'They're both of them paranoid about being outshone by the other, and neither thinks the other one is pulling his weight.'

'What was it this time?'

'Oh, a storm in a teacup. DJ's pissed that we agreed on

the setlist for the wedding and Alex went along with it but now he's changed his mind. Alex is fed up with DJ because he thinks that he's done all the work sorting out this trip and that gives him the right to decide what we play. And, of course, he thinks he's the band leader.'

'It sounds like it's a good job they'll soon be in other places.'

'It probably is,' says Elena. 'Although I think the band would probably break up anyway.'

'Musical differences.' says Mia. 'They're in good company. It happened to The Beatles, The Smiths, The White Stripes, Oasis.'

Elena laughs. 'Yes, but by that time they were world famous and had a fist full of platinum albums. It would be nice if we could go out on a high, though. Theo and Lita's wedding will be a fantastic opportunity to do that.'

If there is a wedding, thinks Mia. She's doubting it more and more. 'What about next year?' she says.

'What about it?'

'Will you carry on with your music?'

'Yeah. Maybe. I'm not sure. It depends on whether I meet other people who are into my kind of thing.'

'It'll be all bagpipes up there in Scotland, won't it?' says Mia

Elena laughs. 'Could be. And whisky too if I'm lucky. I'll carry on with my poetry anyway.'

'Is Alex serious about going to America?'

'I've no idea. Last night was the first I've heard of it. If he does have an uncle in Canada I suppose he might.'

'It must be nice to be able to afford it.'

'He can't. His parents have set up a fund to pay for

him to go to uni but his dad says that's all he can use it for, nothing else. So if he goes on a degree course all his tuition and living expenses will be paid, but if he wants to do anything else he's on his own.'

'Sounds to me like a mixture of generosity and blackmail.' For Mia it's an astonishing insight; she's always assumed Alex had all the money he could spend, and the idea of him being short is a surprise.

Elena stops. Beside the track is a stone bench. She sits down and takes a flat, silver case from her shorts. She opens it and holds it out to Mia. It contains cigarettes.

Mia hesitates. 'I don't smoke, you know.' Despite that, she takes one. Elena flicks a lighter and holds out the flame.

Mia draws in the smoke and coughs. 'A cigarette case, eh? There's sophistication for you.' She coughs again.

Elena turns the case in her hand. 'It used to be my granddad's. I'm trying to ration myself to no more than five a day, so I use this. It holds seven, and that means to keep to my target I have to give two away. You've just helped me by taking one.'

'You're welcome,' says Mia. 'Funny number, seven,' she says. 'I've never seen a packet of seven fags.

'That's what I said when granddad gave me the case. He told me that when he first got it you could buy cigarettes in ones, and he used to top it up from the corner shop.'

'In ones? Really?'

'The good old days,' says Elena.

Mia coughs again. 'I shouldn't be doing this,' she said. 'My dance teacher would murder me. You're ruining your chances, she'd say.' She holds the cigarette away from her face. She decides she's not going to smoke it any more, she'll just let it burn away in her hand.

'Dance chances. I thought you were doing Sport Science.'

'That's what my place is for, but I've been going to dance classes for a couple of years now and I like it. My teacher says I could be good enough to dance professionally and I'm wondering if I can transfer to another course instead.'

Mia has never told her this and Elena is surprised. 'I thought dancers had to be tall. I mean, not that you're...' She runs out of words, and glances down at the smaller girl beside her.

'Not so,' says Mia. 'Shorter girls are usually more agile, have quicker footwork, and we're easier to lift. It's more to do with proportion.'

'So I'm out,' says Elena. She's the tallest of the four of them, taller even than DJ.

'No,' says Mia. 'It takes all sorts. Dance companies do like to have all their dancers around the same size, though, because it looks odd if some of the group are a lot taller than the others. Mind you, you're right, you wouldn't get into any of them. Your tits are too big.' They laugh, and Elena jabs her with her elbow.

They sit on the bench, enjoy the warmth, and take in the view. Elena smokes her cigarette, Mia lets hers burn.

'What a place,' Elena murmurs.

'Fantastic,' Mia agrees. 'Paradise.'

'Yes, though maybe after the apple.'

'Why do you say that?'

Elena pauses a beat. 'I don't know. It seems perfect. The villa's fantastic and the countryside's wonderful, but there's something not quite right.'

'I know what you mean,' says Mia. 'It's something in the atmosphere.'

Elena drops her cigarette and grinds it out with her foot. Then she smooths a small pile of pebbles over it. Mia does the same.

'Perhaps it's not the place,' says Elena. 'Perhaps it's us.'

'What do you mean?'

'It's just that we've never been properly together before. Okay, we've had overnighters at each other's houses, but we've never lived like this, so close for so long. It could be that we're discovering bits of each other that we weren't aware of before, and some of it is coming as a bit of a shock.'

Mia nods. There have always been rows between Alex and DJ but they seem to be worse here. And she and DJ aren't getting on like they did. He doesn't talk to her, and he doesn't appear to want to hear what she says.

'What about you and Alex?'

'What about me and Alex?' Elena feels wary. Can Mia know about what happened between her and DJ on the terrace? Part of her wants to tell her now, to let it all spill out, but she knows that would not be good.

'I mean, are you and Alex getting on better here than you did in England?'

Elena shrugs. Mia knows that Elena's relationship with Alex has ups and downs. They've often talked about it, although not so much recently. 'Oh, you know,' she says. 'Alex is Alex.' She wants the conversation to stop now and not go any further. She stands up. 'Come on,' she says. 'Let's go check this place out.'

She carries on up the hill and Mia follows. The round a clump of trees and less than a hundred metres ahead is Castelvecchio itself, the big house. It sits squarely before them, presiding over the surrounding countryside. So far they've only seen it from a distance; now they're closer they get an idea of its scale.

'Sweet Mary, it's huge,' says Mia.

'Mm. I get the "vecchio" part,' says Elena. 'It's old all right, but it's not a castle.'

It's not. But it is a very large house, formal and solid, on three floors. The worn stonework is yellow ochre, the windows are small and rectangular. In front is a formal garden with tall palms, poplars, topiaries and several statues. Beyond is a grove of olive trees. The garden looks well cared for. A short stairway leads to an impressive door under a timber portico. On the side of the house is an arched colonnade that might have been lifted from an English stately home.

'I can't see a pool,' says Mia. She sounds disappointed.

'There might be one at the back. You'd expect a place this size to have one.'

Mia scans the facade. 'It looks like nobody's home. It's all shut up.'

Elena follows her gaze. The shutters are drawn and everything is still. 'Let's see,' she says.

The two girls go up the steps to the door. There's a handle set into the stonework. Elena tugs it and in the far distance a bell jangles. They wait but there's no response.

'There must be people here,' Mia says. 'Somebody must cut that grass, and water it. Ring again.'

Elena does. 'It could be they're having a siesta, ' she says. 'We shouldn't disturb them.'

'A siesta? It's a bit early for that,' says Mia. She goes down the steps and around the side of the house.

'Better not prowl about too much. Bruno said in his note that the place was alarmed. There may be cctv and all sorts.'

Mia glances up at the eaves. She can't see any cameras, but that doesn't mean there aren't any. She looks along the side of the house. There are two parallel lines of poplars with a narrow track between them.

Elena has joined her. 'I thought the road would stop here but it goes on.' She points to where they can see the terra cotta roofs of more buildings, and the tower of what must be a church in the far distance. 'At least we're not quite alone,' she says.

'They're hardly neighbours. They must be a couple of miles away.'

They continue walking around the outside of the house. At the rear is a cobbled yard that bakes in the sun, and there are a few outbuildings which don't appear to be used. They return to the front.

Elena sums it up for both of them. 'I think we're pretty safe in saying there's no one here. Which is weird. I mean, it's the height of summer. This is a beautiful place, you'd expect it to be busy.'

'If it was mine you wouldn't get me away,' says Mia.

'Alex said the wedding is the day after tomorrow.

Wouldn't you expect there to be a lot of activity? People rushing around to get things ready?'

'Maybe they have been. It could all be set up inside, and they've just closed the shutters to stop the sunlight spoiling things.'

Elena shakes her head. 'This place is empty. It feels it. There's something I don't like about this whole business. We've not seen anyone around. We've not seen the room where we're to play. We don't know when we're to play, or to how many people, or for how long, or when we can get in to rehearse or do a sound check. There's something wrong, there's been a mistake.'

'What sort of mistake?' says Mia. 'The tickets came from Bruno so they must be right. It's not as if Alex booked them and might have got the wrong place or the wrong date.'

'Perhaps the wedding's off. Theo and Lita might have split. There was that guy on *Love Shack* that Lita was supposed to be screwing, the gossip press was full of it. She denied it, but what if there was something in it after all and Theo's given her the boot?'

'Or she's caught him with somebody else and ditched him.'

They both gaze again at the mute facade of the house.

'Come on,' says Elena. 'There's nothing for us here. Let's go back and tell the boys.'

Elena turns away but Mia holds her arm. 'No, look,' she says, pointing upwards. 'The shutter over that window isn't properly closed. If I can get up there I might be able to open it and see in.' The window is on the ground floor but it's well above head height. 'Can I use your shoulder?'

Elena stands under the window. Mia takes two steps and springs at the sill, using Elena's shoulder to give her extra lift. The ledge is narrow and she almost loses her grip, but she manages to scramble up and perch on it. She hooks her fingers around the edge of the shutter and pulls. It swings outwards, almost knocking her off balance but she holds on and steadies herself.

'Shit.'

'What's wrong?'

'I scraped my knee, that's all.' Mia examines it, wets her finger and rubs away the tiny beads of blood. She puts her hand up to shield the light and peers through the glass.

'Can you see anything?'

'A bit. Just a minute. Yes, it's a big room, quite high. There are paintings on the walls. There's a wooden floor, not tiles, and there are some rugs but they're rolled up. All the furniture's piled in the middle of the room and it's covered with dust sheets.' She leans against the pane and the frame gives. 'Hey, this isn't latched.' Mia pushes and the window opens. 'I'm going in.'

'Don't. There may be somebody inside. Or a guard dog or something. Or an alarm.'

Mia ignores her and slides off the sill, landing lightly on the boards. She waits, listening to see if there's any movement from inside. The house is silent and still. She calls through the window to Elena.

'I can't hear anything and I can't see any security. There aren't any of those things on the ceiling that flash at you, like they have at school. Go to the door. I'll see if I can let you in.'

The front door is in the hall and opposite an imposing, marble staircase. It's huge and heavy, with rustic furnishings in black iron. There are bolts top and bottom. They're big and Mia expects them to be stiff but they slide easily. There's a hefty key in a big mortice lock. Mia turns it and pulls the door open. She gives a sweeping bow. 'Welcome to Castle Dracula,' she says in a heavy accent. 'So good of you to come.'

She stands aside. Elena enters and looks around cautiously. 'You're sure there's no one here?'

'Certain. And if there is, we run.'

Elena thinks it's all right for Mia. She's light and fast and could be away in no time; Elena herself isn't built for sprinting.

The two girls explore the ground floor. On the other side of the hallway is another big room like the one Mia described. Towards the rear of the house there are several smaller ones and a large, traditional kitchen.

They go back to the first room. The dust sheets look as though they have been there for some time. Elena lifts one. The chair that it's covering is more ornate than she'd expected, and 19th century French rather than Tuscan rustic. In fact, the whole room has an Empire feel, not at all what they were expecting. The paintings are of men in military uniforms and women wearing impressive dresses adorned with costly accessories. Elena runs her finger along the top of the marble fireplace; it comes away dusty. She stands in the middle of the room.

'This isn't right,' she says. 'No one's been in here for

ages. If they're going to hold a wedding reception they'll first have to get rid of all this stuff, and then clean the place, and bring in some tables and lay them, and some chairs. That'll take ages. And Alex said there were to be five hundred people. You'd get, what, a hundred in here? That would be the max. Where would the rest go? And where would we set up? I know that without a drummer we won't need as much space, but if we play in here how will they hear us in the other rooms?'

'Where are you going?' says Mia as she sees Elena move towards the door.

'I don't like the look of this. Something's up. I think we should tell Alex and DJ what we've found, and then follow Joey's lead and get the hell out.'

'We haven't seen upstairs.'

'It will be the same as this, all covered up and unused.'

'We might as well take a quick peek, while we're here. It could be we'll find something that explains it all.' Mia slips out to the hall and runs lightly up the stairs. Elena doesn't want to follow her but she does.

There's a landing and a long corridor with doors on both sides. The arrangement is very like the house where they're staying but there are more rooms and everything's on an even bigger scale. The first four doors they try are locked.

'Told you,' says Elena. 'There's nothing here.' She goes towards the stairs.

Mia tries the next door and it opens. She looks into the room and freezes. 'Holy shit! Ellie,' she calls softly. 'Come and take a look at this.'

Her tone makes Elena's heart falter. It's going to be something awful. A body? More than one? She turns away from the stairs and goes to where Mia stands in the doorway.

The room is an office. There are some filing drawers, a designer chair, and a large desk. It's what's on the desk that has both girls staring open-mouthed. There's a computer, a keyboard and mouse, several cables, and a large monitor the size of a big TV. Everything is live, switched on. A red light glows on the computer and there are pictures on the monitor. There are nine of them in rectangles, three by three. One of the rectangles is blank but the other eight are live.

'Fuck me!' says Elena.

Each screen contains an image from the villa where they're staying, their house. There's the kitchen and the sitting room; there's the view outside the main door, which also shows the top of the track. Another screen shows the patch of open land before the woods, and the edge of the trees. In one rectangle on the bottom row, the display covers the landing and the top of the stairs; the images in the final three make the two girls gasp.

'My God, those are our bedrooms,' says Mia. There's a view of Joey's room, which is of course empty. Elena's and Alex's is a tip, the chairs, the bed and the floor strewn with clothes and towels. Mia's and DJ's is tidier. DJ is sitting on the bed plucking his guitar. She feels her blood rising as she thinks of what anybody watching the monitor might have witnessed.

'At least they didn't put cameras in the bathrooms!' says Elena.

'This is obscene,' says Mia. 'There's nobody here now, but they could have been spying on us. They probably have been.'

The more they try to process what they've found the more shattering it gets. Mia shudders. Then she feels her anger rising. She takes a step into the room. 'What sort of twisted pervert would do this? It's sick. I want to tear all this shit down. I want to rip out the cables, chuck the computer out of the window and smash that screen.'

Elena's sure she'll do it and she puts a hand out to restrain her. 'I think we should go. All this is likely monitored remotely, and it could be there's even a camera in here that's watching us right now.' She looks around uneasily. 'Maybe everything since we walked up here has been seen. We should get the hell out of here and tell the boys. Then we can decide what we're going to do about it.'

Mia doesn't move. Elena puts her arm on her back and gently eases her towards the door. Then she changes her mind, turns and goes to the desk. With the mouse, she highlights Mia's bedroom where DJ is still strumming. There's an amplifier beside the monitor and she turns up the volume. DJ's guitar is electric and although it's not plugged into anything they can clearly hear the dull, dead notes that he's playing.

'I thought so,' she says. 'Not only full colour video but stereo sound too. Somebody has not only seen everything we've done, they've also heard everything we've said.'

31

The two boys respond differently. Alex thinks it's funny and no big deal. DJ is more concerned.

'I expect how much it bothers you depends on what you've been up to in front of that bedroom camera,' Alex sniggers. 'Seriously, though, it stands to reason that they'd monitor a place as remote as this, especially as they don't know us. And Bruno did warn us that there was security.'

'Yes, but he was meaning in the big house, not here,' says Mia.

Alex ignores her. 'Anyway, relax. There's no one up there to watch it. It could be that it just got left on the last time anyone was inside.'

Mia doesn't think so. She finds the situation alarming, and sinister. 'I think it's horrible,' she says. 'We don't know that nobody's been to the big house. We thought the track stopped there and that anybody going to it would have to pass here on the way, but it doesn't, it goes on. There's a village a couple of miles away. People could have been coming and going from that direction all the time and we wouldn't have known. They could have been watching us from the moment we arrived, and listening too. Ugh.' She shudders again.

'They wouldn't have to be in the house to do that,' says DJ. 'They can probably monitor the system remotely. Hey, there was that movie about a guy who was on reality TV but didn't know it.'

'Yes, *The Truman Show*. I saw it,' says Elena. 'Do you think we're being broadcast? That people are seeing us on their TV screens?'

'We could be a sensation on Italian TV,' says Alex.

'More likely it's some perv watching in a darkened room,' says DJ.

'The security equipment at the gym where I work records too,' says Mia, remembering something else, 'so that if you need to check on anything you can replay it later. Everything we've done and said anywhere in this house will be there to be watched anytime, and we've no idea who'll be doing the watching, or when.'

Elena has a different concern. 'There was a guy who used to come into *The Green Man*,' she says. 'He got done because he had a cottage he rented out on Airbnb and he put cameras in the bedrooms. He made recordings of what people got up to and he sold them online for porn.'

'I've always wondered what it would be like to be a porn star,' Alex says. 'I hear they get paid well.'

'Yes, it's one of the few jobs where the women get paid more than the men,' says Mia.

'You think your bedroom performances are star quality, do you?' Elena says to Alex.

'They could be. Anyway, being watched is in itself a bit of a turn-on, don't you think?'

Elena ignores him; she thinks it's a profound turn off. 'We need to decide what we're going to do,' she says. 'I don't mean the cameras, we can't do anything about those. I mean the wedding. Is there going to be one? Are we staying here expecting there will be, or are we leaving? When I saw that everything at the big house was packed up I thought, okay, nothing is happening so we'll just hang out here for a few more days, enjoy the sunshine and the free food and booze and then we'll clear off. Having seen that video stuff I don't think I want to be here a moment longer. I'm going to pack my things and as soon as it gets light in the morning I want to go.'

Alex is scathing. 'First of all, who says there's no wedding? You've seen shows load in. A gang of people could fix the place up in a day, roadies to sort out the furniture, cleaners and room dressers, a catering crew for the food, no problem. You say we can't do anything about the cameras but you're wrong, we can.'

He points to the camera under the pergola. It's supposed to keep an eye on the terrace but it's covered by Alex's shorts. Elena realises that's what accounts for the blank rectangle, the one of the nine that wasn't showing anything.

'So you think we go round and cover all the cameras with your boxers, do you?'

'Not all of them,' he says. 'Just the bedroom ones. They must be pretty well hidden because none of us has noticed them. They're probably just buttons in the wall, but now we know they're there they should be easy enough to spot. Then we just put a blob of chewing gum on them. Job done.'

The others aren't convinced.

'Look,' Alex continues, 'they probably get all types of people staying here, celebs and all sorts. You've read the gossip. These people can be wild. Whoever manages this place for Theo will want to keep an eye on things. You know, if somebody claims they were raped, or that somebody said something, or they were promised something, they've got proof. It could be very useful in court.'

They're divided. Elena and Mia want to leave, but Alex doesn't. DJ hasn't made his mind up either way but he leans towards staying. They agree that they'll talk about it again and make a decision in the evening, after Gianna has gone. Elena goes upstairs to start packing. Alex and DJ go to the studio. Mia stays on the terrace.

The sun has set before all four of them are together again. Nobody has planned it, but they are all dressed more carefully than on the previous nights. It's as if they've already decided that this is their last dinner together and they've made a special effort for the occasion.

Elena wears a tight, cropped T-shirt and faded denims with strategic rips. Her long hair falls over her shoulders. Mia is in a floral print tiered midi dress. It's girlish and frivolous and shows off her elfin shape. It's obvious the boys like it. Elena is aware that she presents a very different image from Mia. Her chosen outfit displays a roll around her middle. She is torn between self-consciousness and brazen defiance. Fat, she reminds herself, is a feminist issue. DJ too carries extra weight but nobody seems to bother about that, least of all him. It's just the girls who get called out if they're not stick thin.

Alex and DJ have put on clean shirts and chinos. DJ looks well but Alex's face is blotchy and his eyes are red-rimmed. His T-shirt has a single eye in the centre of the chest, outlined in black and with a red pupil. Beneath it are the words *Don't look at me like that*. DJ has a black and yellow Blackbirds shirt, with the number nine and the name Vasilias on the back.

'Creep,' Alex says when he appears in it.

'Not so,' says DJ, his voice low. 'It's to convince anyone watching that I'm one of Theo's fans, keep in their good books.'

'Did you find the camera in your room?' Elena whispers to him.

'Yes and no. Mia worked out where it should be from what she saw on the monitor, and you can see a mark on the ceiling, like a tiny blob in the corner but it's too high up to get at, even on a chair. What about you?'

'Same. Alex thinks he can reach it if he stands on my shoulders but I told him no way. Maybe Mia'll have a go.'

'Have a go at what?' says Mia, joining them.

They explain to her.

Everyone apart from Alex is on edge when they sit down at the table. Elena reflects that there's nothing like thinking you're being recorded to kill conversation.

The meal takes ages but it's another of Gianna's triumphs and as it goes on they relax. They've been treating Gianna rather differently since Joey's speculation that she might not really be deaf. They haven't acted on the plan to test it further, but without discussing it they've all adopted a more careful approach. They've tended to avoid the kitchen when she's there and they don't talk in front of her. They fall silent now as she comes to the table.

'Panzanella,' she says, placing a huge oval dish before them. 'Una specialità della regione.' She makes a sweeping gesture with her arm which takes in the hill behind them, the house, the valley, the forest, and possibly the whole of the country.

'What's she say?' says Alex.

'She says this dish is a speciality of the area. I know it, I had it when I came to Italy before. It's called Panzanella.'

'Yeah, all right. What's in it?' Alex tends to be suspicious of every new dish.

Elena pokes it with her fork. 'Ciabatta, onions, tomatoes, capers, anchovies, and fresh basil, in olive oil and vinegar. Sometimes they put cucumber in it, but this doesn't seem to have any.'

'Thank God for that,' says Alex.

'You can't dislike cucumber,' says Mia. 'There's no taste to it.'

'Exactly.'

'Anyway, you'll like this,' says Elena. 'Just you see.'

'Dovresti berlo con il pinot grigio,' says Gianna, returning to the table with an opened bottle of white wine in an ice bucket.

'She says we should drink this with it,' Elena explains. 'It's pinot grigio.'

'I got the pinot bit,' says Alex. He reaches for the

bottle and studies the label. 'It's local,' he says. He fills his glass. The other three expect he's going to keep it, but he passes it to Elena. She pushes it across the table to DJ, opposite, who hands it to Mia on his left. Mia makes to give it back to Alex and they all laugh. It's good to have something to lighten the mood. Mia keeps the glass and presses it against her cheek, enjoying its coolness. The wine is a delicate, pale green under the terrace lights, and it shines like something polished. She sips. It's delicious, cold and dry, with an acid bite and a suggestion of green apples.

Alex takes a big swig and then raises his glass. 'To absent friends,' he says.

The others join in. 'To absent friends.'

'And Joey,' says Mia.

Alex's pique at the way Joey has left them returns. 'I didn't mean him,' he says. 'I meant our friends in England.'

'You have friends?' says Elena. 'And don't chuck food about,' she adds hurriedly, leaning away and holding up her hand to ward off anything Alex might find to throw at her.

'I wonder where Joey is,' says Mia.

'No way of knowing,' says DJ. He consults at his watch. 'He won't be home yet or anything like it, even if he was lucky with a lift to Florence.'

'I hope he's okay. I just think of him sitting on the roadside hour after hour, thumbing cars that don't stop.'

'It's his own fault,' says Alex. 'Anyway, if he hasn't got a lift yet he'd better find one soon. The wolves will be out before long. And the bears.'

'Bears?' Mia and Elena both speak together.

'There aren't any bears in Italy,' says DJ.

'There bloody well are,' says Alex. 'Brown ones.'

'Really?' says Mia. 'Do you think he'll be all right?'

Alex laughs. 'Of course he will. There aren't many of them. They're endangered and they're only in the national parks. Anyway, why should what happens to Joey bother you?' He looks at DJ. 'Yo better watch yo' bitch, man, 'cos she am eyeing up a noo stud.'

DJ gives Alex a warning look.

'Boys, boys, boys,' says Elena. 'Eat your dinner.'

The panzanella is delicious. They empty the dish and still have room for generous helpings of the next course, mushroom risotto. Gianna brings another bottle of wine.

'Grazie mille,' says Elena, nodding.

'Prego,' says Gianna, with a little bow.

Alex waits till she's left the terrace. 'There, see?' he says in a hushed voice. 'She answered you. She must have heard what you said.'

'Not necessarily,' says Elena. 'I smiled at her and nodded, and she probably realised she was being thanked. Prego is just a formality, like us saying you're welcome. Besides, she may be able to lip read.'

'I think she's talking more,' says Alex.

'She's getting used to us,' says Elena. 'She probably didn't know what to expect from a bunch of foreign teenagers. Besides, the Brits don't have too good a reputation in some parts of Italy. I expect she was just being cautious. Now she knows we're harmless she's thawing out.'

'Mm.' DJ is thoughtful.

'What is it?'

'You could be right, but didn't you notice something else?'

'For fuck's sake,' says Alex, 'notice what?' He's finding DJ irritating.

'When we came to the table there were four places laid.'

'And?'

'Four. Not five. So how did Gianna know that Joey wouldn't be here?'

Nobody else had realised that. There's silence while they all consider what it might mean.

'It's those fucking cameras,' says DJ. 'They must be monitored after all and somebody's seen him go.'

They all turn towards the small, innocuous cube of plastic and metal tucked in the corner against the house. A chill descends as they ponder the possibilities and implications, an almost palpable air of discomfort.

Gianna stays later than usual. She loads the dishwasher and puts the food away just like she has on the previous two evenings, but tonight as well as that she tidies the kitchen, cleans the cooker, and goes through the fridge.

They wait in more or less silence. Everyone is wary of speaking because they feel that anything they say will be overheard and on the record. Alex wants to fill the time with grappa but Elena puts her foot down.

'No,' she whispers. 'We've got some important stuff to figure out. Until we're done with that you can lay off the hard stuff. And no Sphynx either.'

Alex snorts in exasperation. 'It's as if the old cow

knows we're waiting for her to go and is on a deliberate go-slow.'

Eventually, Gianna leaves. They wait until she's clear and then move to the far end of the open ground between the house and the trees. Elena and Mia help pick a spot which as far as they can remember isn't in range of the camera on this side of the house. They reckon that by being well away from the building they won't be picked up by any of the microphones but Elena is wary about going too near the woods.

'Okay, cards on the table,' says Alex. 'Since the girls went up to the big house today I sense a move to leave, so let's find out what we all think. DJ, you first.'

DJ looks at his fingernails, then at Mia. 'I wouldn't mind staying, but I'll do whatever Mia decides.'

Mia doesn't hesitate. 'I want to go,' she says.

'Right,' says Alex. 'I don't. I know you and Elena have been spooked by the cameras, but I don't think there's anything for us to worry about.'

'You don't?' says Mia.

'No, I don't. That system wasn't installed just for us, it's been here a while. Somebody left it switched on by accident, and that's all. I know about these things, we have one at home. The system will record onto a flash drive and it'll constantly refresh by writing over the oldest stuff. That means that any shot is only there for a couple of weeks at most and then it's wiped. We'll probably be long gone before anybody sees what you've been up to in the bedroom,' he says, looking archly at Mia.

'I don't care,' says Mia. 'It's the principle that I don't

like, the fact that equipment to spy on us is there at all and we were never told about it. We wouldn't know now if we'd taken notice of Bruno and kept clear of the big house. Maybe that's why he gave that warning, to keep us away and prevent us from finding out. And another thing, all Ellie and I saw on the monitor were shots of this place. There weren't any views of the big house, none at all. That room has been set up to monitor what goes on here, not there. To watch us. We're being targeted. I want to go.'

Alex bites his lip. He doesn't want Mia to go and he's worried that if she leaves she'll take the other two with her.

'Look,' he says. 'We were invited here to play a gig. We accepted that invitation, and we've been given luxury accommodation, excellent food, and as much booze as we can drink. DJ, Ellie and me have been working hard writing songs and rehearsing. You haven't had to do anything. You're not in the band so you don't even have to be here. It's just a fancy holiday for you, and better than anything you'd manage otherwise. You don't have to sing for your supper. As far as you're concerned it's all take. And now something isn't quite right for you, you want to go waltzing off chasing after your toy boy.'

Elena and DJ are amazed. They'd both thought Alex liked Mia. This vitriol is a surprise.

For a few seconds Mia says nothing. Then she gets up from the grass. She stands for a moment, looking down at Alex. Then she says, very slowly and very calmly, 'You know, it's true what people say about you, Alex. You really are a complete arsehole.' She walks a few paces before she turns to him and says, 'Fuck off.'

DJ makes to go after her but Alex grabs his arm and pulls him back.

'Let her go,' he says. 'She'll come round. And just think. Think what this gig might mean. We'll be playing to a room full of top people – celebs, influencers, sports stars, actors, and maybe even a few musicians. All of them loaded. Just think of the opportunities there. You'll kick yourself forever if you miss it.'

DJ looks in the direction Mia has gone. He's still minded to follow her and he sits down reluctantly. 'Yeah, I suppose,' he says.

'There's one thing you've forgotten,' Elena says.

Alex is curious. What's she talking about? 'What have I forgotten?'

'You haven't asked me what I'm going to do?'

He's surprised. 'I thought you'd be staying. With me.'

'You thought wrong. I'm going.' She gets up and follows Mia into the house.

32

There are twelve of them, nine men and three women. They're in three military Land Rovers. They are dressed in the dark blue operational uniform of the Carabinieri. They have black helmets with face visors. They are armed.

The vehicles stop a little way down the hill from Castelvecchio because it's important for the sleepers not to be disturbed by noise and headlights. The occupants get out and form into two columns. They jog the half mile up the track, their rubber-soled boots making little sound on the dry surface. When they get close to the villa they slow down, approach it in silence and fan out.

Their commander waits and listens. All appears to be quiet, everyone is asleep. She hesitates a moment, then she raises her arm and barks. 'Azione! Azione!'

Pandemonium breaks out as the scene explodes into frantic life. One of the squad fires a burst from his weapon into the air. Its deafening din rattles around the hills. At the same time, another launches a flare that drops in a blazing, white smear. The commander blows a whistle and six of the squad charge into the house and race up the stairs. They're not quiet now. The aim is to drive the occupants into a state of shock and fear, so the raiders shout and stamp and make as much racket as they can.

Two go to each of the bedrooms and hammer on the doors.

'Apri la porta! Subito, subito!' Bang bang bang.

The door of Mia's room opens a crack and a booted foot kicks it back.

'Uscire! Mani al cielo!'

DJ comes out of the bedroom, blinking. He sees the dark figures, sees the guns, sees the gesticulations and raises his hands. 'Stay in,' he shouts over his shoulder to Mia. 'We're being busted.'

'What the fuck? What's going on? Who are you?' This is Alex, struggling out onto the landing opposite. He's pulling a sweatshirt over his head. Elena is behind him.

'You are who?' says the commander.

'I'm Alex.' He doesn't sound so confident now he sees the uniforms and the weapons.

The commander turns to her squad and rattles off something in Italian. Two of them seize Alex, spin him and snap cuffs on his wrists.

'Hey. What are you doing? Get off me! Shit, that hurts!'

The two soldiers, because that's what they seem to be, ignore his protests. They each take one of Alex's arms and march him away.

'Stop it,' shouts Elena. 'What are you doing? He's barefoot. He's got no shoes. Piedi nudi. Senza...' She points at Alex's feet.

The commander understands, and gestures to Elena to get some shoes. She dashes into the bedroom, fetches Alex's trainers and bends to put them on him. Her hands are trembling so much that she can hardly manage to tie the laces. Mia, who's come out onto the landing with DJ, goes to help her but she's pushed back.

Two of the squad go into the bedroom. They're searching for something and they exchange comments in loud voices. One comes out with Alex's backpack. He rummages inside it, shouts, and takes what he's found to show the commander.

'What's going on?' Elena says, still struggling with the shoes and looking up at Alex.

Alex shakes his head. His face is ashen. He's more frightened than she's ever seen him. 'It's a mistake. They've mixed us up with somebody else.'

The shoes are on and the two men who have Alex push him towards the top of the stairs. Another takes his backpack. Elena tries to go with them but she's blocked.

'Find out where they're taking me and see if you can get help,' Alex calls to her as they manhandle him down the stairs.

Some of the raiders must have gone for the Land Rovers because headlights sweep across the ceiling as they pull into the yard.

DJ, Elena and Mia are made to wait on the landing. The girls are wearing only what they had on in bed and one of the squad, who has pushed up his visor, is ogling openly. He turns to a companion, says something and winks. The commander snaps at him and he puts his visor down.

'Cosa sta succedendo per favore?' says Elena, as calmly as she can.

'Your friend is under arrest,' says the commander.

'What for?' 'Why?' 'What's the charge?' The three of them speak together.

'He is being taken elsewhere to be charged. You are to leave immediately, with your possessions. You have five minutes to dress and to stow your objects.'

'Why? What are we supposed to have done?' says DJ.

'You can't do this to us,' says Mia.

'Where are you taking Alex?' says Elena.

Down below one of the Land Rovers starts up again.

'We're allowed to be here,' says DJ. 'We're a band. We've been invited to play at a wedding.'

'We're guests of Signor Sylvani,' says Elena.

'Your minutes are now four and a half,' says the commander.

They go into their rooms. One of the squad makes to follow Elena but the commander waves him away. Inside, she opens her case and starts to cram in her clothes and what are left of Alex's. She doesn't stop to fold things or to separate hers from his, she just shovels in what she can as fast as she can. The room's a mess so it's haphazard. Mia and DJ have been much tidier, living out of their baggage, taking things out as they needed them and putting them back when they've done. They finish their packing and come out onto the landing with their bags.

The commander pushes open Elena's door.

'Il tempo è scaduto. The time is expired,' she says. 'Now you must come.'

Elena stuffs the last few things into her case and joins the others on the landing. All three have put on jeans and T-shirts, the clothes they'd travelled in when they came. All three are shocked and bewildered. For an instant DJ thinks of running but there are two guards at the top of the stairs, their forefingers alongside the trigger guards of their weapons. Mia tries to read their faces but the visors hide their expressions.

'What's this about?' she says to Elena.

'I've no idea. It might be to do with you and me going into the big house yesterday. Bruno's note did say it's alarmed.'

'Yes, but this is really heavy,' says Mia. Her voice sounds thin and scared. 'They don't seem like local police and there must be a dozen of them, all armed. To pick up the four of us? Really?'

'They're like fucking zombies,' says DJ. He's not feeling nearly as macho as he sounds.

'I wonder where they've gone with Alex,' says Elena.

'The local nick, probably. I expect they'll take us to the same place,' says DJ.

The commander returns and motions for them to go downstairs. They pick up their bags and go after her. The stair guards move aside and one follows behind them.

'Fretta, fretta,' he says.

DJ is struggling with his backpack, Elena's suitcase and his guitar, and both the girls are loaded, but none of their captors makes any attempt to help them.

Two Land Rovers remain in the yard. Elena and Mia

are directed to one and DJ to the other. A soldier signs to them to load their baggage. It takes both girls to lift Elena's case into the Land Rover. They climb in after it.

One of the squad sits between Elena and Mia. They're pleased it's a woman, but when they start to talk she briskly shuts them up. They bump down the track in silence. A couple of the men in the front are talking but it's much too fast for Elena to understand what they're saying. She thinks she catches Silvani, and Inghilterra, and sciocche, which she thinks means idiot, but that's all. She can't stop her knees from trembling. She hopes the guard next to her doesn't notice.

They've been going for half an hour when they reach a small town. Elena looks for a sign to tell her where it is but she can't see one. The Land Rover pulls into a car park behind a row of modern shops. It's a scruffy, dirty area with litter and graffiti, definitely not on the tourist route. The two guards in the front come around to the rear of the vehicle and open the doors. They motion the girls to get out, and one of them waves his gun towards a building where lights are showing. DJ's Land Rover draws in just as they reach the door.

They're directed into what appears to be an ordinary office. There are five desks, all empty, with computers, all off, and phones, all silent. There's a row of chairs against one wall. The blinds on the windows are drawn. A clock on the wall shows it's almost 3.00 am. DJ is pushed in and followed by two more guards. The girls are anxious about their belongings and are relieved to see some of the soldiers bringing in their bags and DJ's guitar.

'Something tells me that's it for Castelvecchio,' Mia whispers anxiously. 'I don't think we'll be going back.'

'Well I'm sure as shit not going back,' mutters DJ.

'Nor me,' says Elena. 'That place is far too weird.'

Nothing happens and they're left standing in the middle of the room. It's 3.15 when the commander comes in with a tall, thin man following her. His neatly parted hair, tweed suit, horn-rim glasses, and erect bearing give him the appearance of a stage version of an Englishman. He carries a battered-looking briefcase.

'Where's our friend?' says Elena to the commander. 'We have a right to know what's going on. We have a right to be at Castelvecchio. We were invited to stay there by Signor Sylvani. Contact him and he'll tell you.'

The commander regards Elena as if she's trying to unscramble the ravings of a mad woman. Then she turns to the man in tweeds. 'This gentleman will speak to you,' she says. She leaves the room, closing the door firmly behind her.

The tall man smiles but without enthusiasm, and takes a seat at one of the desks. His face is lined and he looks tired. He could be fifty, or more.

'Please sit,' he says. His voice is as thin as his smile, and crisply public school.

It's not clear where they should sit, so Mia gets herself one of the chairs from the wall and plonks it in front of the desk. The other two do the same. Elena had been trembling, the result of a mixture of fear and rage. She's beginning to feel calmer now, and so are Mia and DJ. Their blood pressure has lowered on the way to wherever this is, and they now have someone who speaks English and who will be able to explain to them what's going on.

'My name is Anthony Webb-Carter,' says the man. 'I'm an attaché at the British Consulate in Florence.' Elena breathes an inward sigh of relief. Somebody in authority, somebody from the Foreign Office who'll be able to sort out this mess. She wants to ask about Alex but thinks it's best to say nothing for the moment.

Webb-Carter puts his briefcase on the desk, takes out a folder, opens it, and studies some papers. He takes a pen from his inside pocket and looks up.

'I take it you are Devon James Bailey,' he says, scrutinising DJ. DJ nods.

Webb-Carter's attention switches to the girls. 'Which of you is Emmelina Jane Noble?'

'I am,' says Mia.

'And so you must be Elena Barnes.'

Elena nods. 'Can you tell us what's going on, please?' she says.

Webb-Carter puts his hands together on the desk and stares at her coldly. 'I would have thought you could tell me that.'

Elena shakes her head. Mia and DJ exchange puzzled looks.

'I have been called in...' he makes a show of studying his watch, 'at three o'clock in the morning, because the authorities here have been informed that you are in possession of List 1 controlled substances, with intent to supply.'

'Controlled substances? List 1?' says Elena.

'The Decree of March 4th, 1992, and subsequent amendments classify legal and illegal substances. List 1 includes opiates and cocaine derivatives, which are illegal. A first offence of possession carries a large fine. Intent to supply carries a prison sentence.'

'It must be the Sphynx,' murmurs Elena.

Webb-Carter looks at her sharply. 'You clearly understand to what I am referring.'

Mia experiences a dread so visceral she almost passes out. How would anyone know about the Sphynx? Then she remembers the cameras. They would have seen it. She never took any of the pills. Would the cameras prove that? There is no possibility that she or her family could ever afford to pay a fine.

Webb-Carter taps his pen on his teeth. 'They could, of course, charge you, keep you in custody and put you on trial,' he says, and pauses while this thought takes root. 'However, they tell me that they can't be bothered going to that amount of trouble for what they refer to as "three spoilt teenagers".' Webb-Carter delivers the quote with some satisfaction. 'Neither do they seek to formally deport you, which of course would go on your records and would affect your reception in other countries of the EU, as well as hindering your chances of ever getting into the United States. Put quite simply, they just want you gone. I am to take you to Florence Peretola airport and put you on a flight to England. If you do not go or if you resist they will arrest you.'

'This is ridiculous.' Mia's voice is no more than a whisper. 'We've done nothing wrong.'

'I'm afraid they think you have.'

'But they've got no proof.'

'I assume the fact that they are taking this action means that they do.' There's another pause. 'I advise you to cooperate,' he says. 'The Italian courts take a very dim view of their time being wasted. If you choose to remain here to run some misguided campaign to demonstrate your innocence it will without any doubt turn out badly for you. The authorities are being very generous.'

'Generous?' DJ explodes. 'I don't want to run into them when they're being mean.'

'Where's Alex?' says Elena.

'Ah, Mr Brandish. I'm afraid his case is different. They say he is more involved than the three of you and they are keeping him in custody while they make further enquiries and consider prosecution.'

It *is* the bloody Sphynx, thinks Elena. Why on earth did he bring it? She told him he was being an idiot. Weren't Italy and the gig and getting away from a wet English summer enough for him? Does he have to bring along some stupid nightclub candy too? 'Can I see him?' she says.

Webb-Carter shakes his head. 'I am afraid they are regulating access rather strictly. He will be permitted a consular visit tomorrow and we will ensure he has legal representation. The Foreign Office will inform his family of the situation as it becomes clearer.' He glances at his watch. 'We must go,' he says. 'I have your 'plane tickets. You have your passports, I presume.' They have. 'Very well. Follow me.'

They follow Webb-Carter to a black Range Rover.

The girls get in the back and DJ is going to join them but Webb-Carter signals for him to take the passenger seat.

'You can ride beside me,' he says. 'I am not your chauffeur.'

The roads are clear and the journey to Peretola takes only an hour. It passes in silence. Webb-Carter offers no conversation and asks no questions. DJ, Mia and Elena are angry, hurt, and resentful; none of them feels like talking. They all at various times think about Alex. DJ thinks he was unlucky to be caught. Mia thinks he's a complete idiot. Elena wonders where he is and hopes he's being treated well. She doesn't like his parents and she isn't looking forward to having to meet them and tell them what's happened, but she supposes she'll have to do that. If Webb-Carter is typical of what they can expect from the Foreign Office she's not confident that Alex will be well served. His dad is going to have to dig his hands deep into his pockets to fork out for a decent lawyer. If he will. He and Alex haven't been getting on of late. He may just leave him to fend for himself.

The airport is busy with travellers arriving for the rush of morning flights. Webb-Carter watches while DJ and the girls load their bags onto a trolley; then he leads them into the terminal. He stays with them while they queue and he presents three tickets at the check-in desk. DJ is apprehensive and thinks of movie clichés of wanted persons being apprehended at airports, but the process goes smoothly. The desk staff are bored and barely glance at the passports before they tag the bags and wish them a pleasant flight.

'The parting of the ways,' says Webb-Carter as they

approach passport control. 'Bon voyage.' He watches them as they go through. Then he makes a phone call.

The three trail through security, and it's not until they're at the departure gate that they see that the three seats they've been allocated are nowhere near each other.

33

I t takes Joey all day to reach Florence. Mia had said that from Castelvecchio to the main road was five miles. He remembered it as less than that. Whatever, he expected that downhill he could cover the distance in not much more than an hour. It takes a great deal longer.

The track is steep and soon his legs are aching. As he gets lower the temperature rises and it becomes hot, even under the trees. Before long the straps on his backpack start to chafe his shoulders and he has to stop. He drops the pack to the ground and rummages for socks to use to pad the straps. The backpack is really heavy. The Coke cans were a great idea but they weigh a ton. He takes one out, pops it open and drinks the warm, sweet liquid. He squashes the can as flat as he can and buries it at the side of the track with a large stone on top of it.

He starts again. His shoulders are better but now the problem is with his feet. His trainers are well-used and worn thin and he feels every pebble. He gets out yet more socks and puts on two pairs. The shoes are now tight and hot but his feet are easier.

It seems much more than three days since they'd all been driven up the hill in the Mercedes. He hadn't then been aware of any forks in the road and if you'd asked him he would have said there were none. However, there are several. There are no signposts, nothing to indicate which route leads to the Florence road, but he reasons that the logical choice is to pick the one that looks to go downhill. Twice that works; then the third time he comes to a dead end at a pair of very forbidding gates. He has to turn around and trudge several hundred meters back up the slope to the junction, where he finds that the road he should have taken ascends in order to get over the shoulder of the hill before continuing its progress down to the valley.

It's early afternoon by the time he reaches the Florence road. He's hungry, so he sits on a pile of stones at the roadside and eats the sandwiches Mia gave him. They taste good, but what pleases him most is Mia thinking of it and making them for him. Was that anything more than just being nice? Could it mean she might care for him a bit?

While he eats he watches the traffic. It comes in waves, a lot of vehicles in a large bunch and then a spell with nothing. Most of the cars and trucks are Italian, no surprise there, but there are several foreign ones too – German, Swiss, French and a few British. One truck that passes shows an address in Ireland. He remembers Mia telling him to ask for Firenze, not Florence, but decides that anyway his best bet is to try to thumb a British driver.

The trouble is that the traffic is going quite fast, and by the time a vehicle is near enough for him to get a good look at the number plate it's past. That's why the lift he eventually gets isn't from a British traveller but from a German car following behind the one he'd thumbed.

It's a woman, older than his mother but much tidier and more trim. She speaks good English and tells him she's been visiting her married daughter in Salerno and since then has worked her way along the coast before heading towards the alps. Joey doesn't know where Salerno is but from what the woman says he guesses it's by the sea and farther south. Her name is Clara. She asks him his name and he tells her Alex. He didn't plan the lie and doesn't know why he does. It just seems fun to be covert.

'And where are you from, Alex?' she asks.

'Birmingham.' Actually the town where he lives is some distance from Birmingham but he expects a foreigner wouldn't have heard of it and he doesn't want to get into a long explanation, so he picks the nearest place he thinks she might know. She does.

'Are you on holiday?'

Joey decided on the way down the hill how he would answer that question if anybody asked. 'Yes. I've been with some friends. They're still here but I've got to go home because I have to be back at work on Monday.'

'What do you do?'

'I'm a chef. Well, not a proper chef yet. I've just started my training.'

Clara is interested and he tells her a bit about *The Golden Bough*. She's impressed that it has Michelin stars.

She asks him where else he's been and what he's seen. He's embarrassed that he's been nowhere and seen nothing, and accounts for that by saying he couldn't get much time off work and has only been in Italy for a couple of days. He takes out his two cans of Coke, offers her one and she accepts it. The conversation flows easily and the time passes quickly. Soon they are on the outskirts of Florence. Now Mia has alerted him to it, he sees that Firenze is the name on the roadsigns. When he saw it before he just assumed it was the name of another place.

'I'm afraid I'm going to have to drop you a little way out of the city centre,' says Clara. 'The traffic will be bad at this hour and I haven't the time to wait in it.'

She gives him instructions for getting to the station, wishes him luck, and tells him he reminds her of her nephew, 'a lovely boy'. He thanks her and watches the BMW drive away.

Joey feels nervous. He's in a strange city in a country where he doesn't speak the language, and he doesn't have much money. Clara was right about the traffic, it is very busy. He heads in the direction she indicated. She said something about catching a bus, but he's not sure where to do that or exactly how they work (ticket first? ticket on the bus?), or what to ask for. He's concerned as well about what it might cost. It's all too difficult. He sees a sign that says *stazione*, which he guesses means station, and he sets off in that direction.

He ends up walking all the way. The signposts are clear and every time he sees one he thinks that the station must be just around the corner. Eventually it is, but that's after a long time and by then he's hot, hungry, thirsty, and his feet ache.

He spends some time studying his ticket and the destination information. The return route that Bruno's assistant has booked is different from the outward journey. He sees that the train he needs is due to leave in forty minutes, which gives him time to buy a McDonalds and another Coke.

There's plenty of room on the train and he settles down. The first change is Milan, which is a couple of hours away: long enough to tempt him to sleep but not long enough to get a decent rest, and he warns himself to stay awake so as not to miss getting off. He fishes out his phone, and curses himself for not charging it up before he left Castelvecchio. With no signal or wifi, he'd put it aside and ignored it. Now the battery is dead so he can't play his games or listen to any of his music.

Someone's left a newspaper on the seat across the gangway. It will be in Italian obviously, but it will be something to look at and he reaches over to get it.

A photo of a radiant couple takes up a good quarter of the front page. Theo Vasilias and Lita Jordan smile out at the reader. Theo is in a suit with a spray in his buttonhole. Lita, on his arm, wears a white dress and a flowery hat with a half veil. What grabs him, though, is the caption. He doesn't understand it but it's obvious what *matrimonio* means. There are more pictures inside the paper, of Theo and Lita and a lot of other people in pairs and groups. In several of them, there are expensive-looking boats in the background.

He can't make much of the article, except that Theo

and Lita have married in Monte Carlo with a lot of famous people in attendance. He's not sure when, but recently. That means they must be on their way to Castelvecchio! They may be there already! If not, do the others know they're coming? He thumps the seat in frustration; he has no way of getting in touch to tell them.

He thinks about Elena and Alex, DJ and Mia on the terrace at Castelvecchio and feels a twinge of sadness. He knows he was right to leave, but he also regrets not being with them.

He thinks about Mia. He's missing her. He wonders what she's doing now. He managed to sit next to her a lot on the journey to Italy, and when he couldn't do that he made sure he was near her. She seemed to him to glow, and he relished the life he felt coursing through her. He savoured her essence. When they left England she had smelled of the country, fresh as clean laundry. As the journey went on this became overlaid with other scents: travel, sleep, sweat, girl. He remembers one time when she'd been beside him and her resting head had drooped onto his shoulder. He'd sat motionless, desperate to be still lest he wake her and she move. He'd remained like that even when his arm went to sleep and he got excruciating pins and needles.

Once they reached Castelvecchio he spent as much time with her as he could. He hated the band practices because she didn't usually join them in the studio, preferring to spend the time on her own, drawing, reading, whatever else she did. Sometimes he sat close to her and sometimes he simply made sure he was in the same room as she was. Did she notice that? Did any of the others? He tried to keep it discreet. She's DJ's girlfriend and he likes DJ, but he likes Mia too. Had she noticed his doglike devotion?

Now her absence hurts. He aches for her. It's not the ache of lust but something deeper and longer lasting. He feels cored, an emptiness inside him that only she can fill.

The evening and night pass in the tedious progress of the journey. In Milan, he has to change stations. He was worried about that, but the signposting is clear and it's very simple. Then three stops on the Malpensa express before a suburban line takes him across the Swiss border to Bellinzona. This train stops everywhere and takes forever. It's almost two hours on another train from Bellinzona to Zurich. Everything is much more complicated than it was on the journey out, and that was bad enough. Of course, he's on his own now and he has to work it all out for himself, rather than simply following Alex and Elena.

It's now dawn, but he's too tired to fully enjoy the spectacular views. He remembers that on the way over Mia was disappointed that she missed seeing the mountains. He hopes she'll see them on the way back. Finally, he gets on to the Paris train and settles down, only to be disturbed by a passport and ticket check.

He sleeps for almost all the four hours it takes to get to Paris. He uses his backpack as a pillow and wakes with his neck and shoulders knotted and aching.

By the time he's reached Gare du Nord and bought a baguette he has only a few euros left, but there's something more he must buy. He's looking for a book stall and he finds a Relay on the concourse. He's hoping that there are still some of the previous day's London editions on sale, and there are. He picks two of the tabloids and takes them with him on to the Eurostar.

Only one of the newspapers has what he's after. The page is mostly filled with photographs of Theo, Lita and the guests at their wedding reception.

The actual report is brief.

Soccer Star Weds Curvy Cutie

Soccer maestro Theo Vasilias (26) married his sweetheart, celebrity model and influencer Lita Jordan (24) yesterday at the Cathedral of St Nicholas, Monte Carlo. As well as a Premiership star, Theo is first-choice striker for his homeland of Italy. Lita is best known for her revealing appearances in Channel 5's *Love Shack*.

Lita wore a clinging dress in white satin and was accompanied by her two nieces as bridesmaids. She was given away by her father, hedge fund manager Xavier Jordan.

The ceremony was followed by a reception at the 5-star Hotel de Paris, with a guest list of more than 500 stars from the worlds of sport and entertainment. Afterwards, the couple boarded the Jordan yacht for a honeymoon cruise.

Entertainment at the reception was provided by Ed Sheeran and supergroup Coldplay.

34

The Land Rover into which Alex is pushed doesn't turn right down the hill; instead, it goes left and takes him the short distance to the big house. The building is no longer in darkness. Lights show at several of the windows, and around the outside.

Bruno is sitting on the terrace in a reclining chair. He's smartly dressed in pressed chinos and a dark blue blazer with a white handkerchief tucked into his breast pocket. His grey hair is slicked into a neat ponytail. When he sees Alex he gets up, but he says nothing as he watches him come forward flanked by two guards, his hands cuffed in front of him.

Alex is bewildered. He feels sick. He's angry and he has to make an effort to control his breathing. When he's ten metres away Bruno gives an instruction in Italian to a guard, who steps in front of him and releases the handcuffs. Alex has seen hundreds of people in handcuffs in movies and on the news, but he'd never realised how painful they can be. His were tight, so that even after such a short time his hands are numb and his wrists hurting. He tries to massage some life back into them. Bruno gives another order and the guards withdraw, one to each end of the terrace, where they stand with legs apart, visors down, and weapons at the ready. They are definitely on call.

'You appear to be somewhat agitated,' Bruno says. The Italian accent that had been so obvious when they'd met at the school has now gone, replaced by smooth, urbane English.

'What's happening?' Alex growls. 'Why have I been brought here? Where have you been? Where are the others?' He looks to the guards. 'What do these people want?'

Bruno is very calm, in contrast to Alex's intense agitation. He sits slowly back in his chair, crosses his legs, and steeples his fingers. They are long, elegant, and adorned with gold rings. He waits some seconds before responding. The result is that Alex feels deflated.

'That is a great many questions,' he says at last. 'I'll start with the first. What is happening is that you have been arrested for the possession of illegal drugs. In Italy this is a serious matter. The police wish to prosecute you. Fortunately, the Vice Questore is a very good friend of mine. I heard of your predicament and persuaded him that the best course is to return you and your friends to England.'

'We can't go to England yet. What about the wedding?'

'Ah yes, the wedding,' says Bruno. He flicks an imaginary speck of dirt from his trousers. Or it could be a mosquito or a moth tumbled from the crowd around the lights. 'Surely you must have realised by now that the wedding was never a serious proposition.'

Alex is horrified. 'What? We brought our instruments. We practised. What do you mean not serious?'

'Oh you may have been serious, but the wedding was never intended to be here. Theo and Lita were married two days ago, in Monte Carlo.'

Alex is thunderstruck. His legs feel weak.

'You look rather pale,' says Bruno. 'Sit down.' He points to a chair.

Alex desperately wants to sit. His head swims and he thinks that if he doesn't he might faint, but he refuses to take orders from this man.

'I beg you to sit down, please.' He does. 'Good.'

Alex is struggling to comprehend the situation, although in a way he's not surprised. 'But you asked us to play, when Lita and Theo heard us at the school. If there's no wedding why are we here?'

Bruno studies Alex intently, weighing him up. He makes a slight adjustment to his cravat. Who the fuck wears a cravat nowadays? Alex asks himself. He finds the steady gaze unsettling.

'Think back,' says Bruno. 'Think back to when I first spoke to you. What exactly did I say?'

'You said that Lita liked our music and wanted us to play at her wedding.'

Bruno slowly shakes his head. 'Not quite. I did indeed say that Lita, now Mrs Vasilias, liked your music. She did. She thought that for students, for amateurs, you played well. Perhaps not as well as she implied, but she is a generous person given to paying compliments. However, I think that if you were to have a recording of our conversation you would find that at no point did I say that the invitation to Castelvecchio came from Lita, or that the wedding would be here. It was I who invited you, and I said that your visit would *coincide* with the wedding. You connected my invitation with the event, I did not.'

'But you agreed to pay us.'

Bruno shakes his head. 'I said I would pay your travel expenses and that you could stay here. I offered you one thousand euros to look after your friends and to take charge of the preparations for your party. I am aware that you did not tell the others of this arrangement, or indeed offer to share the fee with them. I'm also aware that you have done very little for it. All the travel was organised by my staff. Your job was to persuade your people to come here, which you did, and once they were here to ensure they remained, which you have failed to do.'

Alex is furious, and his anger is made worse by being mixed with self-pity. 'So we were screwed, the whole thing was a con.'

Bruno's tone has more edge than his previous replies. 'It was you who perpetrated the "con", as you call it, on your friends. Did you think that Lita would have a band of school students to play at her wedding? Before so many famous persons? The musicians she wanted for that are big-name stars whose diaries fill up many months in advance. They were booked a long time ago. Your vanity convinced you that your group was so outstanding that it was you Lita wanted, and you persuaded the others of this.'

Alex feels as though a hole has opened up beneath him. He can't believe he could have got it so wrong. What had really been said? He can't recall exactly. The euphoria of that evening at the school, the adrenaline from performing for an hour, the sense of achievement after the gig had gone so well, had blurred his perceptions. Bruno had mentioned the wedding, and Castelvecchio, and how nice it would be to play there. He'd never thought to query it. The others hadn't asked any questions either but had jumped at the prospect of a free holiday after all the hassle of their exams. The implication that they might meet some celebs had been irresistible bait.

'Then why bring us to Theo's house?' Alex says. 'Why drag us all the way out here?'

Bruno laughs. 'Castelvecchio is mine. The estate has been in my family for many generations.' He pauses for a moment, then adopts the tone he might use if trying to reason with a petulant child. 'Dragged, you say. As I recall it you didn't need much dragging. And think about it. You've had several days in first-class accommodation in one of Europe's most sought-after vacation areas. Your travel has been paid for. Unlimited food and drinks have been provided, and you have had the services of an excellent cook. You have had access to a lavishly equipped recording facility where you could indulge in your hobby. All this for five young people who have little to offer beyond their own charming personalities. Even if you had come here to play your music, one of your group

319

is not even a member of your band, yet she received the same generous treatment as the rest of you. Do you really think you've been hard done by?'

'You've wasted our time.' Alex is frustrated at Bruno's calm refusal to recognise any grounds for grievance and he's shouting now, leaning forward in his chair, the cords in his neck standing out like cables. He looks as though he might attack Bruno, who regards him with complete unconcern. The two guards are watching closely and edge forward. Alex sees that and forces himself to calm down.

'Wasted your time,' Bruno repeats. 'What is time when you are nineteen? You have so much of it. Would you have used it more profitably at home in England? Or would you have frittered it away, rather as you have done here but in less pleasant surroundings? I would also argue that your time has not been wasted.'

'How come?'

'From being here you have learnt more about yourselves and about each other. Which was part of my intention.'

'Your intention?' Alex is stupefied. 'What was your fucking intention?'

Bruno again delays his answer. It's not until he judges that Alex has calmed sufficiently to pay proper attention that he speaks again.

'I think that I do owe you some explanation for what has taken place.'

'Too right you fucking do!'

Bruno raises his hand. 'Please. Hear what I have to say.'

Alex glares but says nothing. Bruno continues.

'As you know, I own and run a company which represents the interests of sports people and entertainers. I am the agent not only for Theo Vasilias but for several other Premiership players and for some in the Bundesliga and in the Italian and Spanish leagues. We have recently extended our operations to the USA, where soccer is becoming increasingly popular. This is my business, I do it well and I am very successful. However, nowadays the everyday work is done by my staff in my offices in London, Turin, and now Los Angeles. This delegation of duties leaves me free to pursue my other enthusiasm.'

'And what's that?'

'Young people. No, don't look like that. I don't chase after teenage girls, or boys for that matter. I am interested in how young people behave, why they do what they do, the psychology of youth. It's an area that first appealed to me when acting for professional footballers, who can be both immature and volatile. My focus at the moment is on what is important to the young at various stages in their adolescence, and in how this and their personalities change in the few years during which they traverse the path from childhood to becoming adults.'

'You brought us here so you could *study* us?' Alex is incredulous.

Bruno is matter of fact. 'Yes.'

'How have you been doing that?'

'In several ways. Mainly by observing you.'

'Yes, the fucking cameras, spying on us.'

'No, not spying; monitoring your interactions with each other, and your reactions to your surroundings and events. Come.' Bruno rises and walks towards the house. He doesn't check to see that Alex is following him; he knows he will be. One of the guards comes behind at a discreet distance, the other remains on the terrace.

The hallway is dark. Bruno leads the way across it to a staircase. They go up to the first floor, where Bruno opens the door to a room that looks to Alex like a TV control suite. There are screens, speakers, computers, and keyboards. Bruno's fingers flicker over a panel of switches and one of the screens comes to life. It shows rooms in the house, just as Elena and Mia described.

'Oh yes, your Peeping Tom kit,' says Alex, with what he hopes is withering contempt. 'I-Spy in the bedroom.'

'Really,' says Bruno wearily, 'I am not in the least interested in your sexual exploits which, from the little I happen to have seen, are extremely boring and singularly lacking in imagination. This is more the sort of thing that intrigues me.'

He clicks the computer keyboard and another monitor comes to life. Quickly he navigates to a file and a picture fills the screen. It's Alex and DJ in the studio. They are facing each other. Alex's stance is the embodiment of hostility.

Bruno pushes a volume slider.

They don't want that, DJ is saying calmly. *Nobody does. It's shite.*

What do they want, then? Alex is shouting. *Fucking Abba fucking covers?*

Why not? For Christ's sake, it's a wedding.

And you think that just because it's a wedding they leave their brains at the door? They want to hear garbage?

They sure as shit don't want to hear Mr Molester. That would go really well with the champagne and toasts. "Ladies and gentlemen, please take your partners for a song about an old guy who likes to fumble little girls". A deaf moron wouldn't want that.

And you can do better? You write nothing. All the creative input comes from me. You can't even play a simple chord progression without getting your fucking fingers in a knot.

They're both yelling now. Alex remembers it clearly. He also remembers what came from his lips when they broke up and DJ walked out. He hopes it hasn't been recorded, but it has.

Fucking jungle bunny he mutters. DJ didn't hear him but the system did.

Bruno extends a finger and kills the recording. 'Don't you find that interesting? Here is a young man who has been your good friend for many years. You were children together and you have been close ever since. It might be hoped that the fact that he is black would be of no consequence to you, yet when you quarrel your dismissal of him is racist. After all your years together. Why you behaved in that way is the sort of thing that intrigues me.'

Alex is embarrassed. Throughout his life he's managed, with a mixture of smooth talk and charm, to extricate himself from any awkward situation he might have found himself facing. What unsettles him is not the term he used about DJ but the fact that it was recorded. His father has always told him that the best form of defence is attack, so he goes on the offensive. 'You're done now? You've set us up, had your fun, and now we go?'

'You could have gone at any time. I made leaving a

difficult option but it was always there, as Joey demonstrated. I would have preferred it if you could have remained here longer because although the girls and Joey experienced dreams that I found extremely revealing of their characters, you and DJ did not. It would have added to my study if the two of you also had dreamt, but once the girls discovered the surveillance equipment there was no point in you staying. Please, sit down.'

Alex sees that the guard has not come into the room; now it's just him and Bruno. He could go for Bruno and wring his neck, and for a second he seriously considers doing that. Then he realises that there are probably cameras in this room too, and there are the two guards outside. He sinks onto one of the chairs at the control desk. Bruno takes another.

'Much of my work with sportsmen and women has been concerned with the dynamics of groups,' Bruno says, 'how relationships between young people develop and change in situations of stress, and particularly when they are confined for a period in close proximity to one another, as it might be in a team.'

'*Lord of the Flies* stuff.'

'If you like. There's another work which is more relevant to the current circumstances. Have you heard of *The Decameron*.'

'No. Who are they?'

'It's not "they". *The Decameron* is a book by Giovanni Boccaccio, a medieval Italian writer. It's about seven young women and three young men who take refuge in a house in the hills above Florence, as it might be here, to escape the Black Death which is raging in the city.

Although they confine themselves willingly they are in effect prisoners because they lack the means to leave, and anyway if they do go they risk catching the plague. They pass the time by making up stories which they tell each other. These tales reveal insights into the individual personalities, beliefs, prejudices, and proclivities of the members of the group. Your poet Chaucer employed a similar idea for his *Canterbury Tales*.'

'So we're them.'

Bruno smiles wryly. 'Hardly, but the comparison is useful.'

'Why did you trick us? Couldn't you have just asked us to take part in your fucking experiment?'

'No. For my observations to have any value the subjects must be unaware that they are being watched. If I'd told you, you would have been acting to the cameras for at least some of the time.'

'So you're happy with what happened. You're happy to see DJ and me falling out.'

Bruno shakes his head. 'Happiness doesn't come into it. Nothing was planned. All I did was provide stimuli and record your responses.'

'What "stimuli"?'

'I explained that I wanted to look at how young people respond to stress. I saw in your party a group of individuals who I judged to be typical of your age group, social class and nationality. The first thing was to get you here, so I made you a proposal which I was sure you would find attractive. My problem was that you had started to relax. Your exams were over and you had nothing to do but await the results – apart from Joey, who was under some pressure from his new employers. Also, life at the villa is not stressful. On the contrary, it's very comfortable, you had everything you needed. So I had to introduce some adversity in order to create tension.

'The start of that was your journey here. You could have been flown to Florence in a few hours, but that would have been easy for you. Instead, I had my people concoct a long and arduous itinerary. It began in luxury on the Eurostar and became increasingly more wearisome as it went on. It was a good way to start to apply pressure, and it also emphasised how far away from home you were and how difficult it would be to get back.

'Of course, you brought with you some issues of your own, an example of which we saw in the incident in the studio. The relationships between you and Elena, you and DJ, and DJ and Mia are fracturing. That is to be expected as you prepare for the next stage in your lives, but it troubles some of you.

'The fact that you found yourselves alone here, with no way of communicating with anyone else and with no sign of any of the preparations you expected for a wedding left you in the dark about what you thought you had been invited here to do. That was the first of several "areas of uncertainty" that I created.'

Bruno pauses. He's watching Alex's reaction. From Alex's point of view the older man seems extraordinarily pleased with himself. He still wants to punch him, but he's becoming interested in how Bruno has used his home, his wealth and his power to manipulate them, to play with them. 'Go on,' he says.

Bruno smiles. 'Very good. Area of uncertainty number two. I established an atmosphere of threat. I warned you that the woods were menacing. I told you to avoid them, and on your first night I arranged for you to be visited by a pack of wolves.'

'There were no wolves.' Alex realises.

'No. Their sound came from concealed loudspeakers. I was hoping someone would look for the wolves because there were objects hidden in the trees which were to figure later in my plans and I wanted them to be seen. Unfortunately, Joey was the only one who came across them, and he chose not to tell the rest of you what he'd found.'

Alex knows nothing about this, although Joey being secretive doesn't surprise him. Nothing is making sense, but slowly he's beginning to see the complexity of the edifice Bruno has created. 'The studio and control room, locked and then unlocked.'

Bruno nods.

'And Gianna. Not deaf?'

'Gianna is a very intelligent woman who not only has excellent hearing but is fluent in English.'

Alex shakes his head and sighs. He has rarely felt so far out of his depth.

'Then there were the dreams,' says Bruno.

'You *made* us dream?' Alex could accept, just about, that Bruno could use his power and his huge resources to set them up in the way he's described, but to dictate their dreams is beyond belief.

'No one can *make* you dream. Everyone dreams anyway, every night. I did, however, try to *shape* your dreams.' Bruno goes to a cupboard. It's stacked full of identical bottles. He takes one out, puts it on the bench, and points to the label with an elegant fingernail. 'Grappa di Castelvecchio. Grappa is, as it says on the bottle, a distillation made from grapes. It's pleasant tasting and easy to drink. I had high hopes that if I offered it to you at least some of you would drink it. In fact, you all did. The batch at the villa I doctored with hydrocortisone.'

Alex knows about hydrocortisone. 'What for? My mum has that for her asthma.'

'Yes, that is one of its uses. However, the reason I administered it to you and your friends was because it stimulates the production of cortisol, the stress hormone. I wanted to see how, flooded with this hormone, you would respond to danger. The situations could not be truly perilous because that would probably have made you run away, therefore I decided that the best way to do it would be through dreams.'

'And that made Elena, Mia and Joey have nightmares? Why not me and DJ? We drank more of the grappa than any of the others.'

Bruno smiles. 'It was not the grappa on its own. Something more was needed, a trigger for each of you. On your first night a tray of petit fours was provided. One of them was laced with a hallucinatory substance. I didn't know who would take that one, or indeed if anyone would. Elena did, and it brought on a vivid nightmare. On your second night, Mia was targeted. That was easier to arrange. She is a vegetarian, the only one of you who is. It was a simple matter for Gianna to put the same substance in the meal she prepared for her.'

'How did you know one of us wouldn't sample it?'

Bruno shrugs. 'It was a risk that had to be taken. Then we come to the third night. I had hoped that food might provide a further opportunity, that one of you might be gluten intolerant or have an allergy to something, and that would require special catering which could be treated in the same way that Mia's meal was, but you are all disgustingly normal. I was at something of a loss, then you obligingly provided a fantasy-inducing element of your own.'

'The Sphynx.'

'Exactly. It turned out to be just what was required.'

'How did you manage to make them dream what they did, Elena and Mia, and Joey?'

'I didn't. The dreams arose out of their subconscious minds. I merely provided the stage and the setting. And the dreams had to be supervised. Elena really did go into the woods in her sleep...'

'I saw the scratches on her legs.'

'Quite. So you will appreciate that she could not be left simply to wander on her own. A path had to be made for her through the undergrowth, props had to be provided to shape the dream, and she had to be guided back to the house so she could awaken alongside you.'

'And you did all that while she was asleep?'

Bruno smiles. 'Not me personally. My people.'

He still can't believe it. 'But one of us could have woken up and seen what was going on.'

This time Bruno laughs, a teasing chuckle that Alex finds extremely irritating. 'That was a possibility, but you consumed the grappa in such quantities as to make it highly unlikely. The exception was Mia. Apart from the night of her own dream she barely drank anything and therefore she was not comatose like the rest of you.'

'What about DJ and me? Would we have had dreams?'

'I'd hoped you would, but nothing was sure. In dealing with human subjects the element of unpredictability is always a factor.'

'If the Sphynx made Joey dream, why not DJ and me? We took it too.'

'It's a significant point and one I wish I could have followed up. It could be the quantity of alcohol you consumed, or variations in the tablets, or factors in your individual psychologies. It would have been interesting to find out.' Bruno suddenly becomes businesslike. 'Anyway, I am grateful to you for assisting my experiment by providing drugs, and as a mark of my appreciation, I am willing to honour half the financial commitment I made to you. I will pay you five hundred euros. I have no idea what the street value of Sphynx is, but that should buy you a lot more of it.'

Alex is outraged. 'But you promised me a thousand.'

'That was conditional upon you keeping your people here long enough for me to finish my observations. You failed to do that, which means that this particular piece of work is incomplete.'

Alex shakes his head. 'I'm truly sorry about that,' he says, 'totally pissed that I fucked up your precious experiment.'

Bruno ignores the sarcasm. 'Actually, it was rather fascinating. The three of you who did dream created within their own psyches situations far more challenging than the ones I expected, and they were carried over into their waking states in a most illuminating way, blurring the line between dreaming and daytime imaginings.'

'And now you're kicking us out.'

'As I told you, since the discovery of the cameras you're no longer of use to me. DJ, Elena, and Mia are being taken to Florence airport,' he glances at his watch, 'even as we speak.'

Alex is dumbfounded. There's more here than he can cope with. Suddenly he feels very tired.

'So why the charade? Why the midnight raid? You could have just told us to go,' he says resignedly.

'I could, but it's important that what I do here remains confidential. To send you away would have required some explanation. No, this way is best, even if rather elaborate, and expensive. I doubt that DJ, Mia and Elena will want to broadcast the news that they were deported from Italy for possessing drugs and I imagine they will say little about their time here. You alone know the truth. You could go home and enlighten everyone, or you could maintain the fiction.'

'Why should I?'

'Because you have a year to spare and nothing to take you back to England, and you are in a position to help me.'

'Why should I help you?'

'Because it will pay you to do so. This is the first experiment of its kind that I have designed. Until it was cut short it was going well, and that encourages me to do more. Castelvecchio is an ideal location. It is remote and isolated, it is comfortable and appealing. It is also kitted out with all the equipment I need for my observations. The issue is, how do I entice suitable subjects here? It's difficult for me to arrange these things personally, and for reasons that I am sure are obvious to you I am unable to involve my office staff in anything apart from routine travel arrangements and the like. I need somebody who understands my purposes and is in a position to reach out to likely participants. I need an agent in the same age group as those I wish to study, who can approach them in ways I cannot. This person must also see the importance of maintaining complete confidentiality about everything that goes on here. You fit these criteria, and what is more, you are a young man who appreciates the value of money. I could find you a position assisting me.'

'You want me to get more suckers for you,' says Alex. Bruno doesn't reply. 'You realise that because of you my friends probably won't ever speak to me again.' There's another pause. 'What would I do?'

Bruno smiles. He can see that Alex is more than interested. 'Together we would construct several scenarios for luring young people to stay here. You would go to places where our target groups congregate and you would identify potential subjects. You would present those you have selected with an invitation and you would persuade them to accept it. Then you would assist me in managing the operation while they are here.'

'Kind of an event manager.'

'You might describe it like that.' Bruno can see Alex is on the brink of agreeing. 'I would pay you well for your work.'

'How much?'

Bruno nods; his fish is hooked. 'We can negotiate the actual sum later. Why don't you stay here for a few days and we can talk about it? I can make you comfortable, and I have three charming daughters who I am sure would be happy to keep you company.'

He indicates a photograph in a silver frame on one of the shelves. It's of three very attractive girls. Alex guesses that the middle one is about his own age, the one on her left is maybe a couple of years older, and the other correspondingly younger. They're wearing flowing dresses of some diaphanous material. And they appear to have wings.

'They don't always dress like that,' Bruno explains, smiling. 'When this picture was taken they were in costume for a production we put on here last year. It was *A Midsummer Night's Dream*. They were fairies.' He points to them one by one. 'Peaseblossom, Cobweb, and Mustardseed.'

He pushes another photo forward, this time of a single figure, a striking older woman wearing a flowing robe in shimmering blues and greens. 'That is my wife, Tania. She was the queen of the fairies.' He looks at the photo fondly. 'You could say she still is.'

Alex does some quick thinking. There's nothing to take him back to England. There's Elena, of course, but it's becoming clear to both of them that whatever was between them is over. He's in bad odour with his parents and if he's at home they'll nag him mercilessly. Because any withdrawal from his university fund has to be authorised by his father, in effect he has no money. Here is an attractive offer. He does not doubt that Bruno is powerful and wealthy, and can do him a great deal of good. And there are the daughters.

'Okay,' he says, 'Let's talk about it.'

Bruno shakes his hand. 'I have taken the liberty of anticipating your response and a room has been prepared for you. I'll have your things taken to it. There is one condition, and I have one question.'

'Yes?'

'The condition is that until I give you permission you do not contact your friends or your parents, and you do not respond to any attempts they might make to contact you. You may inform Casia, your sister, that you are safe and well, but you are not to tell her where you are, or communicate with her again unless there's an emergency.'

That sounds to Alex like more than one condition but it's not unreasonable. He doesn't want to talk to the others anyway, and he likes the idea of a mysterious disappearance. 'Okay, done,' he says. 'What's the question?'

'The question is this: was it you who stole Mia's money?'

Alex doesn't reply.

'I thought so,' says Bruno. He puts his hand on the small of Alex's back and steers him out of the room. 'I am sure we shall get on very well together.'

A NOTE FROM ELENA

I f you've read this far you know most of what happened, how and why. There are just a few more things to add.

Our journey home from Italy was chaotic. From the time of the raid until we got back to England there was no opportunity for Mia, DJ or me to discuss things. We were either under arrest, or with Webb-Carter, or being rushed through check-in and security. Our seats on the plane were spread apart so we couldn't talk to each other during the flight. We were isolated, and all we had were our individual fears and imaginings. We couldn't compare notes or share our thoughts about what was going on, and by the time we got to Stansted we were in something of a state.

We expected some sort of reception at the airport. Webb-Carter said he would alert our families and we thought there would be someone there to meet us. We were worried we might have to face people from the

Foreign Office or even the police, but there was nobody. The passengers on our flight moved through border control, baggage reclaim, and arrivals, and melted away. The terminal cleared and we were alone.

'What do we do now?' said DJ.

'We go home,' I said.

'How?' said Mia.

DJ was sure there was no point calling his parents because they'd be at work or on call and they wouldn't be able to come and get us. Mia's stepdad has a car but she didn't want to contact him. I was sure my mum would fetch us but it would take her a long time to get to Stansted. The sensible thing was to find a taxi.

Mia had hardly any money but DJ and I had some and we pooled it. The first few of the drivers we approached quoted way more than we had.

'It's not just taking you there, love,' one of them explained. 'It's the return. There's no chance of getting a fare from there back to here.'

Finally, we found a waiting driver who took pity on us and agreed to carry us for what we had. The journey passed more or less in silence. The driver made a few attempts to chat but we didn't want to talk. We had plenty to unload but none of us felt comfortable talking in front of a stranger.

Almost the first thing we did as soon as we were out of the taxi was phone Joey. He told us about his journey, and then dropped the bombshell that the wedding between Lita and Theo had taken place. He told us where and when, and who had provided the music. None of us was surprised.

'I think we knew there was no wedding before we were kicked out of Castelvecchio,' said DJ. 'We were conned.'

'How come we've been so gullible?' I said

'It was Alex,' said DJ. 'He was so up for it and so convincing that he just carried us all along.'

We each dealt with the situation differently. Joey was resigned, I was depressed, DJ was angry, and Mia felt sorry for the three of us. Dealing with the letdown was one thing, but what none of us could explain was *why* we'd been so comprehensively duped.

The days immediately following our return were confused. We didn't feel like owning up to how stupid we'd been, so we agreed that we would say nothing to our families or friends about what had really happened. We'd simply had a great time. The story about the wedding was that although the main reception had been in Monte Carlo there had been a separate party in Italy for Theo and Lita's closest friends. That's where we'd played and it had been great. The mix-up with the police was a misunderstanding; some of the guests had been taking drugs and we got the blame, but we'd had nothing to do with it.

Our families took our accounts in different ways. Mia shared little with hers and there was hardly any response. My mum and dad were relieved that I hadn't been thrown with Alex into an Italian jail. DJ's folks were incensed.

I had no idea what had happened to Alex. I'd come home with a lot of his clothes, which I'd rammed into my case at the time of the police raid. I put them all through the washer, and I even ironed his shirts. Then I folded everything, put it in a bag and went round to his house. I was hoping I'd be able simply to hand them over to Cristina, their maid, and I was disappointed when Alex's father answered the door.

We've never liked each other. I find him cold and unpleasant, and I'm sure he thinks I'm some sort of gold digger whose only interest in Alex is as a way to get at the family's money. However, he invited me in and gave me a cold drink, and I told him about the raid and our arrest. I had to mention the Sphynx because that's why Alex was treated differently from the rest of us. It didn't seem to come as a shock. I was surprised that he hadn't heard anything from or about Alex, and there'd been no contact from the Foreign Office. I was even more astonished that he didn't seem to care.

'My son is a free agent,' he said. 'He's also an adult. He chose to do what he did, so it's up to him to deal with it.'

I didn't stay long after that, and we parted on strained terms.

I met DJ and Mia and told them about the meeting.

'The bastard,' said DJ, describing Alex's dad. 'Why don't we phone Alex?'

'If the police have got him they'll have confiscated his phone,' I said.

'Maybe not. He could be out on bail.'

'Then why hasn't he phoned us?'

We talked about it for a while before deciding that there was nothing to be lost by trying, so I called his number. It rang, and went through to voicemail. I left a message telling him we were all back in England and wondering what had happened to him, and hoping he was okay, and to call me back.

I heard nothing. Neither was there any contact from the Foreign Office or the police, although every day we expected it. We couldn't believe that after all the fuss – the armed raid, our arrest, the direct involvement of the consulate, the flight back to England (who had paid for that?) – it would all be forgotten.

After a few days DJ's dad contacted the Foreign Office directly. He hit a brick wall. Nobody would answer his questions or give him any information, so he tried again. He got the same response and tried once more. This time he got through to somebody who seemed to be quite senior and who told him very tersely that he was wasting their time.

At this point, DJ's mum took over. She knows our local MP and she asked her to help. She was able to discover that there was no one called Webb-Carter working at the Foreign Office and never had been. She also told us that there was no British Consulate in Florence, following a post-Brexit reorganisation which consolidated our representation in Rome and Milan.

It was a relief to realise that we weren't in trouble with the authorities after all, but it was also a shock. Who had we seen on the night we were deported? Why had he taken us to the airport and bundled us onto a 'plane home? What was his relationship with the police? Or with Bruno? I Googled Webb-Carter and found nothing. There were a couple of Webb-Carters but neither was anything like the man we had met, and one of them was dead. It didn't come as a surprise. We were all of us reaching the same conclusion: that what happened on the night we left was not what we'd thought but was part of a game, just like the rest of the trip.

I looked up Castelvecchio and half expected that to be an illusion too, but there it was. The photos showed it was the same place where we had stayed, and there were even pictures of our villa. There was the pergola, the terrace, and the table where Gianna had served us and we'd swigged the grappa and talked about our lives. It made me feel oddly nostalgic. We'd only been there for three nights but it seemed like an age. Wikipedia said that the Castelvecchio estate had been in the Sylvani family for many years. Bruno and Tania Sylvani were well known, both through S.I.R. and Tania's "Action Art". While I was at it I also Googled the Reverend Samuel Forbes, but there was no entry. I searched on Amazon for *Forbes Lexicon of Dreams*; nothing came up. I inquired of a few antiquarian sites but there was nothing there either. When I eventually went up to St Andrews I had one last try in the university library, of course without success.

As the summer trudged towards its end our exam results came out. Mia and I both did well but DJ came unstuck. He missed his place at Bath, but he'd already decided that he didn't fancy Biology. He'd been thinking about becoming a Radiographer and he went through clearing and got a place at the University of Cumbria. He could have gone somewhere much closer to where Mia would be doing her course – Lincoln, Derby, or Sheffield – but by then he'd already concluded that her interest was moving elsewhere, and so was his.

Mia and Joey became an item, although it took them some time. Joey worked hard at *The Golden Bough* and tried to like it, but the management was hostile and bullying and the clientele pernickety. He and Mia talked to each other a lot on the phone but neither had transport, and Joey worked long hours so it was impossible for them to meet, although both badly wanted to. Then Joey learnt of a vacancy at *Margrave Hall*, a country hotel on the Nottinghamshire-Leicestershire border. It wasn't as prestigious as *The Golden Bough* but the work wasn't as hard either, the people were nicer, his accommodation was provided, and he and Mia could see each other. She told me with some amusement that it was not till their third date that Joey kissed her properly, on the lips.

Alex used to rib me about St Andrews, saying that because it's in Scotland it would be wall-to-wall tartans and haggis, but it's not like that at all. The Scots call it "the old grey town by the sea", which makes it sound sombre. It's true that on a rainy day with the wind whipping off the North Sea the place can feel a bit grim, but the university is so lively you couldn't fail to be infected by its exuberance and enthusiasm. I soon settled in there, and the work and social life meant I had less time to think about what happened in Tuscany, or about Alex.

Our relationship had been weakening before we went to Italy. I suppose that was why I had the night, and at that time it was only one, with DJ. The problem with Alex was that he was good-looking and could be absolutely charming when he felt like it, but the occasions when he did feel like it were becoming rare. And he was taking too much notice of other girls, not just Mia. Looking back, I think the real reason why I put up with him for so long was that I was sorry for him. Sorry for a millionaire's son? Yes. I felt sorry for him because of the part he felt compelled to play, acting the rich kid, and I felt sorry for him because of his father.

His father is the nastiest man I have met. Casia, Alex's sister, can do no wrong; Alex can do little right. And his mother is wet and does only what her husband says she may. An example is what Alex told me once about the time when he was a boy and he desperately wanted a hamster. He'd pestered and pestered, and eventually his father had agreed on condition that he take sole responsibility for looking after the animal. Everyone else in the family was forbidden to help. Of course Alex promised, and for a short time things were fine. However, being a kid he didn't keep it up. He forgot to feed the creature, to clean it out, to give it water. His parents and Casia watched and did nothing at all to intervene, while the poor thing starved to death. When Alex found it one morning lifeless in its cage his father had seemed pleased. It explained for me a lot about what Alex was.

I was nearing the end of my first term and for several weeks the shops had been decked in their Christmas garb. Very late one night my phone rang. I'd been working on an essay and dozing at my desk, and I thought it was DJ, who often called me round at that hour. I was amazed to see Alex's name on the screen.

It was one of the oddest phone calls I've ever had, and one of the most difficult. I couldn't understand why he'd called. It was ages since I'd left him the voicemail, which he now told me he'd got. I asked him why he hadn't replied, and he said he oughtn't to be calling me now and he'd be in trouble if he was caught. There were a lot of silences and I thought that either he was drunk or on something, but he said he wasn't well and hadn't been sleeping, and he needed to come clean. We must have been on the phone for well over an hour, and during it, he gave me most of the information you read in the last chapter.

He seemed unhappy, and he sounded lost. The brash, confident, pushy Alex I'd known was gone. I was concerned for his mental health. I told him he should come home but he said he wasn't allowed to leave. Leave where? I asked. He wouldn't say. Who's stopping you? I said. Again there was no response.

The Christmas vacation began. DJ came back from Carlisle, Mia from Loughborough, and we met in my parents' living room at *The Green Man*. Joey had managed a day off from *Margrave Hall* and joined us. Mia was sitting on the floor, leaning against the armchair, her arm resting on Joey's knee. DJ and I were side by side on the couch. We were on our second bottle of Prosecco and well into discussing Alex's phone call.

'I suppose I can believe that Bruno did it,' said DJ. 'but I can't get why.'

'It's hard to understand any of it,' said Mia. 'I don't think it's possible to make people dream what you want them to, like Alex says Bruno did.'

'And even if he did, what were his reasons?'

'Well, Alex says he was studying us,' I said.

'Studying us?' said DJ. 'For fuck's sake. Why us? What for?'

'Maybe he's just a rich guy who gets off on making people dance to his tune,' said Mia. 'A kind of gaslighter.'

'Except Bruno was the real gaslighter here. Alex was gaslit like the rest of us.'

Mia smiled. 'You've still got feelings for him, haven't you?'

I looked at DJ and shook my head. 'Not really. It's just that we go back a long way and I'm sorry for him. He wasn't wanted and his parents have always been tough on him.'

'Perhaps there isn't a proper explanation for any of what happened,' said Joey. 'Sometimes things go on and you can't explain them at all.'

I didn't agree. 'That's not true,' I said. 'There's always a reason for something. You might have to search for it, but it's always there.'

'No there isn't,' Joey replied – he talks much more since he took up with Mia – 'sometimes people do stuff on the spur of the moment and you think, where did that come from? It's the same with accidents. They just happen.'

'Hark at you.' said DJ, and threw a Prosecco cork at him. 'The kitchen boy turned philosopher.'

'DJ, you're such a snob,' said Mia. 'Anyway, it was weird at the time, and even weirder when you think back about it, but we got something from our stay at Castelvecchio.' She took Joey's hand. 'I think all of us changed. Things that we'd been thinking about in the background suddenly came out. I learnt more about myself and what's important to me, and I learnt about the rest of you too. I think it's given us friendships that we'll have for always. Which is not bad, considering we were only there for a few days. The question is, what are we going to do with the experience? Alex said he'd be in trouble if it was found he'd been talking to you. Did he say you shouldn't pass the information he gave on to anyone else?'

'No. I've told you three, haven't I?' I said.

'Right, well I think we should tell the story as we remember it, write it up,' said Mia.

'Good idea,' said DJ. 'Put it to bed, put it behind us.'

'But not share it with anybody,' said Joey. 'Keep it private, or we'll get Alex into trouble.'

'We could publish it as fiction,' said DJ, 'with our names changed.'

There was a long silence while we each thought over the possibilities.

'Who would write it?' said Joey.

Three pairs of eyes turned in my direction. 'Don't look at me,' I said.

'Why not,' said DJ. 'You are, after all, the English student, and you've said yourself that you want to write a novel.'

'But I don't know everything that happened. I know what happened to me and I know what I saw and heard, but how could I know what happened when I wasn't there? How could I know what people said to each other, what you saw, and how you felt about it?'

'You could interview each of us,' said DJ. 'We'd tell

you the story as we experienced it, then you could put it all together.'

'And we'd work with you on the drafts and help you fill in the gaps,' said Mia.

'And you'd have to use your imagination,' said DJ. 'Isn't that what novelists do?'

There was another pause.

'Well, will you do it?' said Joey. 'I couldn't.'

'Nor me,' said DJ.

'I'd have a go,' said Mia, 'but I wouldn't make anywhere near as good a fist of it as you would, Elena.'

I said I'd think about it; seriously think about it. Christmas passed, the vacation ended, and once more we went our separate ways.

Just into the new year, Casia called. She told me that Alex had had a breakdown and was being treated in a private clinic in Bologna. She implied that it was drug-related and I wondered if the "clinic" was actually rehab. She said he was receiving the best possible treatment but that he wouldn't be home for some time. Their parents were hoping to fly out to see him in a couple of weeks. I asked where he was so I could write, but she said their father didn't want his precise whereabouts known. I was sad to get her news. I know Alex can be selfish and manipulative, and anyway I'm with DJ now, but I still have a soft spot for him.

And there it is; I got the job of telling our story. I hope I've managed to convey at least some of the drama, frustration and strangeness of our time in Italy. I've put it down as best I could, based on what I saw, what the others told me, and the phone conversation with Alex. It wasn't easy. Sometimes their recollections of what happened and what was said differed from mine, and from each other. One of the problems was that Alex, DJ and I were stoned, drunk or hung over a lot of the time, so our memories are confused. Mia was the soberest of the five of us but she was drugged one night, and in any case, she keeps herself to herself so missed a lot of what was going on. Joey left before the end. That means I've had to imagine some of the story, but isn't that what we do every day anyway? Make up our own narratives to explain what's happening to us and around us? Ask any five people to describe the same situation and their accounts will differ, often in major ways.

What would have happened if Mia and I hadn't explored the big house and we'd not been sent home? Would Alex and DJ have had dreams on the next two nights? Probably, but what about? And what then? More days, more drugs, more dreams? Joey thinks we would have gone home in our own time without ever knowing the truth about what went on. DJ thinks that Bruno would have let us into his secret and given us a wad of cash to keep quiet. Mia thinks that Bruno might well have told us the truth, but that it wouldn't have ended well for us. We'll never know.

Was it a waste of time? I don't think so. We all of us learnt from it. For my part, I learnt that I don't want a relationship with Alex but I do with DJ. I learnt that I'm inclined to blunder into things without thinking, like in my nightmare trip into the woods. I discovered something I'd suspected for some time: that I can be attracted to another woman, e.g. Mia, but I'm not gay.

However, the main lesson for me is deeper than any of those things. It's that our lives are built not on indisputable truths but rather on what we think we know, and that this is not the same as reality. We know nothing for sure, and what we think we experience has no more substance than a dream. What dreams we had!

ABOUT THE AUTHOR

Thank you for reading my book. Would you leave a review on Amazon? Ratings and reviews are very important to authors because they help to get their works known.

Sign up on my website - www.phillfeatherstone.net - to get on my email list. No more than once a month you'll get an email from me giving news about my books, special offers, and thoughts about books and writing. When you sign up you'll be offered **a free book of short stories.**

facebook.com/PhillFeatherstone-author
twitter.com/PhillFeathers
instagram.com/phillfeathers

IF YOU ENJOYED THIS BOOK...

...you might also like *I Know What You're Thinking*.

Beth and Cameron have known each other since they were children. As they grew up they realised that they have an astonishing gift: each can see into the mind of the other.

A criminal organisation has access to a DNA databank and uses this to target young people as organ donors for wealthy clients. They seize Cameron.

The question is, can Beth use her power not only to find where Cameron has been taken, but also to free him? And if she can, what price must they both pay?

The code will take you to the Amazon page.

Fiction by Phill Featherstone

Novels

 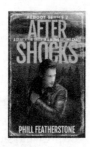  

  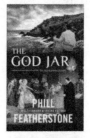

Short Stories

BOOK GROUPS

Are you involved in a book group?

Contact me for special discounted prices for multiple copies of *What Dreams We Had!* You can reach me at phill@phillfeaatherstone.net.

You can download book group discussion questions from my website

ACKNOWLEDGMENTS

I've been asked more than once why I, at one end of my life, should write so much about people at the other. I spent more than twenty years teaching people in their teens, and the first of these acknowledgements is to them, and to record my thanks and appreciation for all they taught me. I hope that in turn they learnt something from me.

Writing is a solitary business. Not only is it something you do alone, usually behind closed doors, but it demands mental as well as physical withdrawal. While working on a book a writer is in at least two places: the real world of family, friends and everyday life, and an alternative world inhabited by imaginary characters. This makes for a rather odd existence and it's good to converse with and receive support from others who experience it too.

There are many writers' groups and I'm grateful to all the ones I've been linked with, but I want to thank especially those who organise, moderate and contribute to Book Connectors, The Indie BRAG, The Alliance of Independent Authors, and Promoting Yorkshire Authors. There is always something interesting on their websites and Facebook pages, and requests for information and help, or just plain grumbles about the irritations and frustrations encountered by the independent writer, always receive a sympathetic hearing and elicit sound advice.

I am again indebted to the close group of loyal readers among my friends who go through drafts of my work and provide helpful comments; Rod and Helen Collett, Justin Ingham, and Emma Dunmore in particular have read early versions of this book and provided feedback, in some cases in great depth. A draft version of this book was serialised by The Pigeonhole.com, and I thank their subscribers for reading and commenting on my text. Mark Edwards did a final check of the manuscript and even at that stage found some errors. I am grateful to him and to them all.

My children, John and Sarah, and their partners, Kathy and Jeff always give me their unstinting interest and support. My UK grandsons, Bruce and Lenny, keep me up to date with at least some of what contemporary young people are thinking about and saying to each other. Bruce is lead guitarist in the band *Juno*, and while they are nothing like *Friendly Fire*, some ideas did come from that source. My American granddaughters, Hailey and Ella, add a USA dimension.

As always, my particular gratitude is to Sally Featherstone, my wife and partner of many years. Not only does she have to put up with the 'split' existence described above, but she is an unfailing source of creative ideas, encouragement and support. She has read much more than I have and is without doubt the most perceptive literary critic I have known.

The first edition of *What Dreams We Had* was written

during the 2020/21 COVID pandemic and especially during the lockdown periods, when real life often seemed stranger than the fiction I was creating and certainly crueller. My final thanks, therefore, go to you, my readers, who have shared this hateful time. I hope that in years to come this book might be picked up by people who only know about pandemics through hearsay.

Phill Featherstone

August 2022, Sheffield, United Kingdom

Printed in Great Britain
by Amazon

40730436R00205